"YOU OUGHT TO DO WHAT MY WIFE'S SISTER'S BOY DID," said Mr. Dougall. "Followed the army till they took him. Ten years old! Wouldn't take no for an answer. He didn't wait to get took on at no recruitment meeting, he went and found the war his own self. Tagged along with a regiment on the march till finally somewheres in Virginia they cottoned on that he wasn't going away, and so they enlisted him."

Jeremy thought about what Mr. Dougall had said. What Jeremy needed to do was head south until he found the war.

THE STORM BEFORE ATLANTA

★

KAREN SCHWABACH

A YEARLING BOOK

Text copyright © 2010 by Karen Schwabach
Cover photograph of boy copyright © Luciano Leon/Alamy.
Cover photograph of earth and sky copyright © Jim Reed/Digital Vision/Jupiterimages.

All rights reserved. Published in the United States by Yearling, an imprint of Random House Children's Books, a division of Random House, Inc., New York. Originally published in hardcover in the United States by Random House Children's Books, New York, in 2010.

Yearling and the jumping horse design are registered trademarks of Random House, Inc.

Visit us on the Web! randomhouse.com/kids

Educators and librarians, for a variety of teaching tools, visit us at randomhouse.com/teachers

The Library of Congress has cataloged the hardcover edition of this work as follows:
Schwabach, Karen.
The storm before Atlanta / Karen Schwabach. — 1st ed.
p. cm.
Summary: In 1863 northwestern Georgia, an unlikely alliance forms between ten-year-old New York drummer boy Jeremy, fourteen-year-old Confederate Charlie, and runaway slave Dulcie as they learn truths about the Civil War, slavery, and freedom.
ISBN 978-0-375-85866-6 (trade) — ISBN 978-0-375-95866-3 (lib. bdg.) —
ISBN 978-0-375-89318-6 (ebook)
1. United States—History—Civil War, 1861–1865—Juvenile fiction.
[1. United States—History—Civil War, 1861–1865—Fiction. 2. Runaways—Fiction.
3. Freedom—Fiction. 4. Soldiers—Fiction. 5. Drummers (Musicians)—Fiction.
6. Slavery—Fiction. 7. Georgia—History—Civil War, 1861–1865—Fiction.] I. Title.
PZ7.S3988Sto 2010 [Fic]—dc22 2010014514

ISBN 978-0-375-85867-3 (pbk.)

Printed in the United States of America

10 9 8 7 6 5 4 3 2 1

First Yearling Edition 2011

To
BOB *and* JOY SCHWABACH
NORBIE *and* MARTHA SCOTT
and
JAMES GUNN
many thanks

THE STORM BEFORE ATLANTA

☆ ★ ★ ONE ★ ★ ☆

JEREMY DEGROOT WAS DETERMINED TO DIE GLORI-
ously for his country. He knew he was meant to be a soldier. He'd known as soon as the war began.

But he was stuck being an indentured servant instead.
Old Silas was supposed to feed Jeremy, clothe him, and
send him to school three months a year in exchange for
Jeremy's labor. By the time Jeremy was ten he was good at
making shingles, planting rye and potatoes, and manag-
ing the stubbornest oxen in all creation. But he had never
had a pair of shoes, he only went to school if Silas could
think of absolutely nothing else for him to do, and he got
fed so little he had to hide potatoes in the woods where
Silas wouldn't look for them, just to get enough to eat.

And besides that, people in the Northwoods were always talking mean about Jeremy's pa. It was no kind of
life at all, so in 1863 Jeremy gave it up and dusted off on his
own hook to Syracuse, where he sold newspapers. He read
about the war in the papers and dreamed of how folks

back home would sit up and take notice once Jeremy was a hero who'd died for his country.

Problem was, none of the blamed officers would let him join up.

"You're too young," said the hundredth recruiting officer Jeremy asked. Or maybe the thousandth.

"Here's a story about a drummer boy that's only nine," said Jeremy, taking it out of his pocket. He'd torn it from an unsold newspaper yesterday.

"Bully for him," the officer said, not taking the paper. He looked over Jeremy's head at the next man in line.

There had been patriotic speeches and songs at the meeting, and a regimental band, and now the men were thronging to join up and fight against the Secessionists, those rebels who thought they could just quit the United States of America anytime they wanted.

"I know how to drum, sir," said Jeremy. He'd found an old tin bucket with the bottom half knocked out, and he practiced on that.

"Come back when you're eighteen," said the recruiting officer.

"The war will probably be over by then!"

"I sure hope so."

Jeremy didn't.

"Move along, you're holding up army business," said the officer.

And at that Jeremy had to step aside and let the man behind him come forward. A grown man with a mustache—

Jeremy envied him. *He* would find a place in the war, all right. Not Jeremy.

Jeremy stomped out of the lecture hall. It wasn't fair. He *knew* he was meant to perish on the field of battle, in a blue Union uniform, and show everybody back home how it was done.

He'd already organized his own regiment among the newsboys. They practiced with a discarded drill manual he'd found on the parade grounds. They could march, file left, file right, about-face—they'd gotten so good at it that they sat on the fence by the parade grounds, their bare feet hooked around the wooden rails, watching the real recruits drill and yelling out helpful instructions to them. The recruits never seemed to appreciate this as much as they should have.

But Jeremy seemed doomed to spend the rest of his life selling newspapers on the streets of Syracuse, New York, and reading about other people's glory.

In fact, it was time to go and pick up the evening papers.

He walked along the Erie Canal, on his way to get the *Courier*. A gang of canalmen was gathered beside the towpath. One of them was sitting on a barrelhead, twanging out a tune on a cigar-box mandolin, and the others sang:

> *On Shiloh's dark and bloody ground*
> *The dead and wounded lay.*
> *Amongst them was a drummer boy*

Who beat the drums that day.
A wounded soldier held him up,
His drum was by his side.
He clasped his hands, then raised his eyes
And prayed before he died.

Jeremy stopped and listened, spellbound. He imagined himself at the Battle of Shiloh. *He* should have been that drummer boy, his shattered drum by his side, one drumstick still held loosely in his pale hand. He imagined lying broken and bleeding in the lap of some faceless soldier, his brave young chest heaving painfully as his lifeblood pulsed out onto his uniform and covered his shiny brass buttons, which would of course have the lyre of the musicians' corps stamped on them.

"Look down upon the battlefield,
Oh, Thou our Heavenly Friend!
Have mercy on our sinful souls!"
The soldiers cried, "Amen!"
For gathered round a little group,
Each brave man knelt and cried.
They listened to the drummer boy
Who prayed before he died.

Yes, that was how it would be—they would all gather around Jeremy, his comrades, the men whom his courage had inspired in life—they would be there to watch his brave, brave passing. Probably they would beg God to save their valiant young comrade. . . . But alas. To no avail. Tears came to Jeremy's eyes.

> *"Oh, Mother," said the dying boy,*
> *"Look down from Heaven on me,*
> *Receive me to thy fond embrace—*
> *Oh, take me home to thee.*
> *I've loved my country as my God;*
> *To serve them both I've tried."*
> *He smiled, shook hands—death seized the boy*
> *Who prayed before he died.*

Jeremy's mother, too, was in heaven (as far as he knew), and that proved that his fate was meant to be the same as the noble drummer boy of Shiloh, who had loved his country so very, very much and gladly died for it—

At this point a mule with no sense of the dramatic wandered past and dropped a steaming pile of un-noble-smelling manure at Jeremy's bare feet. Jeremy hopped back. The canalmen laughed, and Jeremy would have stormed off, but he wanted to hear if there was more to the song. There was. The canalmen sang:

> *Each soldier wept, then, like a child;*
> *Stout hearts were they, and brave.*
> *The flag his winding sheet, God's Book*
> *The key unto his grave.*

They wrote upon a simple board
These words: "This is a guide
To those who'd mourn the drummer boy
Who prayed before he died."

"Who wrote that song?" Jeremy demanded.

"Some fella name of Hays," said the canalman on the barrel.

"Was he there? Did he see it?"

The canalmen looked at each other uncertainly.

"Must of was," one of them said. "Wouldn't of known to write the song otherwise, would he?"

That made sense. Jeremy imagined the unknown Mr. Hays, standing beside that cold, cold little grave, perhaps writing the sad little epitaph on the board—he had probably been one of the soldiers who had cried so manfully at the drummer boy's passing, who had stood amazed at such courage and patriotism in one so young. He had probably seen the poor young patriot's blood soak through the flag, had placed the Bible in the lifeless hands himself.

Jeremy felt that the drummer boy had gotten ahead of him somehow, had taken the heroic death that should have been Jeremy's. He was more determined than ever to get himself into the war.

He walked on along the canal path with the song playing over and over in his head.

The other newsboys were gathered at the loading dock behind the *Courier* office. Jeremy arrived just as Mr. Dougall came out with the string-tied bundles of papers. The boys moved aside to let Jeremy through. Jeremy could read a sight better than most of them, and he would tell them if there were any good stories with lots of death and glory.

He scanned the page. The war had been quiet lately—the South had actually invaded the North over the summer and had to be fought at Gettysburg. Then there had been riots in New York because people didn't want to be in the army—something Jeremy found very strange. Now it was quiet, except for some sort of dustup down around Fort Sumter that didn't look very exciting. Maybe the war was petering out. And Jeremy had missed it.

"Nothing much," he told the waiting newsboys.

Mr. Dougall gave him a sour look. "Folks'll buy these here papers if you sell 'em hard enough."

"I'll take fifty," said Jeremy. If there'd been a good battle or something, he'd have bought a hundred.

He dug in his pocket for the money, which was mostly in pennies and dragged his trousers down.

"Thought you was goin' into the army," said Mr. Dougall as he counted out the papers with his thumb. "Forty, forty-five, fifty." He handed Jeremy the stack of papers.

Jeremy breathed in the smell of ink, which he loved—it meant war news, and money to buy food. Mr. Dougall would have liked Jeremy to go into the army nearly as much as Jeremy would, probably, because by reading the news Jeremy kept the other boys from buying more papers than they could sell, losing money, and going hungry. So Mr. Dougall lost money instead. Jeremy looked at Mr. Dougall's pronounced paunch—he wasn't going hungry, anyway.

"You ought to do what my wife's sister's boy did," said Mr. Dougall. "Followed the army till they took him. Ten years old! Wouldn't take no for an answer. He didn't wait to get took on at no recruitment meeting, he went and found the war his own self. Tagged along with a regiment on the march till finally somewheres in Virginia they cottoned on that he wasn't going away, and so they enlisted him."

"Are you going to sell us papers, or are you going to talk all night?" said Frank, who was in one of the regiments that Jeremy's regiment fought with.

"Just for that, Mister Smart Mouth, you're last," said Mr. Dougall.

Jeremy hurried away to get downtown to where people were coming out of work before the other boys did. But he thought about what Mr. Dougall had said. What Jeremy needed to do was head south until he found the war.

The Yankees hadn't come to Georgia yet, but talk had. For years Dulcie had crawled up under the porch every evening to listen to Mas'r read the newspaper to Missus and then explain what it meant. Then Dulcie would run down to the cabins in the slave quarters to report, and the grown-ups would talk long into the night about what it meant, carefully comparing the stories in the newspapers as Dulcie overheard them with what Mas'r and Missus actually told their slaves, which was usually quite different.

Dulcie had a powerful memory, and if she heard something once she could say it back. She could even repeat back the whole sermon on those Sundays when Reverend Davis, the white circuit rider, preached to the slaves, telling them to mind their masters and mistresses so they could get into heaven. Once, when she'd heard Miss Lottie trying to get her geography lesson straight, she'd unwisely repeated the whole thing out herself. Miss Lottie had read it aloud when she'd first started memorizing it, and hearing it once was all Dulcie needed. When she heard Miss Lottie stumbling, Dulcie blurted right out:

"'What can we say of Massachusetts? That it produces whale oil, textiles, and shoes. What of its people? That they are deluded by a sad fanaticism, a perversion of religion that causes them to attack Southern institutions.'"

Then, as Miss Lottie stared with outrage standing out in high pink spots on her cheeks, Dulcie added, "What does *perversion* mean, miss?"

Dulcie had been whipped with the cowhide for sassin' Miss Lottie, and after that she'd kept her talent to herself around the white folks, and Miss Lottie had eventually gone off to boarding school "on account of the war," and so Dulcie's opportunity to learn about geography was over.

"On account of the war" meant that Mas'r and Missus

had talked to their neighbors and become convinced that girls (meaning white girls, of course) were safer kept in Southern boarding schools until the invasion was over and the Yankees had been sent back where they came from.

"We'll tell the servants that it's to finish off her education," Mas'r said.

"The servants have no business asking," said Missus.

"But they'll wonder, and they'll talk," said Mas'r. "It's what servants do."

(Mas'r and Missus were much too genteel to use an ugly word like *slaves*.)

"Seems like they know the war news before we do half the time," said Missus. "Goodness knows how they find out."

And Dulcie, under the porch with spiderwebs tickling her nose, smiled.

☆ ★ ★ TWO ★ ★ ☆

THE LAST TIME JEREMY HAD BEEN IN THE RAILWAY
station, the clerk had been a man. But now there was a
woman behind the brass grille. She kept picking at her
dress as if she was catching fleas.

"I want to buy a ticket to the war, ma'am," said Jeremy.

She looked up at him, but went on catching fleas with
both hands. "A little boy like you should be home with his
mother."

"I'm not a little boy. And I don't have a mother."

"Then you should be home with your father."

"I'm going to the war."

"You can't go to the war, just like that. You need a passport to get into the Southern states."

She unfolded a map of the United States, crisscrossed
with railroad lines. Jeremy leaned over to look at it. She
spread her hands over the states that had seceded from the
United States. "That's all war, down there. But even if you
have a passport—"

"That's where I want to go," said Jeremy.

"Don't interrupt, boy—your train could be sidelined for days waiting for trains of troops and supplies to pass on the tracks. Or for tracks to be rebuilt." She started catching invisible fleas again. "They blow 'em up, you know."

"What about Gettysburg?" said Jeremy. "I don't need a passport for Pennsylvania, do I?"

"No, you don't," she admitted.

So Jeremy bought a ticket to Gettysburg. And an hour later he was chugging out of Syracuse, ready to find his place in the war. It wasn't his first time on a train, it was his second, so he tried not to stare out the window too much or look around him like he was some hayfoot-strawfoot country boy from the Northwoods. A boy came through the car selling newspapers. Yesterday Jeremy would have envied him. You could make good money selling on the trains, if you were allowed to. But now that he was practically a soldier, he was above envying a mere newsboy.

"Chickamauga!" the newsboy cried. "Secesh win at Chickamauga!"

"Paper!" said Jeremy. He paid the boy a penny.

Where *was* Chickamauga? Right on the Tennessee-Georgia border. More war that Jeremy was missing! And the South had won; that was because Jeremy hadn't been there. He ought to be taking a train to Georgia. He thought of the map the clerk had showed him. Georgia was deep in Confederate territory.

The train went on all day, and into the night.

Then, an hour before dawn, just about the time Jeremy would have been heading out to buy his morning papers, the conductor came through the car calling "Hanover Junction!"

Jeremy sat bolt upright. Hanover Junction was where you got the spur line for Gettysburg.

The train groaned to a stop, and Jeremy got off. He shivered in the cold September morning, but his heart pounded with excitement. He'd been able to see nothing of the land the train had rattled through in the night. They'd passed south of Harrisburg, and he knew the Secesh had gotten as far north as Carlisle—so he might be in territory where there'd been fighting already. And he'd soon be in the thick of it; he'd be in Gettysburg!

The train to Gettysburg seemed too slow. It creaked along, and there weren't enough people on it—a few women, surrounded by sleeping children, an old man, but no soldiers. It was dawn when the train arrived in Gettysburg at last.

The smell hit Jeremy as soon as he stepped onto the platform. It was like that ox hide that Old Silas had never gotten around to nailing up properly, so it had rotted instead of curing.

The other people on the train got off. Jeremy followed a woman with a collection of children up the platform.

"Will we find Papa here?" asked one of the smallest children. An older girl hushed him, and their mother didn't answer.

The station was a two-story building with a small tower on top. There was a clerk at a ticket window, and a man pushing a baggage cart. But no soldiers. There was a wide, dark stain on the wooden floor, and Jeremy stepped around it instinctively.

He walked through the station and out onto the street. The smell was stronger out here, and the street was criss-crossed with wide lines of white powder. A horse came clip-clopping along, pulling a wagon. Jeremy waved to the driver, who pulled up beside him.

"You look lost, young man." The driver was a woman, with stray locks of gray hair escaping from her bonnet.

Jeremy tipped his hat politely. "Yes, ma'am. I'm looking for the soldiers, ma'am."

"Everyone is, who comes to Gettysburg these days." The woman nodded over her shoulder. "They're back that way. Back out of town."

"What's all this white stuff on the streets?"

"Chloride of lime. Disinfectant."

"Oh. Thank you, ma'am." Jeremy lifted his hat again, then walked the way the woman had pointed, careful to stay at the very edge of the street. He had walked barefoot all his life, even in the coldest New York winters, and his feet were as tough as hooves. But he didn't know what chloride of lime was, and he didn't want to step on it.

He saw charred black stains on the buildings, and cannonballs lying here and there. Some of the trees had lost all their branches and stood like stark gray monuments to themselves. The war had been through here, all right.

At the edge of town Jeremy met an old man with a shovel.

"Looking for somebody?" He was hardly taller than Jeremy, bent over as if from years of digging. A wide-brimmed hat covered his head right down to the eyes, and from under it he grinned with a mouthful of maybe six teeth like broken yellow sticks.

"I'm looking for the soldiers."

"Which ones? I'm the man to ask. Been digging for weeks."

He nodded at the field beside the road, which was broken up into brown clods. Jeremy had thought it had just been plowed, but of course it was too late in the year for that. Now Jeremy saw that the field was planted with long lines of narrow boards, ripped from barrels and packing boxes. Near one of them Jeremy thought he saw the toe of a boot sticking up. He didn't see any bloodstained flags, like in "The Drummer Boy of Shiloh," but he assumed they were there underground, along with the Bibles laid beside each unbeating heart.

"Them that's got names, it's written on the boards," the man said, still grinning. "I can find any of 'em that's got names for you. Won't take a minute—they're none of 'em dug in too deep."

Then Jeremy knew what the smell in Gettysburg was.

He was almost sick, but managed to stop himself from giving the strange grinning man that satisfaction. "I'm looking for the soldiers that are still alive!"

"Ah, them. They've all left. Gone to fight the war."

"I'm looking for the war."

"Well, if it's the war you want you'd best go to Washington. That's my advice. It all comes through there, one time or another."

And seeing that Jeremy wasn't interested in his gruesome field, he shouldered his shovel and walked away.

Jeremy went back along the white-powdered streets to the station and bought a ticket to Washington. His money was running out, and if he didn't find the war in Washington he didn't know what he'd do.

☆ ★ ★ THREE ★ ★ ☆

THE OLD MAN HAD BEEN RIGHT. EVERYTHING CAME through Washington, or to it. In the railroad yards Jeremy saw endless trainloads of hardtack, embalmed beef, and coffee. There were hundreds of wagons pulled by horses and mules, and men yelling at the mules and horses to get up, and at each other to get out of the way. There were trainloads of wounded soldiers, some groaning in pain but most grimly silent.

"You lost, sonny?"

Jeremy looked up at a black man with a broom in his hands. He was smiling in a friendly way, but his face looked tight with pain.

"I'm looking for the war," said Jeremy.

"You come to the right place for that," said the man. "This is the war." His nod included the rail yards, the mules, the wounded soldiers, and the rail platform filled with waiting troops.

Jeremy shook his head, impatient. This wasn't the war, not what he'd read about in the newspapers. It wasn't the Drummer Boy of Shiloh's war.

"I want to join a regiment," he said.

"Sonny, I think you better go home to your ma and pa." The man's smile was kind, but he was talking to Jeremy like Jeremy was a little boy, which Jeremy was not.

"I want to join up as a drummer boy," said Jeremy.

"Well, you could talk to them over there." The man nodded across the rail yard. "There's plenty of regiments boarding up for the West out there."

The South, the West—Jeremy had a feeling he was going to go all over the blamed U.S. of A. looking for this war and it would be over before he found it.

"Why aren't you in the war?" Jeremy asked. He knew that black men couldn't join the regular regiments but that there were separate colored regiments. He'd read about them in the newspaper.

"Been in it." A cloud passed over the man's face, and he started sweeping.

"Oh." Jeremy felt uncomfortable. "Well, I guess I'll go over there and talk to the enrolling officers."

"Sure hope they don't take you," said the man, but softly, like he didn't really mean for Jeremy to hear.

Jeremy made his way through the chaos of wagons, ambulances, and shouting men to the platforms where thousands of soldiers were gathered, playing cards, singing, talking, waiting to be shipped out.

An officer was coming down the platform. Jeremy could tell from his insignia that he was a lieutenant, and from New York State. Jeremy stepped into the lieutenant's path and saluted.

The lieutenant stopped, smiled, and returned the salute. "What regiment are you with, soldier?"

"None, sir," said Jeremy, still holding his salute. "But I'm from York State, sir! And I've come to join up."

"At ease, soldier. Can you play a drum?"

"Yes, sir!" Jeremy replied, hardly able to believe his good luck. "I've been practicing for years. I can play reveille, fall in, tattoo. . . ."

"We're short a drummer boy in the 107th New York Volunteer Regiment," said the lieutenant. "Come along with me. I'm Lieutenant Tuttle, by the way."

"Jeremy DeGroot, sir." Jeremy hurried to keep up with Lieutenant Tuttle, who led Jeremy to a little office near the platform where the enrolling officer was.

"We have a drummer boy here who wants to join the 107th," said Lieutenant Tuttle.

Jeremy thrilled at being called a drummer boy.

The enrolling officer looked at Jeremy and took some papers from a stack. "Can you play the drums?"

"Yes, sir!" Jeremy had never actually held a real drum in his hands, but he knew how to play one, he was sure.

The enrolling officer pointed to his desk. "Drum me a reveille on that, lad."

Jeremy put his hands flat on the desk and closed his

eyes to hear the rhythm that pulsed through his blood. He beat the reveille on the desk with his hands. Then, to show them what he could do, he beat a tattoo, and a march time, and a double-quick march, and finally the long roll that called soldiers to battle.

Then he opened his eyes and looked up at the men. Lieutenant Tuttle looked slightly impressed.

"Not bad," said the enrolling officer. "Good enough for you, lieutenant?"

"He'll do."

"Right. We just need your pa's signature on this form, and you're in."

Jeremy's heart sank. "I don't have no pa."

"I'm sorry to hear that. Can you tell me when and where he died?" said the enrolling officer.

Jeremy looked up at Lieutenant Tuttle for help. He had said they needed a drummer boy, after all.

"If you're under sixteen, you need your father's permission to enlist," said the enrolling officer. "President Lincoln says the U.S. Army does not need boys who disobey their parents. Did you get your father's permission to come join the army?"

"Not exactly," said Jeremy.

"Perhaps you just neglected to mention it to him," said Lieutenant Tuttle. "Where do we find your pa, Jeremy?"

"Auburn, New York," Jeremy admitted miserably.

Lieutenant Tuttle pursed his lips. "When you say your

father's in Auburn, do you mean that he is a guest of the State of New York?"

"Yes, sir," said Jeremy. Tarnation! Had he come all this way only to lose his chance?

"What's he in for?" asked the lieutenant.

"Chawed a man's ear off."

"I beg your pardon?"

"Chawed off his ear. He tole him he was gonna chaw his ear off, and then he chawed. He got six years."

Lieutenant Tuttle was beginning to look like he was regretting bringing Jeremy here.

But the enrolling officer said, "Maybe it can be managed. Been arrested yourself, Jeremy?"

Worse and worse. But a soldier had to tell the truth. Jeremy took a deep breath. "Only once."

"What for?"

"Fightin'. My regiment against the Geddes Street regiment."

"Er, did you fight with guns?"

"Rocks. Them and us both threw some rocks."

Jeremy was the only one who'd gotten caught, and only because he'd stayed to make sure that all the rest of his regiment got away safe, over a board fence and down an alley.

The two officers were exchanging looks that said they were about to tell Jeremy to go away.

"They didn't keep me, though," Jeremy said. "They let me out next mornin', on account they said I was too young to be in jail. But I was younger then."

"Old enough for jail now, eh?" said Lieutenant Tuttle.

"Well, now," said the enrolling officer. "The lad shows a good martial spirit. And he seems honest enough, at any rate."

Lieutenant Tuttle gave Jeremy a measuring look, as if he didn't think he was honest at all.

"What about your mother, then?" said the enrolling officer.

"Pa never said nothing about her."

"Is she living?"

"Don't think so, sir."

"Who looks after you, then?"

"Look after myself, sir." Jeremy saw he had better steer the officers away from this line of questioning. Telling the officers about Old Silas would land him in a heap more trouble than he needed. "I sell newspapers."

"Well, that's not a bad thing to do," said the enrolling officer. "Do you want a drummer boy, lieutenant?"

Lieutenant Tuttle twisted his mouth to one side, thinking.

"I'm brave, sir," Jeremy blurted. They didn't hold with flat-out boasting back in York State, but he could see his chance slipping away and he wouldn't let it go. "I ain't scared of nothing. Everybody says so."

He thought of adding that he would be perfectly willing to die like the Drummer Boy of Shiloh, bravely calling out to his mother in heaven while soldiers wept around him. But in the noisy train station the idea seemed somehow far-fetched.

"I guess we'll give him a try," said the lieutenant at last. "But mind, boy! There's no tolerance for misbehavior in the 107th. No tolerance at all."

"Thank you, sir!" said Jeremy.

"Take this, raise your right hand, and read it," said the enrolling officer. "Can you read?"

Jeremy didn't bother to answer that. He'd had over six months of schooling—of course he could read. He raised his right hand, threw his chest out, and read loudly from the card:

"I, JeremIAH DeGroot"—he gave his first name its full, official pronunciation instead of its down-home one— "do solemnly swear that I will bear true allegiance to the United States of America, and that I will serve them honestly and faithfully against all their enemies and opposers whatsoever, and observe and obey the orders of the"— he took a deep breath and read the next words extra loud—"*president of the United States*! And the orders of the officers appointed over me according to the rules and articles for the government of the armies of the United States!"

And that was that. He was down for $13 a month, just like a grown man would get, and just like a grown man he wouldn't see any of it for months and months, because there were always problems moving the money around to where the armies were. He got a uniform, his first-ever pair of shoes, and best of all, a drum.

The drum was glorious. It was painted blue, with an eagle, its wings spread wide, and a red, white, and blue shield. Golden rays surrounded the eagle. The paint was scratched and battered—the drum had already been in the war, and Jeremy wondered what had happened to the drummer boy who had had it before him. Perhaps it had belonged to the Drummer Boy of Shiloh. The quartermaster had painted over the name of its last regiment and painted "107th New York Volunteer Infantry" over the eagle in red and gold.

There were ropes zigzagging around the drum, and as the 107th New York waited its turn to board a westbound train, Jeremy practiced using them to tighten and loosen the calfskin drumhead.

He was sitting on the platform among the men of the 107th New York. Lieutenant Tuttle had left him—after all, an officer was too important to hang around with a drummer boy. The men were singing, telling jokes, sleeping. They all knew each other. None of them paid any attention to Jeremy.

Jeremy picked up one of his new drumsticks and lightly tapped the drumhead. BOOM!

A twitch went through the soldiers. They stopped talking and singing. The sleeping ones woke up. Some of them were halfway to their feet before they saw it was only Jeremy, sitting there investigating his new drum.

"Knock it off, kid!"

"Pipe down!"

"You leave that drum alone or you'll be wearin' it for a collar."

This last remark came from a big, golden-haired man who looked like he could make it stick. Jeremy looked down at his drum. He felt his face burning, and if he hadn't been a soldier he probably would have run away, right off the railroad platform. But that would be deserting. So he looked down at his drum and waited for everyone to forget about him, which after a minute they did.

"Hey, kid. What's your name?"

Jeremy looked up at a tall, skinny man with dirty blond hair.

"Jeremy DeGroot, sir." Jeremy stood up.

"You our new drummer boy? Call me Nicholas." Nicholas extended a hand, and Jeremy shook it.

"Yes, si—er, Nicholas."

"You look a little young. I've had pupils in the first reader that were bigger'n you."

"I can read out of the eighth reader," said Jeremy. He guessed Nicholas was a schoolmaster. But Nicholas seemed relaxed and easygoing, not like any teacher Jeremy had ever had. Schoolmasters came and went pretty quickly in the Northwoods, and since Jeremy had only managed a couple months of school a year, he'd had quite a few teachers.

"You got a mess yet? Want to join ours?" asked Nicholas.

A mess was a small group of soldiers who cooked and ate together.

"Yes, thank you," said Jeremy.

"C'mon over and sit with us."

Nicholas turned and walked away, and Jeremy bent to pick up his drum. He tried putting the strap around his neck—the drum was unexpectedly heavy, and it dragged his head down. He struggled to stand straight. He wished the boys back in Syracuse could see him now—a soldier of the 107th New York, marching along the platform to join his messmates.

And he wished Mr. Dougall could see him—he would never dare give Jeremy dirty looks now that Jeremy was a U.S. soldier. And folks back home in the Northwoods who'd passed remarks about Jeremy being a jailbird's kid. And Old Silas—no, not Old Silas. Jeremy reckoned he'd have to go a bit further before he'd be out of reach of Old Silas.

☆ ★ ★ FOUR ★ ★ ☆

JEREMY WAS FINALLY ON HIS WAY TO THE WAR, rattling along in a boxcar, with his new messmates around him. He didn't actually know where he was going, except that they were headed west. The flat fields of Ohio rolled past outside the open door.

Most of the soldiers in the car had been in the 107th since it was mustered in at Elmira, New York, a year ago. There'd been over a thousand of them then, and now there weren't five hundred. They didn't think much of Jeremy as a soldier—he was pretty sure his new messmates had only accepted him because Nicholas made them. The soldier who'd threatened to put Jeremy's head through his drum back in Washington, Lars, was in the mess too.

"'Member that first night we slept out in the fields outside of D.C.?" said Lars. "We thought we were soldiers then!"

Nicholas laughed at the memory. "Yeah, roughing it, weren't we? Up till then it was always barracks. We had barracks in Elmira."

"Then they marched us right off to Antietam, and *then* we found out what soldiering was," said Dave.

If it'd been anyone else Jeremy would've suspected them of saying this just to make Jeremy feel like he wasn't a real soldier. But Dave was the sort of open-faced, honest character who usually said what he meant. Back home in the Northwoods, people like Dave tended to get beaten up and chucked in the creek a lot.

"Antietam wasn't so bad as the camp fever in Maryland," said Lars.

"At Antietam the river ran red with blood," said Dave.

"But it wasn't our blood," said Lars.

"Not mostly," said Dave. "But it was still blood."

Dave and Nicholas exchanged a look, and then Dave looked out the door. The men had all fallen silent, and Jeremy felt the presence of dead men in the car as his messmates called them to mind.

"Youse 'member that man who came into the camp in Maryland after those two runaway slaves?" said Seth suddenly. Seth was small and wiry, with a curtain of black hair that fell over his face—the sort of person who is often much tougher than they look. And he needed to be, Jeremy thought, looking at Seth's bandaged wound and wincing inwardly.

"Yup," said Dave. "Old Red-in-the-Face."

"Yup," said Nicholas with a laugh.

"That was some fun," said Lars. Lars was huge and golden and acted as if he owned the whole world, or expected to shortly. He had so much self-confidence that it was easy for your own confidence to get crowded out when you were around him.

"I don't," said Jeremy, getting tired of them talking about stuff he didn't know. "I wasn't there."

"Tell the Little Drummer Boy about it, Seth," said Lars.

"Well, it was Maryland, see," said Seth, glancing at Jeremy but clearly telling the story to the whole group. Everyone was eager to relive it. "Maryland's complicated."

"Why?" said Jeremy, even though he was a regular newspaper reader and knew why. At least they were including him in the conversation.

"'Cause they didn't secede, see, but they almost did. Abe Lincoln don't want nothing done that might upset them. That's why he never freed the slaves in Maryland yet."

"He didn't?"

"Don't you know anything?" said Jack, who was the youngest of the men if you didn't count Jeremy—and nobody did count Jeremy, he was quickly learning.

Jeremy decided he'd overdone the not-knowing-things act and said, "The Emancipation Proclamation freed slaves in states in rebellion against the United States. Which don't include Maryland."

"Go to the head of the class, Jeremy," said Nicholas.

Nicholas's natural position seemed to be leaning against the wall of the boxcar, surveying the men around him through half-closed eyes and quietly running the show. Lars thought he ruled the world, Jeremy thought, but if there was a leader in his new mess, it was Nicholas.

Seth frowned at Jeremy. "Right. So there come these two runaway slaves into our camp. And naturally we told them they was contraband of war and could stay there till we figured out what to do with them."

"Young kids," said Dave. "Maybe thirteen, fourteen? Boy and a girl."

"Rosie and Rufus," Nicholas said.

"Rosie and Rufus," Seth echoed, and all the men smiled at the memory of Rosie and Rufus, except for Jack, who as far as Jeremy could tell only smiled about unpleasant things. "So Rosie and Rufus moved right on into camp, and they were doing the laundry for a quarter, half a dollar and whatnot—"

"Done it right smart, too," said Lars.

"And then after a few days come this man who claimed to own 'em."

"Wouldn't have mattered if it hadn't been Maryland," said Dave morosely.

"Right, but it was Maryland, so—"

"He was a big, red-faced man," Dave supplied. "And he got redder and redder."

"Yup. He got redder and redder the more he stormed— they was his property, right, they was worth eighteen hunnerd dollars—"

"Total, not each."

"Right, total. We had no right, the Fugitive Slave Act protected his rights, blah blah blah—"

"Some of the boys was ready to chuck him in the river," said Nicholas.

"Right. And the captain, he said, 'I don't see I have any choice but to let you have 'em, mister, but you're going to have to get the permission of my soldiers to take 'em away.'"

The men laughed at the memory. Get their permission to take Rosie and Rufus, indeed!

"Well, he could see the soldiers—and there was still more'n nine hunnerd of us in the 107th New York then, even after the camp fever at Maryland Heights—wasn't going to let him take his slaves away. So he says to us—"

"It was the *last* thing he thought of—"

"Right, it was the last thing he thought of, not an argument he ever meant to bring up at all, but he says to us—"

"Like he thought it would help!"

"He says to us, 'But they're my own son and daughter! Would you deprive a man of his own flesh and blood?'"

The men nodded. Seth pursed his lips grimly.

"That's when I knew I was agin slavery," said Seth. "I never was sure before but what there might not be two sides to the story—"

"There's two sides to every story—"

"Until that man spoke."

"There are not two sides to this story!" The last man in Jeremy's mess spoke for the first time. As far as Jeremy knew his name was No-Joke. He had only been with the 107th since December—before that, he had been with the 145th New York. He was sallow and hollow-cheeked and serious, and they called him No-Joke because he never laughed.

"There's only one side to slavery," No-Joke said. "And that's that it's wrong."

"There's two sides to every story," Dave insisted. He looked at Nicholas for help.

Nicholas laughed. "If you'd ever been a schoolteacher you'd know there are at least nine sides to every story."

"Did youse let him take his son and daughter back?" Jeremy asked, to get Seth back to the story.

"His slaves, you mean?" said Seth. "No, we din't. We wanted to tar and feather him, but we didn't have no tar and no feathers, so we had to make do with what was to hand."

The men chuckled.

"Yup, we still had Bossy then, and she supplied us with a bit of—"

"—cow manure—"

"—and we covered him up good—"

"—and then took him to the creek for a bath—"

"—and saw him politely on his way—"

"—'cause we wanted to be hospitable-like—"

The men were laughing hard now, even Jack, everybody but No-Joke, and Jeremy laughed too, although he wasn't sure how he felt about treating the man that way.

After all, if he only wanted his son and daughter back—but he didn't, Jeremy realized. He never called them his son and daughter, he called them his slaves.

Pa and Jeremy hadn't always gotten along too awfully well. Pa was a rough customer and no mistake. But at least he knew he was Jeremy's pa and not his owner. It was all pretty hard to get your head around.

"What happened to Rufus and Rosie?" he asked.

"Sent 'em on to Washington," said Nicholas.

Dave frowned. "We should've looked them up when we was there just now."

"Forgot all about it," said Nicholas.

"We've had so many contraband," said Lars. "Who can remember them all? Remember Nathan? Fella that could walk on his hands?"

And they all went on reminiscing about runaway slaves they had known, as the miles clicked past. Their voices and the rattling of the rails lulled Jeremy into a near-doze, and he watched his new messmates through half-closed eyes and listened.

He tried not to be bothered by the way they all looked down on him. After all, they were real soldiers, and his messmates—his pardners.

When he died like the Drummer Boy of Shiloh, they would kneel around him weeping. Looking at his new pardners, Jeremy found this hard to imagine.

★ ★ ★

The boxcars rattled on day and night. They passed through Indiana, and Alabama, and finally into Tennessee, where they stopped. The 107th was put to guarding a railroad, which was no work at all because the railroad never tried to get away.

"Thought they was sendin' us down here for Chickamauga," said Jack. "Not to guard no train tracks."

Jeremy and his messmates were at work building their winter quarters. They'd cut down two great trees bigger around than Lars was, and were working now on cutting off the branches. Jeremy was good at this kind of work. He'd been doing it before he was six years old. So he worked hard and hoped his messmates would notice.

"I'd rather guard train tracks, thanks," said Dave, climbing up on the tree trunk to work at a branch. "Don't mind missing the fun down to Chickamauga."

"*I* mind!" said No-Joke. "The Rebs won at Chickamauga! They drove us out of Georgia."

"Reckon they'd've done that even if the 107th had been there," said Dave.

"No, they wouldn't have!" said Jeremy, shocked that any of his messmates could think this. "The 107th would've driven them clear back to Atlanta!"

"All by ourselves?" Nicholas laughed. "Reckon we'll have our chance come spring. There'll be another push. We ain't leavin' Georgia lie."

"Jeremy'll have his chance to be a hero, like the

drummer boy of Chickamauga." Lars said this mockingly, so it couldn't be anything good.

Still, Jeremy couldn't help asking, "What drummer boy?"

Nicholas frowned. "No need to bring that up."

"Yes, there is," Jeremy contradicted. He turned to Seth, who was the official storyteller of the mess. "How did the drummer boy of Chickamauga die?"

"He didn't." Seth leaned his ax against the tree and sat down on a branch. "He's a little fellow about your age—"

"I heard he's just got captured by the Secesh," Dave said.

"Yeah, he has, but not in the story, all right? He joined up with the Twenty-second Michigan, right, followed them till they took him. And they made a little pet of him and got him his own musket cut down to size, and he rode into battle on a caisson."

Jeremy listened, spellbound. That was what *he* wanted to do.

"Only the battle at Chickamauga didn't go so good, right? So then they're retreating. And this Confederate officer comes ridin' up on a big ol' horse, points a gun at this drummer boy, and tells him to surrender."

"So did he?"

"Nope. He shot him."

"So he did die," said Jeremy. He knew it. *Another* drummer boy had gotten ahead of Jeremy.

"I mean the drummer boy shot the Confederate officer."

"Oh. Did he kill him?"

"Yup." Seth picked up his ax, got up, and started working on the tree again.

"Is that the end of the story?" asked Jeremy.

Seth went on working and didn't answer.

Jeremy went back to work too, chopping small branches off the larger ones. He wasn't sure what to think. In a way he envied the drummer boy, having his own gun to shoot. But actually shooting somebody—he didn't know how he felt about that.

He stopped chopping. "Well, the Confederate officer *would* have shot him," he said.

"I don't know," said Seth. "See, when you go into battle, if you're going to shoot somebody you just shoot 'em. You don't ask him to surrender or nothin'."

"Well, the officer was a slave owner anyway and deserved what he got," said No-Joke.

"No-Joke's one of them bobolitionists," said Lars, as if Jeremy hadn't already figured that out. "He's fightin' to free the slaves."

"*Ab*olitionist," said No-Joke.

"Ain't we all fighting to free the slaves?" said Dave.

"Not me, I ain't fightin' for no slaves. I'm fightin' to preserve the Union," said Lars. "Can't have no states dropping off like the United States was just a singin' club you could quit anytime."

Lars said this with the certainty he said everything

with. Lars had never had a doubt in his life, Jeremy thought. Lars acted like he'd had the whole world figured out since he was two years old.

"I guess that's why I'm fighting too," said Dave, resting his ax on the ground as he wiped his forehead. "For the Union. And so is Nicholas."

Nicholas smiled at Dave answering for him. Nicholas might be the most easygoing man Jeremy had ever met, even if he was a schoolteacher. "I don't mind fighting to free the slaves, too," said Nicholas. "Time those thunderin' Rebs learned to do their own thunderin' work for a change."

"They can't work. Too lazy," said Lars, who was lying on his back against a log, watching the rest of them work.

"That's pretty strange coming from *you*," said No-Joke, hauling aside a branch that he had just cut, so that he could get on to the next one.

"I didn't sign up to die for no slave," said Jack. As usual he had a scowl on his round face. Jack was always angry, as far as Jeremy could tell. Born angry. "It ain't fair to switch it around now and say we're fighting for slaves. If I could get out of this war now I would."

"There's the door," said Nicholas, nodding at the open field around them.

"How about you, Little Drummer Boy?" said Lars. "What would you be fightin' for, if you was fightin'?"

Dave laughed, but then said, "Oh, Jeremy'll be brave enough when he sees the elephant."

Jeremy didn't doubt he'd be brave. But he didn't think

he'd like to shoot a man. Maybe he wasn't as brave as the drummer boy of Chickamauga.

"What's the big deal about the elephant, anyways?" said Lars. "I was at Chancellorsville, never saw him. Gettysburg, never saw him."

"Maybe it's a she-elephant," said No-Joke with a slight frown, because of course he meant it quite seriously.

"'Member when we came down into that sunken road and saw all them dead men bleedin' into the ground? That was the elephant," said Dave.

Seth, who was still working furiously at his tree limb, let out an involuntary grunt of pain.

"Seth's got his elephant right on him," said Lars.

"This? No, this ain't my elephant," said Seth. "When I first turned round to speak to the man next to me and realized he didn't have no head, that was the elephant."

"This" was what was left of Seth's right leg. He'd lost it at Gettysburg, and the stump was still not healed. He had insisted on staying with the regiment anyway. This happened often, Jeremy had learned—wounded men didn't go home, because they thought the regiment *was* home.

It was a shame about Seth's leg. Surely it would be easier to die nobly wounded in battle surrounded by weeping comrades and have it over with. Jeremy tried to think of something encouraging to say to him. He decided to tell him about Uncle Bill back in the Northwoods.

"I've got a uncle who's paralyzed in one leg—" Jeremy began.

Dave winced. Nicholas and Lars grinned in anticipation.

"It don't slow Uncle Bill down hardly at all. He can still—"

"I know!" Seth snapped. "He can still do a tap dance, and walk a tightrope, and ride over Niagara Falls on the top of a dad-blamed barrel singing 'Hail Columbia' with a chorus of dancing girls in pink satin bloomers, all the while doing mental arithmetic out of the eighth-grade book even though he doesn't have a *head*!"

The other men laughed. Jeremy turned away, stung. He'd been trying to be nice. Seth didn't have to take it like that.

"Don't see how you're gonna go on campaign with us on crutches," said Nicholas. "You're gonna have trouble keeping up."

"Don't you worry about me," said Seth, calmer. "I still got my gun. Just save a few Rebs for me, and I'll muster 'em out when I catch up to youse."

Jeremy couldn't help staring at Seth's leg.

"Still want to go to the wars, Little Drummer Boy?" said Lars mockingly.

Jeremy looked straight back at him. "Yep. I do."

DULCIE WAS STANDING BEHIND MISSUS AT THE DRESS-
ing table, fixing Missus's long brown hair, when a distant
boom made her drop the comb on the floor.

"There go the cannons," Dulcie said.

"Nonsense. Cannons! It's thunder, I imagine. Don't use
that comb now it's been on the floor, girl, get another one."

"It sounded like a cannon, Missus."

"How would you know what a cannon sounds like,
girl? Have you ever heard one?"

"No, Missus." Not all winter, anyway. But back in
September she and the other slaves had pressed their ears
to the ground and she had heard, or rather felt, the far-
away shudder of the guns at Chickamauga. It hadn't been
a sound like this. This seemed closer. And something in-
stinctive, the way the sound had rippled down Dulcie's
scalp, made her sure it was cannons. "Maybe it's the Yankees
coming," said Dulcie.

"You'd better hope it's not. You know what Yankees do with colored people."

"Yes, Missus, I'm awfully afraid of Yankees," said Dulcie obediently. Then some inner stubbornness made her add under her breath, "I don't think Yankees *really* eat colored people, though."

"Are you sassin' me, girl?"

"No, Missus," said Dulcie hurriedly, as they both eyed the cowhide hanging by the bedroom door. It was the inevitable end of any trouble with Missus.

The farm wasn't a big one. It was in the hill country, between the mountains and the big plantations of the Etowah Valley. Once, there had been twenty slaves, back when Dulcie was small, but then the war came. First two slaves had gone away when Mas'r and Young Mas'r went away to the war, and then when Mas'r came back to mind the farm the two slaves had stayed with the army.

Everyone said the Yankees would be beat in a week, but that didn't turn out to be true, and Mas'r didn't feel much like staying in the army for longer than that. He liked his new uniform, but he wasn't so keen on sleeping in a tent and having to associate with men lower down the social scale than him. He didn't have to, because the Confederacy passed a law exempting men who owned twenty slaves or more from military service. Later Mas'r sold some slaves—they were worth a lot when owning them could keep people out of the army. So he didn't have twenty anymore, but he paid some money to the government so he could still stay at home. Then some slaves had been sent away to work on fortifications on the coast and around Atlanta. And then, finally, Mas'r himself had been sent away to the defense of Atlanta, even though he had friends in the government and had paid a whole lot of money to different officials to keep him out of the army.

"It's wicked, that's what it is," Missus had said on the porch the night before Mas'r left for Atlanta.

"Well, there's not as much appreciation of people of the better sort as there used to be," said Mas'r with a sigh. "But somebody's got to defend Atlanta."

"Why can't the people in Atlanta do it?" said Missus. "Why does it always have to be you? It's not fair, that's what it's not."

"No," said Mas'r. "But we must all do our part for our country, my dear."

That had been three months ago, during the winter. Now it was well into the spring of 1864, and the war was three years old. The Yankees were likely starting another push for Atlanta. That was what Dulcie heard, and she reported it to the two other slaves remaining on the farm, Aunt Betsy and Uncle John.

"The Yanks are up in the mountains now," Dulcie had said, as the three of them sat on benches in Aunt Betsy's cabin waiting for the corn cakes baking on the hearth. "They might be here in a few days."

"*If* no one tries to stop them. Don't you remember those Secesh soldiers we saw going north?" said Aunt Betsy.

"If the Yanks win they'll be down here on their way to Atlanta," said Uncle John. "And we can pick up and go with them."

"What if the Yanks retreat?" said Dulcie, talking back. "What if the Secesh drive 'em back north again like they did at Chickamauga? Can't we just go and join 'em now?"

"With all those Home Guards and slave patrollers all over the road? No thank *you*," said Aunt Betsy.

Dulcie picked up her corn cake, warm and comforting between her hands, and breathed in sweet corn-cake-smelling steam. Georgians were supposed to be growing corn instead of cotton. The problem was, big plantation owners were ignoring the law and growing cotton anyway, stockpiling it for when the war was over. So there wasn't enough food, not by a long shot. Dulcie had heard Mas'r read in the newspaper about the shortages, the high prices, and the food riots, when white women attacked stores and warehouses to seize food. But none of that had happened to her. The farm grew enough food to feed them all, for now, and the slaves got their share, because Mas'r and Missus had too much self-respect to be known as people who underfed their slaves. They might whip their slaves, of course. Everyone did that. They might lock them in a dark, hot box for days at a time to learn 'em. But underfeed them? Certainly not. Underfeeding was the one thing that could get a slave owner talked about by people who mattered—other slave owners.

"After all, if we don't feed properly then how can we prove to the abolitionists that slavery is a benevolent system?" Mas'r had once said to Missus, and Dulcie, under the porch, had filed away two new words in her head, *abolitionists* and *benevolent*.

Dulcie let her teeth sink luxuriously into the first bite of corn cake. Heaven. There was nothing better in the world, as far as she was concerned, than hot corn cakes fresh off the hearth. She wondered if Yankees had them. "I wonder what Yankees eat," she said aloud.

"Us-all," said Uncle John, teasing her.

She made a face at him. "Seems like they must have trouble getting food, so far away from their own home-place."

"Doesn't trouble them none," said Aunt Betsy. "They just take ours."

They ate in silence for a moment, and Dulcie thought how odd that *ours* was, because nothing belonged to the slaves, not food nor anything else, and yet in a strange way it did seem like if the Yankees came down into Georgia they'd be coming in where they shouldn't and taking what they shouldn't all the same, and Dulcie almost understood that word *ours*.

Dulcie was combing Missus's hair and thinking about this when Missus suddenly said, "What's that?"

The sound of hoofbeats and men's voices came from the yard below.

"Maybe it's Yankees," said Dulcie hopefully, going to the window.

"Hsst! Shut up, girl." Missus was right behind her, sounding frightened. She gripped Dulcie's shoulder tightly.

"It's not Yankees," said Dulcie, wincing under Missus's grip. "It's our side." Again that *our.*

If anything, Missus was more panicked than before. "Run, girl! Hide Begonia!"

"Hide her where, Missus?"

"I don't know where! Do I have to tell you how to do everything, girl? Just hide her! I'll keep the gentlemen busy." And Missus whipped her hair under her bonnet, fluttered herself into shape, and headed for the stairs. Soon Dulcie could hear her making welcoming noises out on the porch.

Dulcie thought fast as she ran to the barn. There weren't too many places you could hide a horse. None of the places the slaves hid things would do—under the floor, up in the roof beams. Down the well was definitely out, and Dulcie had never seen a hollow tree big enough to slip Begonia into.

Dulcie breathed in the sweet hay smell of the barn and took Begonia's halter down from the nail outside her stall. "Come on, Begonia. Good horse. Good girl. Gotta hide you from the Secesh."

Begonia lowered her silver-gray head, made a munching motion with her lips, and shuffled her hooves against the barn floor. She looked at Dulcie with her deep black eyes and let her slip the halter over her head. Dulcie fastened the halter and stroked Begonia's warm, smooth neck; then she took the halter rope and opened the stall door. She tugged the rope, and Begonia clopped obediently after her. At the barn door they stopped. Dulcie heard men's voices on the porch, Missus's gay laugh, and the clink of glasses. Missus must've served them drinks with her own lily-white hands, and now the Confederate officers had to sit and drink them—they could no more have broken the rules of politeness than they could have sprouted wings and flown.

Dulcie looked toward the woods. No, that was where slaves headed when they ran away. Down there to the creek. Then they brought the dogs after 'em. Dulcie didn't want dogs chasing Begonia.

"Come on, Begonia. I know where they'll never think to look. Quiet, now!"

Horses are not good at quiet. Especially when you lead them up wooden steps. With each resounding clomp Dulcie expected the chatter on the front porch to cease. She tried to make up for Begonia's noise by being extra quiet herself, practically gliding across the back porch. Overhead she heard the mockingbirds quarreling in the chestnut trees, and she wished them louder.

Silently she shut the kitchen door behind them.

"*Good* girl." She put a hand up to stroke Begonia's solemn silver-gray face. Begonia blinked one calm black eye at Dulcie and flicked her tail.

There was a resounding crash.

"I'll see what it was. That girl is always dropping things," Missus's voice sang merrily down the hall. Dulcie tried to hide behind Begonia's thick, warm body. She saw what had smashed—a big clay pot of sorghum molasses, done in by Begonia's tail. A sticky, burnt-sugar-smelling pool leaked across the scrubbed pine floor. Dulcie, who seldom got anything sweet to eat, knelt down and stuck her finger in it.

"What—" Missus gasped, then swallowed the sound quickly. She grabbed Dulcie's arm and wrenched her to her feet. "Get that horse out of this kitchen at once!" she hissed.

"Yes'm."

Dulcie held her breath until Missus was out on the porch again.

"—don't even have a horse anymore, I'm afraid, gentlemen," Dulcie heard her say. "Though I surely would like to help out the Confederate cause, and do my duty by giving it up, if I did have one. You're welcome to look in the barn—it's around here. . . ."

Stupid! Southern politeness would prevent them from contradicting Missus, but it wouldn't keep them from seeing, as soon as they looked in the barn, that a horse lived there.

Begonia was eating a bunch of collard greens from the kitchen table. Dulcie didn't try to stop her; she figured Begonia had a right to them. She looked out the back door. She could see them out there—two Confederate impressment officers, in mostly gray uniforms, and Missus hovering anxiously beside them, her hoopskirt bobbing like a duck on a river. There was no getting Begonia out that way—they'd be seen at once. Anyway, it isn't that easy to turn a horse around in a kitchen.

"Come on, Begonia."

Begonia followed obediently, clattering and slipping over the polished wooden floor of the hallway and the parlor. She whickered a greeting to the Secesh officers' horses, whose reins were looped around the porch rail. Dulcie heard the heavy plop of something landing wetly on the parlor carpet.

She decided not to think about this.

"Come on, girl. Can't go out the front door, they'll be back there in a minute."

The stairs weren't easy. Begonia could manage a few steps, but a whole staircase she thought was a mountain. She really wanted to gallop up it, but Dulcie was in the way. It took a lot of patience and stumbling on the part of both girl and horse before they finally reached the top and trotted into Missus's bedroom.

"Well, we sure are sorry you haven't got a horse, ma'am." Dulcie could hear the officers outside, returning from the barn. "What with so many of our troops being unmounted cavalry now, and our wagons sitting still for lack of anything to pull them."

"I surely do wish I could help out," Missus fluttered.

"Course if you did have a horse and we didn't get it, the Yanks'd have it soon enough," said the other officer. "They aren't twenty miles northwest of here, if you follow the railroad."

"But surely our brave, noble soldiers aren't going to let them get any closer!" said Missus.

"I surely hope not. Be hard to stop 'em when we don't have horses, though, ma'am." They were on the porch now. "Oh no, let us take those trays in for you, ma'am."

Downstairs, the front door opened. There was a sound of footsteps in the parlor, and then a long, heavy, considering kind of silence.

Upstairs, Begonia started eating Missus's candlewick bedspread.

Dulcie could almost taste the Confederate officers' dilemma, as they stood in the parlor below. On the one hand, they saw—and smelled—clear evidence of horseness before them. On the other hand, good manners and the nature of the evidence struck them dumb.

"Stop eating that, Begonia." Dulcie reached to pull the bedspread out of Begonia's mouth, and Begonia shook her head angrily and backed into Missus's dressing table, which went over with a crash.

Footsteps came pounding up the stairs.

"Well, I never!" said Missus.

"I did," said one of the officers under his breath. "Third horse in a bedroom this week."

"I certainly never told her to!" said Missus. "Dulcie, how dare you try to hide Beg—er, a horse, this horse, wherever you got it from, from the Confederate government!"

Dulcie looked at the officers. They looked back. Dulcie looked at the cowhide hanging by the door. Missus would whip her later, of course. Not in front of the officers. Missus was too well-bred for that, but she would add in extra effort to make up for the wait. Well, Dulcie had had enough. She was through. She walked around the officers, and around Missus. At the top of the stairs she turned and curtsied. Then she went down to the kitchen and took a measure of parched corn and what was left of a ham and tied them up in a napkin. Then she walked out onto the back porch, and kept on walking.

Somehow she'd known she was going to do it as soon as she heard the cannons in the distance. She didn't stop to say goodbye to Aunt Betsy and Uncle John. They wouldn't have to say they'd seen her leave. She went to the stream, the way people did, and she walked into it, the water cool on her bare feet. Northwest, they had said. West like the sun that sank over the mountains each evening. North like the North Star at night. Dulcie followed the stream that way.

☆ ★ ★ SIX ★ ★ ☆

AT LEAST SHELBYVILLE, TENNESSEE, WAS SOMEWHERE different, Jeremy thought. People talked differently, the trees were different, the streets and the way the wagons were hitched were different. Jeremy was seeing the world, and that was something. People from the Northwoods had always been going out into the world, heading west to get rich. Usually they came back as poor as they went, but richer by the things they'd seen—the plains with endless herds of buffalo like living rivers, Indians on horseback watching them from the prairie hilltops, the great snow-capped Rockies, the goldfields of California and the un-steady streets of San Francisco. Jeremy longed to see the world, and now he was seeing it.

But to his great disappointment, Shelbyville was a Unionist town. Tennessee had been the last state to secede from the Union, and the people in Shelbyville hadn't wanted to secede at all. It seemed like everyone there loved the Union and loved its soldiers. There wasn't an enemy in sight all winter long. The U.S. soldiers spent much of the winter being invited to dinner parties by Tennessee loyalists, and having them to dinner in their camp in return. The men danced the Alabama Flatrock with the Tennessee ladies, and when the ladies couldn't make it to the dances some of the soldiers pretended to be ladies, and they danced anyway. Jeremy refused to be a lady, because the soldiers hadn't got around to realizing he was a man yet. The only other person who refused to be a lady was No-Joke. But No-Joke didn't have Jeremy's excuse. No one doubted he was a man. It was just that No-Joke was never any fun.

Jeremy played marbles with the boys in Shelbyville—he wore his Union musicians' corps uniform and basked in their admiration. When it got really cold, so cold the river froze over, which none of the Shelbyville boys had ever seen before, he pretended it was nothing and showed them how to slide on the ice on a board. In January, he turned eleven years old, but no one noticed. He learned to play base ball, a new game that he'd heard of but never seen.

Finally, at the end of April 1864, orders came for the 107th. They were to become part of a new corps, the Twentieth Corps, led by General Hooker. They were to reduce all their possessions to what they could carry. They would be traveling as light as possible—they weren't even supposed to carry tents. They were not told where they were going or why. It wasn't a soldier's business to know that.

Jeremy felt a thrill at being a real soldier—he wouldn't know what was happening till it happened before his eyes.

"Better send your things on home," said Dave gloomily. "I sent stuff to the government warehouse before, and I ain't never seen a stitch of it again."

Jeremy didn't have a home to send his things to, so he gave away what he had, which was mostly some marbles—he gave them back to the boys he'd won them from—and a couple of dime novels, and a copy of *Uncle Tom's Cabin* that a missionary lady from the tract society had given him. All three books he had read, lent out, and reread several dozen times. He kept a blanket, his canteen and mess kit, and, of course, his drum.

The 107th had marched out of Shelbyville a week ago. They were in Georgia now, and as far as Jeremy could tell, the state was all mountains and trees. No people lived here.

He beat his drum for the march when he could. Most of the time he couldn't. They were marching over steep mountain roads that seemed more like trails, and it was hard enough just to keep on his feet and carry a pack and a heavy wooden drum, never mind play it.

It was noon, and Jeremy was hot and tired from marching over the mountain passes. His company was waiting its turn to cross Pea Vine Creek. They had been waiting all morning. There were wagons and ambulances crossing ahead of them. Most of the mules balked and wouldn't put their feet in the water. It was hot and dusty and everyone from the mules to the officers had gotten fussy and snappish. Jeremy's messmates were acting like they didn't like having a drummer boy hanging around them, and so was everyone else, and Jeremy was missing his friends back in Shelbyville already.

Jeremy's canteen was empty, so he wandered upstream to fill it. The soldiers had been warned not to drink muddy water. Around a bend and out of sight, Jeremy found a clear place. He crouched down at the edge of the creek, trying to tilt his canteen enough to get the water to run into the neck of it without stirring up silt from the river bottom. Suddenly he became aware of someone on the other side of the creek.

He looked up. A boy was looking back at him. The boy was tall and scrawny and older than Jeremy. He was dressed in a gray homespun shirt and a pair of too-big Union trousers, with a red patch on one knee cut into the shape of a steam locomotive. He wore a belt cinched tight with a buckle that said C.S.—except for the letters, it was just like Jeremy's belt buckle.

C.S. for "Confederate States." Jeremy froze, his canteen in his hands. He was in the presence of the enemy.

And Jeremy was all alone. He wondered if he should yell for help. But what kind of coward would do that, faced with one lonely enemy soldier, and not even a full-grown one at that? He stared at the enemy. The enemy looked back, an amused half-smile on his face. The enemy didn't have a weapon, as far as Jeremy could see. Neither did Jeremy, except his pocketknife. The thought of sticking his pocketknife into someone had never occurred to him before, and now that it did he didn't like it.

"What's your name?" asked the enemy.

"Jeremy DeGroot, drummer boy, 107th New York, Second Brigade, called the Red Star Brigade, First Division, Twentieth Corps under General Hooker, Army of the Cumberland, Department of Ohio under General Sherman," Jeremy blurted.

That didn't intimidate the enemy any—he just laughed. "A bit free with the information, ain't you? Name's Charlie Jackson."

"Are you a drummer boy?" Jeremy asked, to cover up his embarrassment at having said so much.

"Nope, full-in soldier."

"Tell me another one."

"It's true," said Charlie. "Been in it since Shiloh. I have seen the elephant. Unlike some people." He smiled, to take the sting out of the words, and Jeremy had an awful feeling that he could like this enemy.

"How do you know I ain't been in battle?" said Jeremy.

"People look different after. In their eyes. They've seen the elephant."

Jeremy looked at Charlie's eyes and tried to see any reflection of elephant there. Charlie's eyes were brown and amused, and yes, there was a knowing look to them, but Jeremy had seen that look in lots of people's eyes, and he wasn't sure it had anything to do with elephants.

"Reckon y'all are coming into Georgia to see him, though," said Charlie, still friendly enough. "We'll show him to you. We'll eat the 107th New York for breakfast."

"At least you'll have something to eat then," Jeremy said, noticing how big the C.S. buckle was on Charlie's tightly cinched belt.

Charlie picked up a pebble from the riverbank and tossed it at the opposite shore, making it fall in the water a few feet short of Jeremy. "We got plenty to eat."

"What've youse got to eat over there?" said Jeremy. Only a week out of Shelbyville he was already tired of camp rations.

"Corn bread. Goobers. All kinds of stuff."

"Really? You got corn bread?"

"Yup. Got some right here." The boy reached into his shirt pocket and pulled out a leaf-wrapped cake. "What've you got to trade for it?"

Jeremy felt his mouth water. But he had to admit the awful truth. "Hardtack."

"Really?" Charlie's eyes lit up. "Show me."

Jeremy dug out a thick cracker about the size of a playing card and not much different in taste. "You really want this?"

"Nah, but I'll do you a favor," said Charlie. "Seein' as how you want the corn bread." He was already splashing across the creek, and Jeremy noticed for the first time that Charlie was barefoot.

"Bread," said Charlie, smiling at the hardtack like a long-lost friend.

Hardtack was bread like a fossil was a fish. But Jeremy was too busy eating the corn bread to argue. There were bits of grit that stuck in his teeth, but at least his teeth could get into it. He luxuriated in the chewability of it. Charlie, meanwhile, was squatting down, soaking the hardtack in the creek.

"There's probably bugs in it," Jeremy pointed out, with his mouth full.

"If they stay clear of my teeth they won't get hurt," said Charlie. "You don't have any coffee, I suppose."

"Not on me," said Jeremy.

"Reckon you could get some?" said Charlie. "I could trade you tobacco for it."

Jeremy didn't use tobacco, but it was hard to resist the longing in Charlie's voice. "Sure. We got tons of coffee. I'll bring you some."

"Really? Capital!" Charlie stopped soaking the hardtack, put it in his mouth, and tried to bite it. He winced.

"Sometimes we boil the hardtack," said Jeremy helpfully. "That softens it up good, and the worms float to the top."

"When can you bring the coffee? Where y'all headed?"

"I don't know," said Jeremy.

"You don't know at all?"

"Well, they don't tell us," said Jeremy.

"Well, I can tell you that, anyway. Y'all are aimin' for Atlanta," said Charlie. "Ain't gonna get there, 'cause we're gonna stop you, but that's where you're headed."

"Oh," said Jeremy.

"That's Taylor Ridge up there," said Charlie, pointing. "Y'all are probably figurin' to cross at Buzzard's Roost."

Jeremy shrugged. The land ahead was all green mountains to him, something they were supposed to get over somehow.

Charlie squatted down to soak his hardtack some more. He reached into the water and pulled something out. At first Jeremy thought it was a big rock.

They both looked at what Charlie was holding.

"Whush!" said Jeremy.

"Chickamauga, you reckon?" said Charlie, giving it an appraising frown.

"Are we on the Chickamauga battlefield?" Jeremy hadn't known that.

"Close to. Hard to say, really. Battles go on for miles and miles. Could be this fella was wounded and came here to get a drink of water."

Jeremy stared at the thing Charlie had found: a skull, green with algae, and missing its lower jaw. Jeremy felt something drain out of him, and he had an awful feeling it might be his courage. "Is he one of yours or one of ours?"

"Kind of hard to tell now, isn't it?" Charlie looked

amused again, which seemed to be his permanent expression, as if the world was just about to let him in on the joke and he could see it coming. He poked around in the water. "Don't see no bits of uniform or anything here."

"Where's the rest of him?"

"Maybe downstream, or maybe animals dragged the bones off." Charlie put the skull back in the water. Then he stuck the hardtack cracker in his pocket. Jeremy was relieved, at any rate, that Charlie wasn't going to go on soaking his hardtack in the creek. Jeremy himself decided he would empty out his canteen at the first opportunity. But he didn't want Charlie to see him do it.

"Why'd they let you in the army so young?" Jeremy asked. If Charlie wasn't going to worry about the skull in the water, Jeremy was blamed if he was going to look like he did.

"I was a drill officer. They brought us from the military academy to drill the recruits. Then when they tried to take us back, I wouldn't go."

"How old were you?"

"Twelve." Charlie shrugged. "Old enough, I reckon. And now I'm near fifteen."

"I'm eleven," Jeremy confessed. "But my pa's in jail." He wasn't sure why he added this. Maybe to make up for being so young.

"Really? What for?"

"Chawing a man's ear off."

"That's all?"

"Well, Pa don't believe in gougin' out eyes."

"Seems a bit thin to send a man to jail for gettin' in a fight."

"Well, they *said* he was stealin' a horse," Jeremy admitted. "But he wasn't. It was his own horse. Only this fella said he traded it with him and Pa didn't, or at least he was drunk and didn't mean it."

Jeremy wished now that he hadn't started the story. You could tell when Pa had got drunk, because he always came home with a horse that wasn't his own, and it was always a worse horse than the one he'd left home on, and he was always laborin' under the misapprehension that it was a better one.

"Sounds like he should've got him a better lawyer," said Charlie.

Just then Jeremy heard voices coming from upstream. "There's more soldiers coming—on my side," he said. He realized he was warning Charlie, that he didn't want him to get caught.

Charlie looked upstream at the trees. The voices came closer, but there were still no soldiers to be seen. Without looking particularly worried about it, he turned and splashed across the creek. When he was across he turned to look back at Jeremy. "We'll meet up again to trade for that coffee, all right? I'll find you by the water."

"What water?" said Jeremy.

"Any water." Charlie lifted a hand in farewell. "Been

a pleasure meetin' with you, Jeremy. Hope to make your better acquaintance."

Jeremy was surprised at the polite words and was still trying to think of the correct response as Charlie vanished into the woods on the other side of the creek.

☆ ★ ★ S E V E N ★ ★ ☆

AN ARMY ON THE MARCH GOES ON FOR MILES. MILES from front to back, miles from one side to the other. General William Tecumseh Sherman entered Georgia with 98,000 soldiers. Ninety-eight thousand soldiers take a long time to pass by, no matter how you spread them out. And then there were wagons, hundreds of them, pulled by six mules each, and a vast herd of cattle, to be eaten as they went along— Jeremy tried not to look them in the eye. There were ambulances, with drivers and stretcher bearers. And there were hundreds of civilians. There were soldiers' wives, keeping well back because Sherman didn't allow women, and children hawking cold drinks and fruit to the soldiers. There were sutlers, morticians, and the officers' servants, most of them contraband, and more contraband, and people who didn't appear to have any particular reason to follow the army but were just doing it anyway. And then there were dogs, and a pet pig, and some buzzards circling overhead.

An army isn't an easy thing to hide. But it isn't an easy

thing to find, either, spread out across the high mountains of northwest Georgia, making its many ways along high, twisting trails and roadways, seething through the mountain passes. The Rebs were somewhere to the east of them, and the two armies sent out scouts to look for each other, trying to predict where the other was going next.

"I don't reckon Johnny Reb will put up a fight," said Dave. "We're not likely to see any fighting till we get to Atlanta, if you want my opinion."

"Oh, this is just a demonstration," scoffed Jack. "We're not going to Atlanta, we're just out to show the Johnnies our strength, and then we'll go back to Chattanooga."

"I hope we don't go back!" said No-Joke. His eyes shone black in his narrow, hollow-cheeked face. "If we take Atlanta, the Secesh will know we mean business!"

"They already know we mean business," Lars said. "Hey, Little Drummer Boy, why ain't you drumming?"

They were on the march, if you could call it that, along the west side of a stony mountain ridge that rose stark and gray above them. There was no point in drumming; the men couldn't have kept time if they'd wanted to, scrabbling for footholds on the steep hillside. Jeremy wished Lars at perdition.

Once, Dulcie had seen a runaway slave caught by dogs. Her name was Anne, and seven dogs had brought her down, and bitten her again and again—they were trained to do that. To bite without tearing out the flesh. Dulcie had been five then, and had buried her face in her mother's skirts to hide from it. They hadn't let the dogs kill Anne. Instead they'd let the bites heal, then whipped her two hundred lashes in front of all the slaves. Dulcie had tried to hide her head in Mama's skirts again, but Missus had grabbed her away from Mama and turned her around and made her face Anne. They had brought in an overseer from another farm to do it. Dulcie closed her eyes tight, but she could still hear the gunshot crack of the whip, even now, six years later, as she walked through the cool running brook in her bare feet.

That was when she'd first realized that she, Dulcie, belonged to Mas'r and Missus and not to Mama and Papa. Mas'r and Missus had complete control over their lives, and though the preacher might come sometimes and tell the slaves that God wanted them to obey Mas'r and Missus, Dulcie found it hard to believe that anybody, even God, had more power over her than Mas'r and Missus did. She understood that Papa belonged to a different mas'r and missus, and then they had sold Papa further south, and they could do that too. They could kill you if they wanted. It would be against the law, but there wasn't a chance in a hundred the law would say anything if they did.

Dulcie remembered the doctor saying that to Missus about Anne, later. "Even if she does die," he had said, kneeling on the clay floor in the cabin amid the flies and the smell of infection, "since it occurred naturally, in the course of condign punishment, it's not a crime."

And Missus had smiled a secret, satisfied smile that Dulcie found terrifying.

Not long afterward Mas'r sent Dulcie's mama away. He hired her out to someone as a cook. "I never break up families," Dulcie remembered him saying to the white man who came to take Mama away. "But this is only temporary, and anyway, the girl is nearly six already."

And Dulcie never saw her mama again. A letter had come once, that someone had written for Mama and that Mas'r had read to Dulcie. But there had been no more letters, and when Dulcie asked when Mama was coming back Missus told her to stop complaining and get back to work.

After that Dulcie hated Mas'r and Missus, and hated being a slave, and determined that one way or another, one day, she was going to be free.

And now she was running away to the Yankees.

Dulcie walked all night. They would have missed her by now, but Missus would think she was just hiding from the inevitable beating. Mas'r and Missus thought they'd succeeded in making their slaves afraid of Yankees. But their slaves never believed anything Mas'r and Missus told them, on general principle.

When the gray mist of dawn came, Dulcie scrambled up the cliff-steep bank of the stream, eager to find out how far she had come. At the top she looked down. Below her she could see a white clapboard house, and a yard with a dog in it, fields green with new corn, and a cluster of slave cabins. . . . Dulcie knew those cabins. She'd grown up in them! She'd barely come any distance at all, after walking all night, and her feet were stone-bruised and wrinkled from the cold stream.

She needed to leave the stream, to move faster. But which way to go? Quickly she climbed a hemlock tree— she had always been good at climbing. She stood on the highest branch she could get to, the bark rough under her bare feet, and looked out over the surrounding land. To the west of her lay a wagon road, two red lines of Georgia clay stretching into the distance. Clouds of red dust rose all along the road. One dust cloud meant a traveler. Dulcie had never seen dust clouds like this. A whole army was moving along that road. But it was moving away from Dulcie—so it was probably the Secesh.

A railroad track gleamed silver in the sunlight. Both road and railroad led northwest, in the direction Dulcie believed she had heard cannons from yesterday.

She heard the distant clap of guns again. It went on and on. Dulcie clambered down. She had to decide which way to go, and fast. The railroad seemed to go in the direction the guns were coming from. And where those guns were, Dulcie would find Mr. Lincoln's soldiers.

Keeping to the trees and listening hard for sounds of pursuit, Dulcie headed toward the railway tracks.

By her second night on the railroad tracks, Dulcie's feet were blistered and might have been bleeding—she couldn't see them in the dark. Her stomach hurt from the unaccustomed diet of parched corn, and she was thirsty. She kept her ears perked for the sound of trickling water.

Hoofbeats! Crunching over the railroad ballast, beating hollowly on the ties.

Dulcie made a dash for the bushes, but the horsemen were around her in an instant. Strong hands gripped her arms, her head was forced back, and a lantern glared in her face. Dulcie could see nothing but the light, which made her squint her eyes shut painfully, but she could smell horses and sweat and unwashed clothes.

"Gotcha," said a voice. "Who are you, girl? Who do you belong to?"

"Don't belong to nobody," said Dulcie. "I'm a Free Person of Color."

"Right. Tell that to the marines."

"Where are your free papers, then?"

"Whatcha doing skulking along the railroad at night?"

At least three different voices. Dulcie didn't dare ask them who they were—even Free Persons of Color were expected to answer questions, not ask them—but she was sure there must be more than three. Whatever they were—slave patrollers, Home Guards, Secesh army, militia—they would be traveling in a pack of at least half a dozen.

Her eyes adjusted to the light. She could see the man holding the lantern now—boy, rather. He couldn't have been more than thirteen years old. He was dressed in ragged homespun and a slouch hat. Dulcie couldn't see any of the others. Many hands were holding her, so tightly that she couldn't move her head. But she knew from their voices that at least some of them were grown men.

"Where's your free papers?"

Big hands began groping at Dulcie's apron pockets, and she said hurriedly, "I left them home."

But nobody ever left their free papers home. She knew the men didn't believe her and that she would probably be safest if they thought that she belonged to someone who might give them a reward.

"Belong to John Butler," said Dulcie, picking a name anyone might have. "In Chattanooga. I been visiting my ma and I'm headed home now."

"Well, we'll help you out," one of the men said. "We'll take you to the calaboose and lock you up safe, and your mas'r can come and get you."

A shot split the night. Dulcie heard the heavy thud of a body hitting the ground. One of the hands that held her tight was gone.

"The Union forever!" yelled a voice. More voices cried, "Georgia and the Union! The Union! The Union!"

The men let go of Dulcie as they scrambled to face the new threat. "Homegrown Yanks!"

Dulcie didn't stick around. She ran, faster and harder than she had ever run in her life. The railroad ties vanished beneath her swift bare feet. Behind her she heard more cries, shots, and then, as the men had all emptied their guns, the sickening smack of the rifle butts against flesh, groans of pain. Dulcie paid it no mind. She just ran.

Finally she had to stop, out of breath and with a stitch in her side. She could no longer hear the fight behind her. Maybe they'd all killed each other. If not, the survivors would be looking for her soon. She had to get off the railroad.

A half-moon had come out, and she could see a little now. The train tracks ran through a gully. To her right was a sheer rock cliff. To her left the bank was steep and rocky, but not perpendicular. Here and there a sapling stood out black in the moonlight. Slowly Dulcie began to climb up the cliff. Once, she dislodged a rock and heard it tumble down and thump on the ground below, and she froze, listening. But she only heard the night sounds of crickets and frogs.

At last she reached the top of the bank. Her toes were sore, and one of her hands was bleeding from a cut on a jagged rock. She pressed the cut against the hem of her apron.

She was in a forest, dense with underbrush. She started walking in the dark, pushing her way forward against twigs and stickers that caught at her clothes and jabbed her face and eyes. She meant to be going the same way as the railroad tracks had gone, but she couldn't see the sky, nor the ground beneath her feet. She couldn't see anything, and fighting against the clinging branches made her tired. She almost wanted to sit down on the ground and cry. But she wouldn't give up. There was no way they were going to catch her and take her back to Missus to be whipped two hundred times. No way in the world.

Somewhere above her a bird sang, and another answered back. Dawn was coming—Dulcie couldn't see it, but the birds always knew. Imperceptibly the woods grew lighter, and Dulcie could see the trunks and branches all around her, and the sharp holly leaves that had made scratches all over her skin during the night. A flying squirrel glided past right in front of her face, making her jump.

Then she heard voices ahead of her. She froze. Men's voices. She smelled mules, and wood smoke. She saw flickering orange firelight through the trees. Surely this was an army encampment. But was it Mr. Lincoln's soldiers, or the Secesh?

She meant to go just close enough to look, but the woods ended suddenly and Dulcie tumbled right out into the camp.

A white man in a gray uniform and kepi hat looked up at her without much interest. "What are you doing in there, girl? Go get me some water." He nodded at a bucket that sat next to a white tent.

Secesh. All that running and hiding and she'd fallen right into a Secesh camp.

There were hundreds of white canvas Sibley tents. Thousands of people moved among them, busy cooking breakfast around hundreds of campfires that sent orange sparks upward into the dark dawn sky. The tents and the men seemed to go on forever. The murmur of conversation mixed in with the neighing of horses and mules, and somewhere someone was singing.

We are a band of brothers, and native to the soil,
Fighting for the property we earned by honest toil.
And when our rights were threatened, the cry rose near
   and far,
Hurrah for the bonnie blue flag that bears a single star!
Hurrah! Hurrah! For Southern rights hurrah!
Hurrah for the bonnie blue flag that bears a single star!

"Hurry up with that water, girl," the soldier repeated. "We're moving out in an hour."

Dulcie picked up the wooden bucket and put it on her head. She didn't know where the water was to be found, but she knew a good disguise when she saw it. She walked off, in the casual, no-hurry fashion in which masters expected to see their orders obeyed. Most masters believed that slaves were afflicted with the slows and couldn't move fast even if they wanted to. And that was fine, because a slow-moving slave wouldn't run far.

Dulcie walked deeper into the camp, looking around her. There were many black men and women moving about—slaves, Dulcie knew—toting firewood, hauling water, tending the mules and horses, hitching up the teams to the wagons.

Dulcie held the bucket steady on her head with one hand, her eyes cast down, and walked as if she knew exactly where she was going. She looked down at herself. Her dress, which had been threadbare to start with, was torn nearly to shreds. There were bloodstains on her apron from her various cuts, and red dust coated her all the way down to her sore and dusty feet. She would have liked a bath, as well as something to eat and something to drink, but all of that was less important than getting through the Secesh camp and finding the Union side.

The smells of cooking made her stomach growl. Nobody around the tents and campfires seemed to notice her. And then, to her horror, she felt someone tug at her sleeve. Dulcie froze.

"Whoa, there, little sister." A man's voice.

Slowly Dulcie looked up from under the bucket at a tall black man with a broad nose between narrow, considering eyes. The kind of eyes that go "snap, snap" because they are taking everything in, like a camera, and remembering it.

"Ain't seen you around here before." The man spoke softly, not to be overheard by anyone else. But people all around them were minding their own business, or each other's. They had no time for Dulcie's.

"People don't notice me so much, sir," said Dulcie, looking down at the ground again.

"I notice everybody," said the man. "Name's Nahum."

"Pleased to meet you, Uncle Nahum," said Dulcie, still looking at the ground.

"Got a name yourself?"

"Dulcie."

"Well, Dulcie, I'ma show you the way to the river, in case you should be needing to cross it."

"I'm just going to fetch water, sir," said Dulcie. Did he mean that the Union Army was on the other side of the river?

"Follow me, and I'ma take a roundabout route, and when we get to a footpath I'ma leave you, and you can keep on walking it."

"Yes, sir," said Dulcie.

Dulcie had never heard of a black person turning in a runaway slave. When it came to running away, everyone was your relative and everyone would help you—except white people, of course. Still, Dulcie had a frightful feeling in her stomach, knowing her life was in this strange man's hands. And she didn't like the way he'd noticed her when no one else had.

Nahum was carrying a bundle wrapped in canvas on his shoulder, and he walked away from Dulcie without looking back. Dulcie hesitated a bit, to let him get a ways ahead of her, and then she followed. She kept her eyes on his feet, which were wrapped in rawhide sandals that had flies buzzing around them.

They made their way through the spaces that had been left to separate the regiments. The different states weren't too awfully fond of each other—just enough to fight for each other but not enough to sleep near each other. After about half an hour they reached a tent where Nahum put the bundle down and picked up another. Then they changed direction, wended back the way they had come for a while, and then changed direction again and went on. They came out on the edge of the camp at last, and Dulcie saw the footpath.

"At the end of that path is the river," said Nahum. "There's no crossing here, but downstream a few miles there's a railroad bridge. Problem is, it's guarded. It's safer to swim across here. On the other side of the river is a mountain. Start walking toward it. The Yankees are camped out in a mountain pass a few miles to the northeast of the river, but you should meet their pickets or scouts before that. Go up to them and tell them you are a slave who has left her master. Now, do you understand what you're to do?"

"Yes, sir," said Dulcie, looking up at him. "At the end of the path is the river. There's no crossing here, but downstream a few miles there's a railroad bridge. Problem is, it's guarded. It's safer to swim across here. On the other side of the river is a mountain. Start walking toward it. The Yankees are camped out in a mountain pass a few miles to the northeast of the river, but I should meet their pickets or scouts before that. Go up to them and tell them I am a slave who has left my master."

Nahum looked at her sharply through his narrowed eyes, and Dulcie put her hand to her mouth. Strangers didn't know about her memory and would think she was sassing them.

"Interesting talent you have there, girl. Now off. The Lord keep you."

"Thank you, sir, it was a pleasure to make your acquaintance," said Dulcie. Good manners were the one gift that slaves could afford to give each other. She curtsied and walked away from him.

She didn't bother to tell him that she couldn't swim.

☆ ★ ★ EIGHT ★ ★ ☆

JEREMY HAD BEEN CARRYING HIS COFFEE RATION TIED up in an empty tobacco pouch looped to his top shirt button, waiting to run into Charlie again. He knew Charlie was an enemy, and he was vaguely aware that you could be shot for communicating with the enemy. But he hadn't talked to anyone even close to his own age since they'd left Shelbyville—the other drummers in his regiment were really grown men, not boys at all—and he was getting awfully tired of being called Little Drummer Boy.

He tried not to show that it bothered him, because he knew that that would just make things worse. One of his teachers back in the Northwoods had once told him that if he ignored people who were picking on him, they would stop. He had found that his teacher was one hundred percent and entirely wrong about this.

Pa, on the other hand, had had a different suggestion for dealing with the problem. "Kick 'em in the teeth," he'd said.

The trouble was, Lars was built like the front half of a Percheron horse. You couldn't kick him in the teeth. You'd have a deuce of a time even jumping high enough to slap him in the teeth, and after that you'd probably be searching in the grass for your own.

"You skeered yet, Little Drummer Boy?" Lars asked him. They were in Snake Creek Gap, corduroying the road. Originally they had been supposed to cross the mountains at Buzzard's Roost Gap, following the tracks of the Western and Atlantic Railroad, which Sherman meant to use as their supply line back to Tennessee and, beyond that, the Union. But the Rebs had dammed a creek and flooded the road up to the gap, and they had artillery in the gap and on either side of it, perched on high crags above Buzzard's Roost—and besides that there were hundreds of buzzards. Roosting, of course.

"Waitin' for us," said Seth. "The Rebs'll strip us nekkid and the buzzards'll eat us."

So the whole army was to go through Snake Creek Gap, further south, instead, and pass through the town of Resaca. That meant the road through the gap had to be stabilized with tree trunks laid out crosswise, a corduroy road to keep the wagons and horses and men from sinking in the deep mud. The 107th was finishing up a stint of chopping trees and hauling them down to be laid in the muddy track through the high stone walls of the gap.

Beyond the gap lay a battle.

"Little Drummer Boy's skeered," said Lars, shouldering his ax as the men headed back to where they'd set up camp. "Don't know if he can stand the gaff. What do you think, Jack?"

Jack sneered. "I think he'll run cryin' for Mama at the first smell of powder, that's what I think."

"Stop teasing him, both of you," said No-Joke. "Everyone is scared at their first battle, and after that they get used to it."

"Every bullet has its billet," said Dave.

"That's not so," said Nicholas, to Dave's visible dismay. "Most bullets fetch up in tree trunks or in the ground. Not one in a hundred hits a man."

"Those could still be billets," said Dave. "I didn't say it had to be a person that was a billet's ballot. I mean a . . ." He stopped, confused.

"A bullet's billet," No-Joke said kindly.

"Yeah."

They began building a fire from pine knots and branches cut from the corduroying logs. Pine knots burned like oil and were the thing the soldiers liked best about Georgia so far. It wasn't time to eat yet and it wasn't time to drill, and there were no orders for Jeremy to beat out on his drum, and when there was nothing to do, Lars and Jack always decided to amuse themselves with Jeremy.

Jeremy was sick of it. He got up and wandered away.

He wanted to see if there were any signs yet of this battle that might soon take place.

He made his way along the squelchy track between the stone ramparts, trying to stick to the side where there was some grass growing that hadn't been stirred up too badly yet. Men were still laying logs across and trying to embed them deeply in the mud so that they wouldn't skid away. Someone had managed to get a cannon stuck up to its iron hubs in mud, the mules knee-deep in the mud in front of it, and soldiers were using more logs to try to pry the wheels loose while a contraband mule driver talked softly to the mules, trying to calm them down.

Jeremy walked on between the high cliff walls of the gap. Up above, a shadow against the sky, he saw a soldier signaling with flags. It was important for armies to hold mountaintops, Jeremy knew, for two reasons—because you could see the enemy's movements from a mountaintop, and because they were good places for signal flags to be used, provided there was another mountaintop nearby where the signals could be received.

The problem with signal flags was that the enemy could read them too. General Sherman had a moving telegraph station in a railroad car. But because the Secesh held the railroad tracks at Buzzard's Roost, that telegraph station was stuck behind the lines for now.

As he watched the signaler's arms go up, out to the side, down, up, Jeremy noticed dark clouds gathering. There was a distant roll of thunder. Jeremy hoped the rain would hold off.

That night it poured rain. The mud liquefied, and the corduroying might as well not have been done—every time you stepped on a log it either sank a foot deep into the mud or skidded out sideways, and down you went on your fundament.

For some reason it was decided that this was a good time for the 107th to move forward through the gap.

"In the night," said Dave, marveling. "We set around all day, then they order us to march through this muck in the nigh—Thunderin' Hannah!" He skidded along a log and fetched up facedown in the mud.

"Go ahead and laugh," he said, picking himself up. "It'll happen to the rest of youse in a minute."

And it did. Thunder rolled overhead, and lightning flashed, and every time it did Jeremy had a weird instant's lit-up view of the men of the 107th falling on their backsides, frontsides, and every other side in the mud of Snake Creek Gap.

"Let's sing a song," No-Joke suggested.

"Perdition take your songs!"

"Play something on your drum, Jeremy."

Jeremy looked at No-Joke as if he was crazy, which was something he'd half suspected anyway. "It's soaking wet. It won't play."

"Well, then let's sing." And to everyone's amazement, No-Joke began to sing, in a loud, tuneless tenor that carried over the pouring rain and was only drowned out by the loudest crashes of thunder:

> *We are coming, Father Abraham, three hundred*
>   *thousand more,*
> *From Mississippi's winding stream and from New*
>   *England's shore.*
> *We leave our plows and workshops, our wives and*
>   *children dear,*
> *With hearts too full for utterance, with but a silent tear.*
> *We dare not look behind us but steadfastly before.*
> *We are coming, Father Abraham, three hundred*
>   *thousand more!*

The men laughed. They had all figured out long ago that No-Joke was crazy. No-Joke was, Jeremy realized, something of a joke in himself, and maybe he got picked on just as much as Jeremy did. But it never seemed to bother him. He appeared never to notice. Maybe he was just ignoring it. If so, it was further proof that ignoring it didn't do any good. The more No-Joke ignored people laughing at him, the more they did it.

Except, Jeremy realized suddenly, maybe it did some good to No-Joke to ignore it.

Soon all the men were singing and laughing as they slipped, slithered, and fell, and now the scene was like nothing Jeremy expected he'd ever see again—the thunder crashing, Jeremy and everyone else soaked through, their clothes clinging wetly, their whole bodies slick with mud, and lightning showing the crazy scene in sudden flashes like mad tintypes.

Jeremy laughed too. What else could you do? The whole thing was just crazy.

"We don't have any tents anyways!" shouted a soldier. "We might as well march in this muck as sleep in it!"

> *In eighteen hundred and sixty-three,*
> *Hurrah, hurrah!*
> *In eighteen hundred and sixty-three,*
> *Hurrah! says I,*
> *In eighteen hundred and sixty-three*
> *Abe Lincoln declared the slaves were free,*
> *And we'll all drink deep, so*
> *Johnny fill up the bowl!*

And they laughed and laughed, and they wouldn't be laughing, Jeremy realized, if it wasn't for No-Joke.

The path down to the river was steep and slippery. It must have rained the night before. Dulcie's bare feet gripped it tightly, feeling for tree roots to keep from sliding. She kept a sharp eye out for snakes and scorpions. At the river's edge she stopped and clung to a dead tree branch, thinking. Green, muddy-smelling water slid past below her. The river was at least fifty yards across, smooth and swift and probably too deep for wading, because no driftwood trees or branches stuck up from the bottom. Certainly not something you wanted to risk when you couldn't swim. Dulcie looked down the river as far as she could, but saw nothing like a bridge or a boat or any way to get across.

Upriver something was happening on the opposite bank. There was a crowd of people and mules and some big things that looked like clumsily constructed boats. The people were doing something—trying to reach across the river with the boats. They were pontoons, Dulcie realized— she had heard of this from the newspapers Mas'r read to Missus. They were building a pontoon bridge to cross the river. Were those Mr. Lincoln's soldiers? If they were, they might help Dulcie across if she went to them and asked. But if they were Confederate soldiers she by no means wanted them to notice her. How could she find out which they were? At this distance she couldn't see their uniforms.

Maybe she'd get a better view from higher up. She turned and quickly climbed the tree she'd been holding on to. Climbing was something she was good at, and her bare feet and hands felt for holds and pulled her upward easily. She stood up on a branch that went over the water, the bark rough and solid under her bare feet. She held on to a higher branch to steady herself. She inched out over the water. The branch swayed under her feet.

Now she could see that the men were wearing blue uniforms. That should mean they were Union soldiers. The problem was, as Dulcie had seen in the Confederate camp, a lot of Confederate soldiers wore blue uniforms too. They wore bits of Union uniforms mixed with bits of Confederate uniforms—Dulcie had heard one of the soldiers call them multiforms. Cautiously, Dulcie inched her way further out on the branch, looking for signs of gray in the uniforms. She could almost see well enough to tell—if she just went a little further out, and let go of the branch above her—

She heard the branch crack ominously under her feet. She grabbed at the branch over her head and missed it. She slipped and lost her footing on the branch beneath her. She threw out her arms and caught hold of it, and it broke off, and she plunged down, down, down into the deep, cold, green waters of the river.

☆ ★ ★ NINE ★ ★ ☆

EVERYONE IN THE 107TH NEW YORK COULD FEEL THE waiting. The air was heavy with the uneasy knowledge of a coming battle. Most of General Sherman's army was massed now in Snake Creek Gap and in Sugar Valley below it. The 107th had been moved through the gap. Most of the men were writing letters. Jeremy had no one to write a letter to—he and Pa had never gotten into the habit of writing, somehow. Pa didn't know where Jeremy was, as a matter of fact, and it occurred to Jeremy for the first time that when he died like the Drummer Boy of Shiloh, Pa would not know where to come to visit his grave. At least, not unless somebody wrote a song about it.

On the other hand, if he wrote to Pa in Auburn Prison, then Old Silas might find out where Jeremy was. Prisoners' letters were probably opened and read. If they were even allowed to get letters. Jeremy didn't know if they were. A runaway bound-boy was a fugitive, and Old Silas might have contacted the warden at the prison in Auburn, telling him to watch for a letter from Jeremy. It was too risky.

Jeremy had other unfinished business to attend to. He had been carrying coffee around in an empty tobacco pouch to give to Charlie. When the battle started Charlie would be on the other side, but in the meantime Jeremy had promised him coffee, and he didn't like to break a promise. Especially on what might be his last day on earth.

Jeremy wandered away from camp, toward where he thought the rebel lines might be. Charlie had said they'd meet near water. Well, water was downhill; anyone born in the Northwoods knew that. He headed down into the forest.

A soldier was not supposed to leave camp without permission. He was supposed to get a written pass from his superior officer. Jeremy felt about that exactly the way all the other soldiers in his company felt about it. He was a free American citizen, and he didn't need *nobody's* permission to go *nowhere*.

Anyway, he wasn't really leaving the camp, he reasoned, if he didn't go past the pickets. He had to get past the guard, but that was easy enough, especially if, like Jeremy, you had years of experience walking through forests and had practiced since you were a child to do it silently. The guards were mainly focused to the east, toward Resaca, and Jeremy slipped behind them easily.

Jeremy found a stream where he expected to find one, downhill. The water ran swift and smooth. He looked across it. No Charlie. Well, what did he expect, really? They'd been moving over miles and miles, there was forest and mountains all around them, and there were thousands of Union soldiers—hundreds of regiments besides the 107th New York. How would Charlie ever find him again?

Nonetheless, he followed the stream down, clinging to trees for balance as he walked along the banks, scanning the woods on the other side.

He came out of the woods onto a plain beside a wide river. He looked around him. Upstream he could see a mass of soldiers, working at something—building a pontoon bridge, it looked like. They were Union soldiers. So he was still inside Union lines, and thus not really straying too far out of camp after all. He hoped he would get to march across the pontoon bridge when it was finished, playing his drum.

He squinted, scanning the other side of the river. He saw someone over there—a boy wearing blue Union trousers with a flash of red at the knee and a gray Confederate homespun shirt. Could it possibly be Charlie?

Jeremy waved.

The boy waved back. He cupped his hands and called, "Meet me in the middle!"

Jeremy looked at the river. He could swim well, of course, but it was only May. That water would be cold.

He kicked off his shoes and took off his trousers and fatigue blouse. His drawers he left on. They would get wet and be uncomfortable later, but he had a feeling you didn't take your drawers off when you were parleying with the enemy.

He waded out. The water was warmer than he'd expected, and had that muddy-water smell that rivers back home had. Mud squished up between his toes. He fell forward and started swimming.

He swam toward the middle, letting the current carry him downstream as he went. In the middle he met Charlie.

"'Ere i' is." He trod water, the bag held between his teeth.

"Capital!" Charlie reached out and took the bag. "Won't it be wet?"

"It won't hurt the beans," said Jeremy. "You have to roast 'em over the fire, then grind 'em. Pound 'em up with a rifle butt, that's what we do."

"I meant to bring you some tobacco, but I haven't got it yet."

"Oh, that's all right," said Jeremy. He would've said he didn't use tobacco, but he didn't want Charlie to think he was a child.

"No, I don't want to be beholden. Let me bring you some next time we meet."

Jeremy was proud and flattered that the older boy considered him a friend and wanted to keep on meeting him, even though they were enemies. "All right. We can meet at the next river."

"Next one either way, depending on whether we push y'all back the way you came."

"That ain't gonna happen," said Jeremy. "Whush, what's that?"

Treading water, they both looked at something floating toward them from upstream.

"It's a dog, I think. Is it alive?"

"Nah, it ain't a dog, it's a log," said Jeremy.

"It ain't neither! It's a slave!"

At this Jeremy started swimming hard toward the figure clinging to the log.

Slaves were Union business! But it wasn't easy swimming against the current, and Charlie was bigger and stronger than him. The result was that Charlie reached the slave first and grabbed his arm.

"Whoa, there. Who's your master, girl?" Charlie said, grabbing the girl's arm—because it was a girl, Jeremy saw.

The girl coughed and sputtered and said nothing. Jeremy scissor-kicked to stay upright and let the pair and the log drift toward him. He reached out and grabbed her other arm. The log floated away.

"Contraband!" he said. "I claim contraband of war!"

"You can't! This is somebody's property, and in Georgia's own sovereign land."

Jeremy did not know about the legalities of this. All he knew was that it was part of the Union war effort to get the slaves away from their masters.

"She's running away to us. She knows she don't ought to have no owner."

The girl was still coughing. Holding tight to her arm, Jeremy started scissor-kicking toward the shore where he had left his clothes. Charlie kept hold of her other arm and swam in the other direction. Charlie was stronger, and Jeremy struggled with all his might, kicking hard and dragging at the girl's arm.

The girl flailed out suddenly with both fists. "Let go of me!"

Startled, they both did. The girl sank straight down and vanished in the water.

"She's mine when she comes up," Jeremy said.

"Tell that to the marines."

"What do you want her for? She's not your slave, is she?"

"Course not. But I defend a Confederate citizen's right to his own valuable property. On Confederate soil."

"You can't own a person—a person can't be property," said Jeremy, who had never put this into words before but now saw that he believed it. "A person is a person. She belongs to herself, we'll have to ask her what she wants to do." No one had asked *him* what he wanted, when he was indentured to Old Silas.

"Well, I can tell you what she wants to do, she wants to escape. But I ain't lettin' her."

"Why does she want to escape?" said Jeremy. "You slaveholders are always saying that slaves are well off."

"Well, they are! Better off than the wage slaves in your Northern factories."

"Then why do they want to escape, huh?" Jeremy repeated. He felt he had hit upon a pretty strong point here.

"Because they're cussed-headed!"

Something else occurred to Jeremy. "She ain't comin' back up."

Jeremy dove. He went deep, letting the current carry him as it would have carried the girl. He swam past the warm surface into the cold depths, with his arms spread out before him, his fingers splayed, groping in the green darkness to try to find the girl. At last his hand met flesh, and he seized on it and pulled it upward. The girl fought upward too, and they broke the surface of the river together, gasping.

Only it wasn't a girl Jeremy had ahold of, it was Charlie. The girl was still down there somewhere.

They both dove again. Jeremy dove down even deeper than before, feeling his way through the cold in every direction, but he encountered nothing. At last, his lungs burning, he kicked to the surface.

And he saw that Charlie had the girl and was swimming toward the nearest shore. Jeremy had to kick hard to catch up, and he couldn't get a hand on her, so that in the end it was Charlie who rescued the girl and pulled her up onto the red mud bank.

"What do we do now?" said Jeremy.

"Roll her over a barrel," said Charlie.

"There ain't no barrels here."

"Then I dunno. Turn her upside down and shake the water out of her."

The girl sat up and coughed up a great quantity of river.

She was about eleven years old, Jeremy thought, with hair cut very short. She wore a blue dress that was sopping wet and torn nearly to shreds. She wiped her nose on her sleeve and scowled up at both of them with eyes sharp as bayonet points.

"You one of Mr. Lincoln's soldiers?" she asked Jeremy.

"Yes, sir," said Jeremy, because that was the kind of voice she said it in. "I mean, yeah."

"I am a slave who has left her master!"

"Yes, good," said Jeremy. "Er . . ."

"Who's your master?" said Charlie.

She turned her bayonet eyes on him. "Are *you* one of Mr. Lincoln's soldiers?"

"He ain't. He's Secesh," said Jeremy quickly.

"Then what are you doing with him?"

"He's my friend," Jeremy explained. Somehow this girl had taken command of the situation. He felt that this was wrong. "Come on, I'll take you to my regiment. You're free now."

"No, you ain't," Charlie quickly countered.

"Yes, she is," said Jeremy. "Because happen you brought her out on *our* side of the river."

The girl got to her feet. "Yes, I am free," she said with

great determination. She turned to Jeremy. "Take me to your regiment, then."

"But I'm the one who rescued her," said Charlie.

"You let me sink in the first place," said the girl. "What are you fightin' for slavery for? You don't own any slaves."

"How do you know he doesn't?" said Jeremy.

She spared him a glance. "He ain't the sort." She turned back to Charlie. "My mas'r didn't have to fight in this war, because he owned twenty slaves. How you feel fightin' for his property rights while he sits home?"

Charlie had the same half-amused expression as always, but Jeremy could tell the girl had scored a hit. It was just a flicker in Charlie's eyes, that said Charlie didn't like fightin' for another man's property rights *at all*.

"Beats me why you're fightin' for slavery," said the girl. "You know your own business best, but if I was you I'd head on home to wherever you come from."

"We're fightin' for Southern rights," said Charlie. "But I ain't got time to argue with no runaway slave turned lawyer." He smiled. "Reckon you better take her, Yank."

Whush—the girl had argued Charlie into a corner and Charlie was backing down. And she'd done it when she was half drowned, too. Jeremy wanted to ask Charlie how he really felt about fighting for slavery, but there was the girl to take care of—he had to get her back to camp.

"See you later, Yank," said Charlie. "Remember—at the next river." And he turned and walked back into the river and started swimming to the opposite shore.

"My name's Dulcie," said the girl. "I'm pleased to make your acquaintance."

"Oh. Right. I'm Jeremy." Jeremy couldn't say that kind of polite stuff that Southern people said; he'd feel like a fool. "Come on. I'll take you back to camp."

★★★ TEN ★★☆

JEREMY KNEW HE DIDN'T USUALLY MAKE MUCH OF AN impression on his messmates, let alone on the company as a whole. He was slightly more important than the dogs that hung around the camp, because unlike them he had two names. But people sure sat up and took notice when he walked into camp leading a soggy runaway slave. The girl seemed a little less full of herself now that they were in Jeremy's territory, and so he took her hand paternally and led her forward.

"Got contraband here," he said importantly. "Need to take her to the captain."

"We need to get her into some dry clothes first, is what we need to do," said No-Joke. "She'll catch her death."

Jeremy felt a bit deflated as No-Joke took over his contraband, hustling her off to find dry clothes. When they came back a half hour later, the girl was dressed in a Union combat blouse, the cuffs rolled up around her wrists, and a petticoat that looked like it was made from two pieces of sacking hastily stitched together.

"Hungry, contraband?" said Seth.

The girl looked at him in confusion.

"She's called Dulcie," said Jeremy, trying to regain his authority.

Seth reached into the fire and pulled out a piece of red-roasted meat tied to a stick with a piece of string. An appetizing smell of roast meat and wood smoke rose from it, and Jeremy would have liked a piece of it himself, but Seth held the stick out to Dulcie. "Put yourself around that, Dulcie."

Dulcie curtsied. "Thank you, sir."

"I'm hungry too," said Jeremy.

"You can wait for dinner," said Seth. "Where did you find this contraband, anyway?"

Jeremy felt this subject was best not discussed, since he'd been far away from where he was supposed to be. "Where did you get the pork?"

"From a Secesh pig," said Seth. "It refused to take the oath of allegiance."

Dulcie had never, in all her life, had to make choices before. The decision to run away was the first decision she had ever knowingly made. Now she was free, and the knowledge coursed through her veins and gave her strength she'd never had. She had told the boys to let go of her, and they let. She said she wanted to go to the Union camp, and she went. She hadn't called anybody Mas'r, just their names or sir, and nobody had even noticed.

The boy Jeremy and the soldier they called No-Joke took her to Captain John F. Knox. Dulcie studied the two out of the tail of her eye as they walked. The boy was small and black-haired, probably part Cherokee, Dulcie thought, or part some kind of Indian, anyway. So, for that matter, was the man. Dulcie spent more time studying him, because there was something funny about No-Joke. He burned, that was it. There was a fire inside him, and it had hollowed out his cheeks and left his face and his whole body spare and half-starved-looking, while his eyes were bright with divine fire. His expression reminded Dulcie of Aunt Ruth back home, just before she had died of consumption. But No-Joke didn't cough, and as far as Dulcie could tell he wasn't sick. He just burned.

"The captain's headquarters is up here," said Jeremy.

"There ain't no tents," said Dulcie, not quite daring, despite her freedom, to form it as a question.

"Nah, Crazy Willie wouldn't let us bring no tents on this campaign."

"*General Sherman* said we were to travel light and ready for battle," said No-Joke severely.

Dulcie thought they would regret this when the rains came, but she kept it to herself.

Captain Knox was reading through some papers laid out on a trestle table in front of him. He had an aide beside him. Behind him stood a young black man, a servant, Dulcie supposed. Or a slave? Surely not a slave. Jeremy and No-Joke stood to attention and saluted, and Dulcie, not sure if it was expected of her, saluted as well. The captain returned the salute.

"Contraband, sir," said No-Joke. "She just came over from enemy lines."

The captain looked interested. "What's your name, young person?"

"Dulcie, sir."

"Got a second name?"

"No, sir."

"How about Knox? That's my last name. Would you like Knox for a last name?"

"I'll think about it, sir."

"Who do you belong to?"

At this question Dulcie's heart sank. Were they going to return her to Missus after all?

"Don't rightly know, sir," she hedged.

The black man behind the captain made a little gesture sideways with his head. Dulcie looked at him. What did he mean? Was he telling her that the captain could be trusted? Dulcie didn't want to risk it.

"Is your master in rebellion against the United States of America?"

"Yes, sir."

"Ah, then, you're mine now." The captain smiled, but Dulcie felt like turning and running.

The black man made a little gesture with his lips, and Dulcie thought he was saying that it was all right.

"Where did you come from?"

"Down around the Etowah, sir," said Dulcie cautiously.

"And did you pass through troop movements on the way up here?"

"Yes, sir. A whole big camp of Confederates. By the river down there."

"How many Confederates?"

Dulcie didn't know how to answer this. It seemed to her that there had been an awful lot. "They went on forever, sir."

"Hmm. And where were they headed, do you know that? Did they say? Rome? Resaca?"

Dulcie thought.

"She doesn't know anything, sir," said the captain's white aide.

Dulcie took some more time thinking. Of course she knew something. She remembered every single word that she'd heard as she passed through the Reb camp. It just took her a minute to sort through everything, the songs, the jokes, the complaints, the men teasing each other about their sweethearts.

"They said that their commander, General Johnston, thought that y'all were going to Rome, Georgia," she said. "But now he thinks you are going to attack Resaca. Most of his army is headed to Resaca now, and they are fortifying the town. But some of them are going downriver, because they know that y'all are trying to make a pontoon bridge across the river there and they aim to stop you."

"Just what I said they'd do all along."

The captain waved the aide aside. "What else did you see, Dulcie?"

"Didn't really see much, sir. I had a bucket on my head. But anything I hear once, I remember it."

"I told you they had the intellectual capacities of white people!" said the captain to his aide.

Dulcie had never heard of a white person with a memory like hers, but she held her tongue.

"Write her a pass," said the captain. "Let her stay in the camp now if she chooses. She can look for a job if she wants." He turned back to Dulcie and her companions. "Dismissed."

No-Joke and Jeremy and Dulcie saluted again, and the captain returned their salutes.

Dulcie lingered. The words "if she chooses" and "if she wants" were said in an offhand manner, but they sounded huge and loud to her. She wanted to talk to the black man, to ask him what she could believe, who she could trust, and most of all, what she should do.

That it was simply her choice, that she was free now, she could almost get herself to believe—but what were the choices, and how did you make one? Where did you go?

No-Joke and Jeremy turned and started back to their camp. Dulcie slid away from them. The black man noticed her lingering. He shot her a questioning look. She waited for him to come over to her.

"What do I do now?" she asked.

"Whatever you want," said the man.

"What—" She almost said *What do I want?* but that sounded like such a dumb question. "What do *you* do?"

"I'm the captain's servant. He hired me back in Tennessee. I was in one of the contraband camps for a while." He shuddered. "Don't go to a contraband camp."

"Why not?"

"Too crowded, not enough food. They're hirin' the kids your age out to farmers as servants for their food. No money, just their food. And there's camp fever. One in three died last winter."

Dulcie tried to imagine that. One in three. It sounded like somewhere she didn't want to be. Especially if they were going to turn around and give her to some farmer as a "servant."

"When you say you're the captain's servant . . . ," she ventured.

"He pays me."

"Oh. And—how do I get someone to pay me?"

"Just ask. All the officers hire servants. They're lookin' pretty often, because sometimes the servants leave."

"Run away? Why?"

The man smiled. "They don't run away. They leave."

Dulcie thought about the difference. You could leave

when you wanted. Any day. There was no running away, no pursuit, no being dragged down by dogs and whipped two hundred times. You wanted to leave? You left. Imagine.

"You got a big smile on your face, girl," said the man, smiling in return. "Why don't you try the surgeon? His servant just left him. Reckon he could use another pair of hands."

"All right."

"Here's your pass. Carry it with you all the time."

Dulcie took the paper and held it in her hands. Some of it was printed with a printing press; there were blanks that were filled in with writing. Dulcie could not read. "Is this my free paper?"

"Not exactly. You don't need a free paper, you just free. That's a pass—everyone in the war zone has to have one. Even the soldiers, if they go outside the camp."

"Thank you," said Dulcie.

The man nodded and gave Dulcie a little wave—he was going back to his duties. Dulcie curtsied in return and, clutching the pass tightly in her hand, turned to follow Jeremy and No-Joke. Because she chose to.

Dulcie found Dr. Flood, the regimental surgeon for the 107th, under a chestnut tree, reading a book.

She saluted. "Excuse me, sir."

He looked up from his book. He was old, Dulcie saw. Too old for a soldier, really.

He had silver hair, cut close to his head, and a stern, square-looking face. "Where have you sprung from?"

Dulcie didn't know how to answer this, so she skipped past it. "They told me you're looking for a servant."

Dr. Flood looked Dulcie up and down. "A boy."

Dulcie didn't know what to say to this. She was brought up not to argue, and anyway she couldn't be a boy. That was not possible. She looked down at the ground.

"An army on the march is no place for a girl," Dr. Flood explained. "You ought to go back behind the lines."

"Where behind the lines, sir?"

"I don't know. One of the contraband camps." Dr. Flood frowned. "But they're no place for a girl either. No place for anybody."

Dulcie stood in front of him, waiting.

"Can you cook?"

"Yes, sir."

"Can you wash clothes?"

"Yes, sir." Dulcie could do lots of things. It was just that being a boy was not one of them.

He sighed. "Well, I suppose I'll give you a try. Five dollars a month, and your food, such as it is. How does that sound?"

Dulcie knew nothing at all about money, except that in the old days, before the war, the adult slaves used to get a silver dollar at Christmas from Mas'r and Missus. The children got a dime or a quarter. After the war began there was no money, as far as Dulcie could tell. Mas'r and Missus talked about this a lot on the porch.

"It sounds good, sir."

"It's not," said Dr. Flood with a sudden smile. "If you work out well, I'll make it six."

☆ ★ ★ ELEVEN ★ ★ ☆

JEREMY HAD LEARNED MONTHS AGO TO WAKE BEFORE dawn, so that he could join the other drummers in the regiment's drum corps to beat the reveille at five a.m. Now that they were on the march, reveille came much earlier, usually at three or 3:30 a.m. The night of the twelfth of May, he couldn't sleep. He knew that soon he would be beating the long roll—"Wake up, and be ready for action." He had only practiced it before—first back in Syracuse, and then all winter in Shelbyville with the drum corps. He knew it perfectly, and it beat in his head all night, making him toss and turn under the open sky.

The 107th was going into battle. Even the few things they'd brought had been handed over to the quartermaster for safe keeping. They'd been issued three days' cooked rations and sixty paper cartridges, neat packages each containing a charge of powder and a leaden minié ball. Forty went into their cartridge boxes—their "forty dead men," the soldiers called them—and twenty into their pockets.

Sixty bullets was a lot. The soldiers' Springfield rifles had to be reloaded after each shot. A battle where a man could use up all sixty rounds would be an unusually rough one.

Jeremy got the cooked rations, which he stowed in his haversack to carry into battle with him, but he didn't get any cartridges, of course. Because he wouldn't be carrying a gun into battle—he would be carrying his drum.

Into the cool night darkness the lead drummer played the first drumroll, to awaken the drummer boys. Jeremy wasn't asleep. He leapt to his feet, hurriedly pulling on his shoes. He put his head through the strap of his drum and grabbed his drumsticks, the drum banging against his legs as he climbed up the slope to join the line of drummers who were stumbling into place, ready to wake the camp. He held his head high and looked out over the black out-lines of the wooded valley below. The sky was full of stars; not one had faded out yet. The first bird had not yet chirped. Dawn was a long way away.

This was what he had dreamed of all these years.

The drum major gave the signal, and the drummers began to beat the long roll. It echoed up through Snake Creek Gap and down the valley below, filling Jeremy's ears. The drummers were calling the 107th New York Volunteers to war.

Around them on the mountainside and up in the gap, other drum corps wakened other regiments in the night. The drum rolls went on and on all around, how far Jeremy couldn't tell.

Below them men stumbled, grumbling and swearing, to their feet. Fires flickered into existence. Jeremy went down to join his messmates, who were making coffee.

"So, off to the wars at last, eh, Little Drummer Boy?"

"He doesn't like it when you call him Little Drummer Boy, Lars," said No-Joke, not helping.

"Everybody got a identifier?" said Dave.

"I don't," said Jeremy, suddenly realizing it. Of course, if he fell like the noble Drummer Boy of Shiloh, he wouldn't need his name and address on a piece of paper in his pocket. The mourning comrades kneeling around him would know who he was.

"It's no good to put your name in your pocket anymore," said Nicholas. "The Rebs aren't leaving a stitch of clothes on the bodies, except sometimes the drawers."

"It's safe if you tie it on a string round your neck, though," said Dave.

"Do we have to talk about this?" said Jack.

"You're not marching with us, are you, Seth?" said No-Joke, worried.

"Nope. I'd throw the line off. You fellas do ninety steps a minute, and I'm down to forty-five. But once I catch up I'll muster out any Rebs youse leave for me."

"Fall in!" called the captain.

There was a rush to assemble kits and throw bedrolls together.

And then they were marching, pouring down through Sugar Valley, the 107th Regiment, the Twentieth Corps, the Armies of the Cumberland, the Tennessee, and the Ohio, tens of thousands of men, all in files, all following their regimental banners, all marching to the throbbing beat of hundreds of drums, and Jeremy was caught up in the rhythm, his drumstick hitting when the other drumsticks hit, at the precise moment that the men's feet hit the ground, thousands at once, and the whole valley throbbed with the war beat.

A shot rang out. Then another. Jeremy almost dropped his drumstick. The sound of the shot echoed in his heart and all the way down to his feet, which wanted him to stop marching and run away. Jeremy had heard thousands of gunshots before, but these ones were different. Suddenly he knew he was part of an invading army and that someone was objecting to the invasion.

The syncopated clap of gunshots interrupted the beat for a moment, and Jeremy lost the rhythm, but the drumming continued. Jeremy quickly joined back in. The guns went on, a pause to reload here and there. Jeremy didn't know where they were or even whose guns they were—the Rebs' or the Federals'. Both, he reasoned. If they're firing on us, we're firing back. But where? Up ahead? Right beside him? Jeremy's company kept marching, uninterrupted.

"Center on the colors!" the captain called, and Jeremy and the others looked up at the regimental flag, which bore the names of the great battles the 107th had fought in—

Chancellorsville, Antietam, Gettysburg, and the rest. Thousands of gunshots, thousands of bullets.

Out of the corner of his eye Jeremy was aware of two stretcher bearers slogging past, up the hill, carrying a stretcher between them with a man in a blue Union uniform on it. With a jolt Jeremy realized that this was real. Real Rebs were shooting real bullets and real men were being hit. This was seeing the elephant.

"Close up that file!" called a sergeant to Jeremy's right.

The gunshots had stopped. The regiment marched on.

The sun climbed high overhead, and it began to get hot. Jeremy could feel sweat trickling down his back inside his fatigue blouse, and he would have dearly loved to stop and take a drink from his canteen.

Finally the captain called "Company halt! Fall out!"

Jeremy was surprised to see it was already noon. The men stopped with sighs of relief. Jeremy threw his drum down on the roadside and sat on it, as drummer boys did. He pulled out his canteen and took a long swig. Then he ate some of his cooked beef. He didn't look for his messmates. Around him men were talking. Some were singing. But Jeremy found he didn't want to talk to anybody. The moment seemed too big for anything but his own thoughts.

The order came to fall in again. The yellow sun beat down on them. The drumming began again, and then the marching. They moved on.

Then the deep, hollow boom of cannon fire slammed against his ears. For a moment Jeremy could hear nothing, and thought he had gone deaf. Then gunshots answered, and the cannons roared again. The company stopped, then started, then stopped. They didn't know why they were stopping; they didn't know what was going on up ahead of them, except that it involved cannons. They moved when they were told to, kept on marching forward. Sometimes they passed fields, more often they passed through dense woods, and Jeremy knew that rifle fire could erupt from among the trees at any moment. The red dust stirred up by the march got in the men's faces and made them cough. Twice Jeremy made hasty hops to avoid marching in horse droppings. Still the cannons and the guns sounded up ahead.

Then, to Jeremy's confusion, they left the road and began marching across the broken ground, among pine trees and hillocks. It was hard going, and he had to stop drumming. It was enough work just to keep moving, stepping high over fallen tree trunks, pushing through the undergrowth and the branches that kept trying to dislodge his drum. After a while they wheeled right. Jeremy had no idea what they were aiming for. All he could see around him was trees. Still the cannons sounded up ahead, but the order came to halt, and Jeremy stopped to beat it out on his drum. They were ordered to fortify their position.

"But we haven't got to the battle yet!" said Jeremy.

"There ain't no battle yet, I don't think," said Dave.

"What's all that up ahead, then?"

"Just skirmishing, I think," said Dave.

"When does the battle start?"

"It don't run on a timetable. It starts when it starts. Don't be impatient. We'll get our turn. If not now, later on."

But Jeremy wanted his turn now. The air vibrated with the crash of cannons and guns up ahead, just out of sight; the smell of gunpowder drifted through the trees toward him. He was too worked up to do anything but see the elephant, and when he joined the men in cutting and dragging trees to front their trenches with, he felt it was a distraction from the real work that lay up ahead.

No more orders came, so they kept fortifying. They dug their trenches deeper, using their bayonets and bowie knives to dig with. Still no orders came.

"Might as well cook, even if we are dug in for battle," Nicholas decided.

The mess was gathered in the rifle pit they'd dug, behind a wall of logs and red clay.

"When do we get to go in?" said Jeremy.

"Never, I hope. We're being held in reserve. Enjoy it," said Nicholas.

"Little Drummer Boy wants to get into the battle and be a hero," said Lars. He started humming "The Drummer Boy of Shiloh."

"Leave him alone!" said No-Joke. "Who's brought a mess kettle?"

"Nobody. You don't bring a mess kettle into battle," said Dave. "We got cooked rations."

"Little Drummer Boy's got a canteen. Hand it over and we'll blow it up," said Lars.

"I told you to stop calling him that!" No-Joke said.

"I told you to stop calling him that!" Lars mimicked, copying No-Joke's hoarse, raspy voice, which always sounded as if his throat was doing the talking and his mouth was just trying to keep up.

Hurriedly Jeremy pulled his canteen strap up over his head. He didn't want to see his messmates fight, least of all over Lars teasing him, which was an embarrassing thing to have discussed. He watched with interest as Nicholas swigged down the last of the water and then stuffed a charge of gunpowder into the opening.

"Jeremy!"

Jeremy turned to see Dulcie. "What are you doing here? It ain't safe!"

"Dr. Flood wants you to sharpen these." She was carrying a wooden instrument case and a whetstone. "He says I don't have enough elbow grease."

"Sharpen them?" Jeremy repeated.

Dulcie sat down on the edge of the trench and flipped the instrument case open. It was lined with red velvet, and an assortment of saws and long, wicked-looking knives lay within, pressed into neat compartments made for them. They reminded him of the tools used in the Northwoods at hog-killing and deer-hunting time.

"He says he needs 'em ready for the battle, so if you could do it double-quick he would be much obliged."

"All right," said Jeremy, still staring at the instruments. The steel blades were stained black in spots.

"He says that the sharper they are, the easier it will be for the soldiers, if you know what he means."

BLAM! A sudden explosion made Jeremy jump, and when his ears cleared again he heard his messmates exclaiming over the remains of his canteen, and Dulcie was saying ". . . to sharpen a saw blade?"

"What?" said Jeremy.

"He said to ask you do you know how to sharpen a saw blade?"

"Oh. Of course."

Dulcie left. Jeremy coughed as the smoke from his exploded canteen drifted into his mouth. He turned around. His canteen was in two blackened halves, and his messmates were building a fire on the edge of the trench and digging out ingredients—hardtack, raw bacon, cooked beef, more hardtack.

"Was you gonna eat that bacon raw? Why'd you bring raw bacon?"

"Thought we might have time to cook up. Nothin' wrong with eatin' bacon raw if you got the stomach for it."

"Is too. It'll kill you."

"Is not. I read it in the surgeon's book. Said it's good for you."

"Don't you remember Eary? He died in Virginia of raw bacon."

"I thought it was a putrid fever."

"Nope, raw bacon. What you wanna make, skillygally? Slumgullion?"

"Anybody got any of them desecrated vegetables?"

"*Desiccated* vegetables, Dave." That was No-Joke, of course.

"We don't need all that hardtack. Use mine, it's got more worms in."

"Mine got so many worms there ain't no hardtack, just pressed worms."

"Desecrated worms."

"I need something to break up this hardtack with— gimme some more gunpowder."

Jack reached across Jeremy and grabbed one of the surgeon's stained knives out of the case and started hacking away at the hardtack with it. Jeremy sat back and watched the construction of the meal. First the bacon was cooked in the canteen halves, and when there was a good lot of hot grease there, the hardtack bits and beef were thrown in and fried, pressed together into a thick cake, and then divided up among the messmates.

The result was . . . edible. Largely. At least there was plenty of grease to make it stick to the ribs. Jeremy ate his slowly, because he'd learned that was the best way to stave off a raging stomachache. He tried not to think about things like soft bread and hot beef stew. This was soldier food, and he was a soldier, and proud to be eating like one. The song about the Drummer Boy of Shiloh had never mentioned the courage that was needed to face camp food. Jeremy wondered what Charlie had to eat, over on the other side. Probably nothing near as good as this. Thinking of Charlie, Jeremy tried hard to take a sip of the coffee that was offered him, letting it slide back between his molars in hopes of getting it to his throat without having to pass the bitter taste over his tongue. It was no good. He just didn't like the stuff. It was his biggest failing as a soldier, he felt.

After dinner he sharpened the surgeon's instruments. This was good because it drove Lars away.

"I can't listen to another second of that," said Lars. "Aren't they sharp enough yet?"

"Nope," said Jeremy, pleased to have found a way to really annoy Lars. "They gotta be really sharp. Surgeon's gotta be able to slice in quick-like. And the saws..."

But Lars gave a grunt and was out of the trench and away.

"Aren't you supposed to be to the rear?" No-Joke said suddenly. This was the thing about No-Joke. He was perfectly capable of defending Jeremy to Lars and then lighting into Jeremy on his own account.

"Nope. S'posed to be up here, ready to drum out the officers' orders during the battle," said Jeremy.

"I thought drummer boys were supposed to be stretcher bearers."

"Not anymore. Ambulance corps are stretcher bearers now." Jeremy was sure that No-Joke knew this, and was just being annoying.

No-Joke grunted and took his Bible out of his shirt pocket and began reading it.

From a rifle pit farther down came the sound of other men in the regiment singing:

Just before the battle, Mother,
I am thinking most of you,
While upon the field we're watching,
With the enemy in view.
Comrades brave are round me lying,
Filled with thoughts of home and God,
For well they know that on the morrow
Some will sleep beneath the sod.

"I hate that song," said Jack. "What idiot made up that song?"

Dr. Flood came himself to get his weapons—his instruments, Jeremy corrected himself.

"You sharpen a good saw, Jeremy," said the surgeon. "I haven't had such an edge on my blades since my assistant mustered out two months ago."

The next morning began with the sound of guns, not birds, and then cannons. The woods shook with cannon fire, and the 107th New York stayed in the trenches. The firing went on and on, and no orders came. Jeremy wavered between being very excited and very bored. Would they never get into the battle? It was all around them, to their left and right, ahead of them . . . miles of battle. Behind them on the hilltops the artillery boomed again and again, firing over the heads of the infantry into the enemy ranks beyond.

"Are they never going to let us into the battle at all?" said Jeremy.

"Oh, shut your bazoo, Little Drummer Boy. Go find some more saws to sharpen."

"We're being held in reserve, and we like it like that," said Nicholas.

"Don't worry. When the front regiments are all shot to pieces, they'll call us in."

Jeremy knew he shouldn't be eager for the battle if other people had to be shot to pieces first for him to get in. But he *was*. He wanted to get it over with. He wanted to see the elephant and to find out that he wasn't afraid. He had always been tough. He knew he was brave; he wasn't scared to walk on roofs or jump off the fifth-highest branch of the tree into the swimming hole back home. But going into battle was different, and deep inside of him was a terror that he might run away, and then have to be shot for desertion.

Finally, in the afternoon, the regiment was ordered to fall in. Jeremy and his messmates climbed out of their rifle pit and joined the other men of the 107th New York, forming ranks. Jeremy beat his drum, at least to start off with. Then they were moving, up a steep hill and through entangling pine branches. Something like a large bumblebee whizzed past Jeremy, and when it smacked straight into a tree above his head he realized it was a bullet. It gave him a chill, and he reminded himself of what Nicholas had said—not one bullet in a hundred hits a soldier, was that it?

They climbed higher, fighting their way through clinging thickets. They were behind their own cannons now, and Jeremy had a moment of mingled hope and fear that they were leaving the battle altogether. But no, they were moving along behind the line of battle, past one artillery placement after another, and to his right Jeremy kept hearing the FWOOMP of cannonballs leaving the barrel, the smell of gunpowder drifting over a moment later. He tried not to look toward the artillery placements. He had to keep his mind on his part of the battle.

Dulcie walked along the road, in the opposite direction from the marching soldiers.

"Are those our new flags, girlie?"

"What's the *H* for? 'Here we are'?"

Dulcie ignored them. She'd already learned that soldiers teased officers' servants all the time. She stopped and stuck one of the yellow flags into the red clay. Then she walked on, still ignoring the calls of the soldiers. She stopped and looked back. She had gotten far enough away that the yellow flag was just a dot back in the red dust stirred up by the soldiers marching and the cannon and wagon wheels turning. She stuck another flag in.

Put the flags all the way back to where they were setting up the field hospital, Dr. Flood had told her. She had started at the dressing station that Dr. Flood was setting up near where the battle was about to begin. It had a tent, because dressing stations and hospitals were one of the purposes for which General Sherman had acknowledged that tents might be necessary. When the battle began, wounded soldiers would come or be carried to the dressing station. There, Dr. Flood would try to patch them together. If they could walk, he would give them a pass, to prove that they weren't deserting, and send them back to the field hospital to have their wounds treated. Dulcie's flags were important. Without them, the soldiers might get lost, never find the field hospital, and come to harm in the woods.

When she was done with this, she would place more flags between the dressing station and the battle lines, in enough different places that, one way or another, the injured who could move might be able to make it back to the dressing station. Their comrades wouldn't be allowed to stop and help them.

"That's . . . ," Dulcie began, when Dr. Flood explained this to her. Then she stopped. Her opinion was undoubtedly not wanted.

"That's not very nice?" Dr. Flood asked her. "Well, war's not very nice, Dulcie. If every soldier stopped to help a wounded one, we'd soon have no one on the field of battle, and the Rebs could overwhelm us and capture our soldiers, our dressing station, you, me, and everything."

"Yes, sir," said Dulcie. She knew she didn't want to be captured by the Secesh. Not now that she was free.

"Now repeat to me again what you're to do during the battle."

"Don't go too close to the enemy lines," Dulcie quoted. "If I see a soldier coming toward me, I should go out and guide him in if he looks like he needs help. If I see him fall, I should tell the stretcher bearers. Otherwise I should make sure that you always have an open carton of bandages and that the morphine bottle is full."

"My words exactly!"

Dulcie made a slight curtsy to acknowledge the compliment, and wondered how she would do when the wounded soldiers started pouring in and the smell of blood filled the hot tent. She remembered Anne being brought down by the slave hunters' dogs, and she shuddered.

☆ ★ ★ TWELVE ★ ★ ☆

THE 107TH MOVED FORWARD, THROUGH THE TREES, ON a path trampled by soldiers going before. Broken branches and spent shells lay all around them. Once they passed three dead men, neatly lined up side by side.

Then the battle came into view.

A charred, burnt valley spread out below them. On the hills opposite ranged the Confederate barricades, mounds of red clay fronted with logs, and from the barricades gleamed bayonets, rifle barrels, and the mouths of cannons. As Jeremy watched, orange arcs of flame shot out from the cannons and iron missiles sailed across the valley. Bullets whizzed back and forth like mad wasps. Between the two lines lay men, some of them twisted into unnatural positions, not moving.

All the trees in the valley had been cut down, and those that weren't used in the Confederate barricades had been burned. A bitter smell of charcoal underlay the overwhelming smell of gunpowder. Jeremy never got a clear view of the Union side, because the regiment was ordered to wheel left and move in behind. Again they halted, still not in the battle, although from here they could see and hear much more than they had been able to before.

The afternoon wore on, and at last the order came to march again. Jeremy beat the drum. The men assembled into ranks. The wild-eyed, fork-bearded General Alpheus Williams rode down along the regiments, sword in hand, exhorting the men. There was something different this time. Jeremy's heart beat fast. This time they weren't being maneuvered, weren't going to be held in reserve some-where else, but were going to fight.

They were marching, and Jeremy had a better view of the battle than before. It filled the valley below him. Thou-sands of men, the smoke and din of rifles, men lying on the ground, groaning and writhing or not moving at all. There was a smell Jeremy instantly identified with a slaughterhouse he used to pass on his way to pick up his newspapers in Syracuse. Each roar from the cannons tore a line of death through the oncoming attackers. The sight made Jeremy feel ill, but he fought the feeling—he was a soldier, and this was war.

The front line of the lead brigade of Jeremy's division fired their rifles, then dropped to the ground to reload so that the rank behind them could fire. It took Jeremy, who was a long way to the rear, a few minutes to figure out what was going on—the cannon battery was a Union one, and the attacking soldiers trying to capture the cannons were Confederates. He guessed this mostly from the direction they were coming from, out of the woods on the opposite side of the wagon road that ran down the valley. Almost everyone on both sides was wearing some form of Union uniform, or parts of one.

The next line fired and dropped, and the next. The Confederate soldiers turned and fled, running back toward the woods at the other side of the valley. A cheer went up from the men around Jeremy.

"Take that, Johnny Reb!"

"Don't you wanna stay and play?"

"When you get to Richmond give Jeff Davis a kiss for us!"

Jeremy fought disappointment. "We didn't even get into the fight," he said under his breath.

"Who cares?" said the man next to him, a soldier named John Decker. "We saved the battery."

But Jeremy felt cheated all the same.

Later, after they had dug their trenches and eaten in the dark, he felt better.

"Ain't no Reb that can stand up to the Twentieth Corps," he said expansively. "Did you see them run like rabbits?"

"Yeah, and I seen us run like rabbits sometimes too," said Dave.

Lars scowled. "What're you taking their side for? LDB is right. They *did* run like rabbits."

"Stayin' alive to shoot us next time," said Dave.

Jeremy thought he could live with being called LDB. It was better than Little Drummer Boy.

There had been no firing for over an hour. A voice called out of the darkness, from the other side of the valley. "Hey! Hey, Yanks! Why don't you come bring us some of your coffee?"

"Come get it yourself!" Lars called back. "Ain't you got nothing to eat over there?"

"Send one of your slaves over!" suggested No-Joke angrily.

"Why, you need a new colonel for your regiment?" another voice called back. "Did we shoot yours?"

"No, you didn't!" said No-Joke. He wasn't very good at this sort of thing.

"How much are your slaves worth now?" Nicholas called.

"More than any Yank I ever met."

"How much is your gray-backed money worth now?"

"Hey, are you General Hooker's men?"

"Yes, we are!" said Dave proudly.

"Don't tell them that," No-Joke hissed. "That's divulging intelligence to the enemy."

Jeremy remembered how, when he had first met Charlie, he had told him his division, brigade, regiment, and about everything else he could think of. He felt a pang. Well, Charlie was only Charlie, hardly an enemy at all.

The firing began again at dawn. The cannon that the Red Star Division had saved last night boomed above them, the Confederate cannon boomed in answer, and all down the line, for many miles, cannons and rifles fired. The men in Jeremy's mess fired their rifles. Jeremy had nothing to fire. No-Joke suggested that he ought to go to the rear, but Dave said sensibly, "If he leaves the trench he might get hit, No-Joke."

Then in the afternoon the order came to move. They made their way ducking and shoving through the clinging thicket and pine trees, tumbling into ravines and clambering up the other side—it wasn't marching, it was scrambling. Jeremy slung his drum over his shoulder and wished he didn't have to drag it along. A cannonball crashed through the trees near him, knocking off several branches, and Jeremy hugged the ground in terror. Then he got up, embarrassed. He had momentarily forgotten his ambition to die nobly in battle. He could tell there were other men in the trees around him, making their way forward, but he could no longer be sure they were the men in his company. He was practically all alone. A bullet smacked into a tree next to him, and Jeremy realized it had come from behind him.

"You're firing on your own men!" he yelled.

Then an instant later he wasn't so sure the bullet had come from a Union gun. Could be he'd gotten turned around. Maybe he was facing the Union with the Confederates behind him. He thought of climbing a tree to see better, but there were too many shells and bullets flying around up there. He could see no other soldiers clearly.

Around him he heard men's shouts; he heard the command "Center on the colors!" But he couldn't see the colors, his own or any other company's or the Rebs'. All was chaos, the scream of bullets and shells and the trembling of the woods, and then a sudden groan off to his left, and a man's voice: "I'm hit!"

He made his way over to this last cry, on his hands and knees. He found a man lying on his stomach on the ground. The man was wearing Union breeches and a Union fatigue blouse—that didn't prove he was in the Union Army, though. Jeremy had to force himself to creep closer to the man. He didn't want to, didn't want to see. He reached his hand out and touched the man. Instantly the man's hand shot out and gripped Jeremy's tightly. Jeremy didn't know what to do. He stayed still, and in a moment the grip slackened. He leaned forward, forced himself to look at the soldier's face. Union or Confederate—Jeremy still couldn't tell—the man was dead.

There had been no comrades gathered around crying, no time for a prayer or for the soldier to say how he loved his country as his God—whichever country it was. Not like the Drummer Boy of Shiloh at all.

Around him branches and trees splintered amid the crash of cannons and rifle fire. Jeremy no longer had any idea which direction he'd come from. He unslung his drum, set it on the ground between his knees, and beat out the Dead March, to make up to the dead man for the lack of weeping comrades.

Then he got shakily to his feet. This was no way to behave. He was a soldier, and his company was in battle, and he was supposed to be in battle with them. If he wasn't, he might as well be a deserter, and deserters sometimes got shot. Of course, probably not as often as *non*-deserters got shot, he realized. He closed his eyes and tried to sort out the sounds around him, tried to figure out which way the battle was. No good. The battle was all over the place. The best thing was to try to retrace his steps.

This was hard to do. Not only did the woods and the ravines all look the same, but they looked a sight more shot up than they had an hour ago. Nothing looked familiar. At last Jeremy saw a man in a Union uniform.

"Yank or Reb?" Jeremy asked, out of breath.

"Provost marshal," said the man.

Jeremy gulped. A provost marshal's job was to drive fleeing men back into battle, to arrest anyone who was trying to escape the battle behind the lines. "I got lost."

"I'll say you did," said the provost marshal. "You don't belong in this at all. Get to the rear."

"I'm a soldier," Jeremy protested.

"Then you won't disobey a direct order. Get to the rear."

Jeremy nodded. He didn't know where the rear was. The provost marshal pointed, and Jeremy stumbled that way. But as soon as the provost marshal was out of sight, he turned around. He knew the battle must be in the opposite direction from where the provost marshal had pointed him, and so he went toward the battle. He crashed and fought his way through clinging branches and brush. Sometimes his feet weren't even touching the ground as he punched and kicked and forced the forest to let him through. At last the trees grew thinner and he burst out into the actual battle.

In the valley below was a railroad track, and on the near side of it the Union Army was arrayed in battle. Artillery boomed from the hills. Rank upon rank of soldiers fired into the forest on the opposite side of the tracks, where the enemy was hidden. Jeremy tried to find his own regiment, but it was impossible to pick out the blue flag of the 107th New York in the chaos below. As Jeremy watched, a volley of shells came from the Confederate side and an entire Union regiment lay down on the ground and didn't get up again. At first Jeremy thought they were dead, but then he saw some of them moving. And there wasn't much blood, either. They were lying down because they were afraid to get up. Jeremy was indignant. At least he knew *that* wasn't the 107th New York.

Then the Rebs moved out of the forest, advancing in ranks toward the Union lines. The Union soldiers fired on them like so many targets set up for practice. Jeremy watched in horror as the soldiers fell. But they were enemies, he reminded himself. It was good for them to die. He wished they would stop marching forward. Still they kept marching, and they kept dying.

Finally, to Jeremy's intense relief, the remaining Rebs turned and ran back into the woods. But then more Rebs came out, fresh ranks from the woods, marching and dying. Closer and closer they came to the Union lines, but that just made them easier to shoot. This was *insane*. On a bright, sunny May afternoon, in a country that had trains and telegraphs and newspapers and every other kind of modern invention, people were lining up and shooting each other to death. Someone should stop them!

Jeremy hastily banished this unpatriotic thought from his mind. At last the Rebs retreated into the woods, except for a group who came forward under a white flag to surrender.

That night there was no calling back and forth across the lines. The Confederates weren't that close. They must have all retreated into the town of Resaca, Jeremy's messmates supposed.

"Not everyone can face a real battle," said Lars, looking at Jeremy as he said it.

"I got lost!" said Jeremy, indignant.

"Sure. I've known plenty of soldiers who get 'lost' when their regiments go into battle," said Lars.

"Leave him alone, Lars!" said No-Joke. "He's just a child."

"I'm a soldier!"

"Reckon this battle's over," said Dave, changing the subject. "Reckon the Rebs have absquatulated."

"Wish the whole blamed war was over," said Nicholas.

"The war must not be over until slavery has ended!" said No-Joke.

"Well, you've got your Emancipation Proclamation, ain't that good enough for you?"

"Only if we win," said No-Joke.

"How can we lose?" said Jeremy. He thought of what he had seen that day, of the Rebs coming out of the forest and then running back into the forest. He erased from the picture the sight of them being mowed down like hay under a scythe in summertime, because that wasn't so pleasant to think about. "The 107th is invincible!"

"You got that right, Little Drummer Boy," said Lars.

☆ ★ ★ T H I R T E E N ★ ★ ☆

AFTER THE FIRST DAY, DULCIE HARDLY NOTICED
the sound of muskets and grapeshot anymore. She was too
busy dealing with the results.

The cannons she still noticed, because each time they
boomed she could feel the ground tremble under her bare
feet. But she didn't have time to think about it.

The first man she saw coming out of the battle
wounded was not walking, he was crawling. Dulcie ran
toward him. He wasn't headed toward the field dressing
station; he couldn't see. Blood ran down his face into his
eyes. The smell of the blood took Dulcie back to the farmyard, to Anne being whipped two hundred times . . . being
bitten by dogs. . . . She willed the memory away. She had
a job to do.

She approached the man and gingerly laid a hand
on his shoulder. "This way, sir. The dressing station is
over here."

He made no response, but kept crawling in the wrong direction.

Dulcie risked a look down. He had been shot in the leg. It was horrible. She looked away hastily. She wanted to run back to the tent and get someone else to handle this. One of the orderlies, or Dr. Flood.

No, they were busy. She had to handle this herself.

She gripped the man's collar and pulled him gently toward the tent. To her relief, he yielded to the pressure and started crawling in the right direction. She kept pulling, he kept moving. It was like how you had to drag Redtop, the old dog back on the farm, when he needed a bath. Dogs. Don't think of dogs. Anyway, Redtop wasn't that kind of dog.

One of the orderlies, Jake, was running out of the tent toward them, holding a length of cloth and a stick in his hand. Pushing Dulcie aside, he rolled the wounded soldier over onto his back, wrapped the bandage tight around the man's leg just above the knee, and put the stick through the bandage. He wound the stick around and around, until the tourniquet cut deep into the man's leg. The bleeding slowed to an ooze. Dulcie forced herself to watch. This was important.

"Tourniquet," Jake said to Dulcie. "Go get Tim and tell him to bring a stretcher. And then grab a tourniquet yourself. They're by the door."

Dulcie did as she was told. She saw that she would be

expected to apply the next tourniquet herself. She hoped she wouldn't mess it up.

When she came out of the tent again, they were everywhere . . . men stumbling, men crawling. One man was walking, but he suddenly keeled over frontward. Dulcie ran toward him, her tourniquet in her hand.

There was nowhere to put the tourniquet that she could see. A pool of blood seeped from beneath the soldier. Dulcie knelt beside him, wondering what to do.

"Leave him!" A man's hand gripped her shoulder— one of the orderlies. Bill. He hauled her to her feet. "Go help those who can be helped!"

Dulcie looked up at him, horrified. This soldier beside them was still alive. Bill scowled back at her. "This is war, girl."

Dulcie ran off to help another man who was stumbling blindly. She draped his unresponsive arm over her shoulder and guided him to the tent, where Jake took him off her hands. She wanted to ask how the first soldier she'd found was, but there wasn't time. She had to run out and get more wounded soldiers.

It's us against the battle, she realized. *And we have to save as many as we can.*

There must be others who weren't able to stumble out of the battle, who are lying wounded under the gunfire. She forced herself not to think about them right now.

"You're not wounded!" Dulcie heard Bill yell.

She turned. He was screaming in the face of a dazed-looking soldier.

The soldier stared vaguely back at him.

"Get back to the battle or you'll be shot for desertion!" Bill turned the unresisting soldier around, back toward the explosion of guns and cannons, and gave him a little shove. The soldier fell over flat on the ground and, as far as Dulcie could see, did not move.

There was no time to think about this. She ran to the next soldier. His arm was bleeding copiously. Tourniquet. Dulcie fumbled with it. Quick. She wrapped the bandage around the man's arm. The more she tried to hurry, the more she grappled with the bandage. She dropped the stick. The wounded man watched her curiously all the while, as if she and his wound were in a painting hanging on a wall somewhere, nothing to do with him.

When it came time to turn the stick, though, he helped her. Together they turned it round and round, the soldier wincing in pain, and he held it while she clumsily bound it in place with the bandage.

Not all the soldiers were quiet and calm. The groans and howls of the wounded were all around her, filling her ears more insistently than the boom of the artillery and the crack and whistle of rifles. She tried not to feel anything. Feeling got in the way of action. She needed to be everywhere at once. There was never a moment to slow down and take a breath. She hated Bill's instruction to help only those who could be saved—especially because she had no idea which ones those were. She kept gathering fresh tourniquets and heading out to guide in the walking and crawling wounded. She tried not to look at the others. If they were stretcher cases the stretcher bearers would deal with them. Let them make the decisions about who could be saved.

She also tried not to look at a space under a wide-spreading chinquapin tree where some of the wounded soldiers had been gently laid down in the shade. She thought they were not dead—yet. She tried not to think about it.

Darkness fell. The shooting was less now, but it was still going on.

"Light some more lanterns, Dulcie."

It was Dr. Flood who spoke. He was damp with exhaustion, the silver hair hanging down in strings over his forehead. His arms were spattered in blood, and he held a bloody knife in his hand.

Dulcie found the lanterns, lined up—candles in perforated tin boxes. She struck steel and flint together and lit them, one by one. Dr. Flood, she saw, already had several candles around him as he worked on a patient on a rubber blanket laid out on the ground. Beside him sat Seth, with his good leg tucked under him and the stump sticking out in front. Silently Seth passed the doctor bandages and bloodstained instruments. A bucket of water stood at his side, and sometimes he took a rag from the bucket and wiped blood off the instruments with it.

Dulcie took the lanterns to the orderlies. She kept one for herself and headed out, again. Now she had to locate the wounded by their groans, and she could no longer look away from the worst cases, because she didn't know who they were until she was up close, shining the lantern's yellow dots of light down on them.

A soldier was crawling toward her. Dulcie could see no wounds on his arms and legs, or head.

"Where are you wounded, sir?" she asked.

The man looked up at her, his teeth clenched in pain. He couldn't have been more than eighteen years old. "Gut," he said tightly.

Dulcie thought of what Bill had said. She ought to leave him and help those who could be saved. She knew gut-shot soldiers couldn't.

But she was free. Did she have to obey Bill just because he was white? No, she did not. She made her own decision. She leaned down and put her hand on his shoulder. "Come on," she said. "The dressing station is this way."

Nobody working at the dressing station had gone to sleep the night before, and Dulcie had only eaten a small piece of salt beef that Seth had shoved into her hands. He'd given her a hardtack cracker, too, but she hadn't been able to make a dent in it. Now it was afternoon, and No-Joke came in, helping a man from the 107th.

Dulcie had had several years of medical experience

since the day before, and she saw at once that this man could not be saved. He was still almost walking, in a dazed sort of way, but the front of his blue fatigue blouse was dark with a spreading bloodstain and the look in his eyes was blank and distant. No-Joke half guided, half carried him along.

Dulcie went out to help. She didn't tell No-Joke the man should be left for those who could be saved. Together they guided him toward the tent.

"All right, Jerome," No-Joke was saying. "All right there. You'll be all right."

Things had quieted down a little. No-Joke reached up and ducked Jerome's head down as they stepped into the tent, and Dr. Flood rose wearily to meet them. He shot Dulcie an accusing look, and Dulcie understood it to mean *Why did you bring me this one?*

But she pretended not to understand, and went out of the tent with No-Joke.

"Is there any water?" said No-Joke.

"Over here," said Dulcie, leading him to one of the buckets she'd found time to haul up from the river. She watched him kneel and drink, straight out of the bucket because there was no dipper handy. There had been one, but Dulcie had taken it over to the tree where the men who couldn't be helped lay, when she had found time to give them a drink of water.

When he had drunk he sat down wearily on the ground. He looked exhausted, and Dulcie knew how that felt. His face was blackened with gunpowder, especially around the mouth from biting cartridges open.

In the distance the rifles crackled, and Dulcie and No-Joke both looked toward the front lines. "We're not in it right now," said No-Joke. "We've been in it, and Jerome Newton was hit." He nodded toward the tent.

"Is Jeremy all right?" said Dulcie.

"The drummer boy? Yes, he's fine. He got lost in the woods, but he found his way out."

Dulcie nodded, glad to hear this.

"How's the medical work suiting you, Dulcie?"

"All right," said Dulcie, not really thinking about whether it suited her or not. It needed doing; she did it.

"Do you reckon you want to be a medic, now that you're free?"

"I don't know, sir," said Dulcie. No-Joke's intense eyes bothered her. She wasn't used to people taking such an interest in her.

"I have a sister about your age. Look." No-Joke reached into his fatigue blouse and pulled out a small tintype.

Dulcie took the metal photograph. She saw four white people, all looking rather like No-Joke—a middle-aged man and woman, a girl of about nine, and a young woman of about eighteen. The two women both had No-Joke's narrow, hollow-cheeked face and expression of burning intensity.

"That was a couple years ago. She's eleven now. Her

name's Hattie. My parents mean her for a teacher, but I don't know if she wants to be one."

"Oh," said Dulcie.

"You have to do the work you're meant for, the work you're born for, even if they tell you you're born for something else. Even if you're a girl."

Dulcie nodded, again uncomfortable with No-Joke's fervor, which she saw reflected in the photograph. "Is this your whole family, then?"

No-Joke pointed with his pinky. "My ma and pa. They're abolitionists too."

"Who's the young mis—the young lady?"

No-Joke looked away. "Oh—my other sister. Eliza."

From his tone Dulcie could tell there was something wrong about this sister. They didn't get along, maybe. Maybe she had married someone No-Joke didn't approve of. Or maybe she wasn't an abolitionist. Aunt Betsy back on the farm always said it was sad when families fell out.

"How come you're not in the picture?"

No-Joke looked away. "Oh, it was taken after I left."

Dulcie figured she was right—No-Joke had quarreled with his sister, and maybe his whole family. She flipped the photo over and saw there was writing on the back.

"Can you read?"

"No, sir."

No-Joke sighed. "Of course. It's illegal to teach slaves to read in Georgia, isn't it?"

"Yes, sir. But some can read," she reassured him. "Not

many, but some. Willie on our place could read. I mean, he probably still can. They sold him away."

"We're going to need thousands of schools when this is over," No-Joke said. "Thousands and thousands of schools for freedmen."

"When this is over," said Dulcie, "I want to go and find my ma and pa."

"Where are they?"

"I don't know, sir."

No-Joke sighed again and got painfully to his feet. "I'm going to check on Jerome before I go back to my company."

He went into the tent and came out again a moment later, shaking his head. Jerome hadn't made it. Dulcie could've told No-Joke he wouldn't.

☆ ★ ★ FOURTEEN ★ ★ ☆

THE FIRING WENT ON UP AND DOWN THE LINE
through the second evening. Some of it sounded miles
away to the south. Jeremy had never realized before how
big a battle could be—how much land it could cover. The
battle was bigger than Syracuse, probably. The last distant
cannon fire died away around midnight. In the morning
the firing did not begin again, and Jeremy and his messmates waited for orders to come. Jeremy wasn't as restless
as he had been before the battle. He knew now that you
had to wait your turn to go in. You had to wait for orders.
Their turn would come.

The morning dribbled away and still no orders came.
Around ten a.m. a soldier came along whom Jeremy knew
vaguely by sight, one of the westerners. Jeremy saw from
his insignia that he was from Wisconsin.

"Any news?" Lars greeted him.

"No more battle today, boys. The Rebs have absquatulated."

"They flew the coop?" Nicholas said.

"Dusted off in the night! Isn't that just like a Reb."

"Just when we were starting to have fun."

Everyone seemed very lighthearted, and Jeremy felt that way himself. Maybe not so much because the Rebs had run but because they were *gone,* and didn't need to be fought anymore right now.

"We were too many for them," said Jeremy. "Can't no Reb stand up to us. The Reb hasn't been born who can stand up to the 107th New York."

"Did you see how many of them were surrendering?"

The man frowned. "Twenty-three of them surrendered to us. We took 'em prisoner, then we asked them if they remembered Fort Pillow, and then we used 'em up."

There was a moment's silence, in which the man looked at them all defiantly.

"You what?" said Dave.

"You can't do that," said Nicholas.

"They did the same to our men," said the man. "Or don't you remember Fort Pillow?"

Dave shifted uncomfortably. "Well, those were colored prisoners that the Rebs killed at Fort Pillow."

"They were American soldiers," said No-Joke. "Union soldiers."

"So that makes it all right to kill Reb prisoners?" said Lars. "That's too thin, even for you, No-Joke."

Jeremy listened to this in confusion. He had grown up with war, he had known war since he was eight years old, he had studied war and cherished it, and he knew its rules. You didn't kill your prisoners. And yet here was a man standing in front of them claiming to have done just that, and not appearing to feel particularly bad about it.

"It's *not* all right," Jeremy told him. "You can't kill prisoners that have surrendered to you."

"You got that right, Little Drummer Boy," said Lars.

"Someone's got to teach those Rebs a lesson!" said No-Joke. "They slaughtered the colored soldiers who surrendered at Fort Pillow! They didn't even see 'em as human beings. Somebody's gotta teach 'em."

"Can't teach nobody nothing by killing 'em," said Dave.

"That's the trouble with fanatics like you, No-Joke," said Lars. "Nothing matters to you but your cause. You don't care about the war."

"Care about it!" said No-Joke angrily. Red spots of color rose in his sunken cheeks. "Care about it! You, sir, have no idea!"

The man from Wisconsin frowned down at them in their trench. "I don't see why you're acting like you're some pumpkins. You'd of done the same thing yourself. Especially if other people was doing it. I talked to one fella, him and his pardners caught a Reb that had Fort Pillow tattooed on his arm, and they tore him to pieces."

Fascinated, Jeremy turned over in his head the idea of "tore him to pieces." Then he thought of his friend Charlie. What if someone were to treat Charlie that way? What if they *had* treated Charlie that way? What if Charlie had been one of the twenty-three prisoners this man had killed?

"If we don't show these Rebs what war really means, they're never going to surrender," said No-Joke. "And I know General Sherman agrees with me about that!"

"Big of him," said Nicholas.

"So do you think a man who was shooting at you five seconds ago, just because he stops and waves a white flag, you suddenly aren't allowed to shoot back?" said Jack.

"Yep. That's exactly what I think," said Nicholas.

"*Were* they shooting at you five seconds ago?" Dave asked.

The soldier from Wisconsin didn't answer.

"If he's surrendered he ain't gonna shoot you no more, and shooting him is flat-out murder and nothing else," said Lars firmly.

"I don't need to stand here and be slangwhanged at by no paper-collar soldiers from back East," said the soldier from Wisconsin, and went on his way.

"I hate when them westerners call us paper-collar soldiers," said Nicholas. "I never wore a paper collar in my life."

"Me neither," said No-Joke.

Dave frowned, still puzzling over what the western soldier had said. "I guess there are two sides to the story."

Nicholas laughed. "I told you. There are hundreds of sides to every story."

Dave, as usual, looked hurt that Nicholas disagreed

with him. Jeremy tried to imagine what Nicholas would have been like as a schoolteacher. He couldn't. All the teachers he'd ever had were strict, frowning, wielding a hickory stick to keep the students in order. Nicholas was relaxed, and laughed all the time. But then, most of the soldiers seemed to laugh all the time.

Maybe it was what war did to a man.

"Your eyes look different," said Jeremy to Dulcie. "You've seen the elephant."

The Secesh had abandoned Resaca, leaving behind entrenchments and many dead Rebels. The surgeons and their assistants were patching up men to be sent back by train to Union hospitals in Tennessee, now that the railroad was secured again. Just before what Jeremy now knew had been the Battle of Resaca, a contingent of the Union Army had managed to capture Buzzard's Roost, through which the railroad ran.

The train ride would be long and slow, and every jolt would endanger the injured soldiers' lives. Jeremy and Dulcie were cutting pine boughs to lay on the boxcar floors, to protect the men from the worst of the bumps. Above the pine boughs they planned to put a layer of straw, and then they would cover the straw with whatever blankets they could find.

To Jeremy Dulcie looked very different. She was still wearing a Union fatigue blouse and a skirt made of flour sacks, which was now stained and crusted with mud and blood. Her face looked older, though. Her eyes still stabbed like bayonets, but they seemed to know things now that they hadn't before.

"I have seen the elephant," Dulcie agreed. "In the dressing station, behind the lines. The elephant was there."

"Do my eyes look different?" Jeremy asked.

Dulcie didn't answer for a minute, and Jeremy felt her scrutiny as he went on chopping at a pine bough, right where it met the tree.

"No."

"What?" Jeremy threw his ax down as the branch broke free. A warm smell of pine sap rose from the cut. "But I've seen the elephant!"

"Maybe you have, but your eyes don't look different."

Jeremy went on to the next branch as Dulcie picked up that one and dragged it away. Well, what did a girl know about seeing the elephant, anyway? He was sure when he saw Charlie again Charlie would be able to tell that he had seen the elephant.

He was carrying another packet of green coffee beans for Charlie. The thought crossed his mind, not for the first time, that Charlie might have gone to a place where coffee beans were no longer useful. Jeremy had avoided looking at the Confederate dead as the 107th marched past them across the battlefield and into Resaca. A Union burial detail had already been working on a long trench to lay them in.

When Dulcie came back he took his mind off the subject by telling her about the battle.

"I heard you got lost in the woods."

"Anyone could've got lost in those woods. Besides, I found the battle again in the end." He thought about the dying soldier whose hand he had briefly held. He decided not to tell Dulcie about that. It didn't seem like a good war story for a man who had seen the elephant to tell.

"You should've seen those Rebs run," he said instead. "They kept coming out of the woods, and when we fired they turned around and ran like scared rabbits."

"I hope the war is over soon."

"Why?" Jeremy felt exasperated. Girls! As far as he was concerned the war had finally begun, and he liked it fine. He was pretty sure he did, anyway. Mostly.

"I want to find my ma and pa."

"Oh, it'll be over soon. It can't last that long."

"Yes, it can. The Hundred Years' War between England and France lasted from 1337 to 1453."

"Whush!" Jeremy couldn't help smiling. She was a funny girl, really—imagine knowing something like that. "That must've been some war. Why'd it last so long?"

"I don't know. There was a plague and stuff. And the Thirty Years' War lasted from 1618 to 1648."

"How do you know all that?"

"From listening to Miss Lottie's lessons."

"This war won't last that long," Jeremy assured her. "We thought at first it would only last a week."

Why that should mean that it couldn't last a hundred years, Jeremy wasn't exactly sure, but he felt it. He knew he could never be that lucky.

He looked at Dulcie again. She ought to have a proper dress to wear, he thought, instead of ragged flour sacks. There had been dresses that some of the men used to wear to the Gander Dances they'd held last winter in Tennessee, when they couldn't find any ladies to invite—but those had all been left behind, along with everything else that wasn't needed in the war zone, and anyway, they had been dresses for grown-up ladies. A dress wasn't something you could easily acquire in an army on the march. The Union commissary didn't supply them.

Jeremy looked for Charlie when the 107th crossed the Coosawattee River. Charlie had said they'd meet at the next river. But he wasn't there. Jeremy looked for him again each time they came to a stream or a river. He didn't find him. He told himself that didn't *have* to mean anything. After all, the Union Army was huge; the Confederate Army probably was too. The road they were taking wasn't the only road that Union soldiers were taking. In the miles and miles of countryside that the armies were moving through, how could Charlie manage to find Jeremy again? If he even wanted to, because let's face it, Charlie was older than Jeremy and had seen many more elephants. He might think himself above being friends with Jeremy.

Charlie's absence didn't have to mean that he was—that anything had happened to him, Jeremy told himself. He tried not to think of all those Secesh dead in Resaca. And he kept on carrying the little packet of coffee beans.

One foggy evening, while they were making camp (which was pretty quick work without tents) and the pickets were being set, Jeremy walked along a small stream from which silver mist rose like ghosts in the twilight. He walked until he sensed someone else walking on the other side, invisible through the fog.

It could have been anybody, friend or enemy. But Jeremy said, "Charlie?"

"Evening," said Charlie. "That you, Jeremy?"

"Course," said Jeremy.

"Can't hardly see anything for this fog," Charlie said. "Why don't you come on over and visit?"

"Why don't you come over here?" said Jeremy cautiously.

"You got any other Yanks over there?"

"Only within hollerin' distance," said Jeremy.

"Gettin' awfully suspicious, ain't we?" But there was a splashing sound, and a moment later Charlie emerged from the fog and climbed up onto the bank beside Jeremy. He was a little dirtier, and a little more ragged, but he held a pair of shoes in his hand.

Jeremy was feeling rather sorry for him. The Rebs mowed down by Union fire as they came out of the woods kept popping back up and falling over again in his dreams. And dozens of Rebs had surrendered when they could have just run away—some had even surrendered with their weapons in their hands. It must be really embarrassing to be a Reb and have to live with that, Jeremy thought sadly.

"Got these from a Yank," Charlie said, waving the shoes in his hand and then setting them carefully down on the bank.

"Er," said Jeremy. "He gave them to you?"

"Not exactly," said Charlie. "But he wasn't using them anymore."

"Was he a prisoner?"

Charlie looked at Jeremy like he was crazy. "What are you talking about? He was a stiff 'un."

"When you found him?"

"Of course!"

"You didn't . . ."

"Didn't what? He looked like he was hit by a cannon shell. You don't think I'd kill a prisoner, do you?"

"Course not," said Jeremy, uncomfortable.

"I heard some Yanks'll do that, but I don't think you would."

"No, I wouldn't!"

"Well, neither would I."

Jeremy felt ashamed for having doubted this. "I brought you some coffee," he said.

"Capital! Thanks, Jeremy. You're a real friend."

"It's nothing," said Jeremy, embarrassed.

"Course it's something. Here, I brought you some tobacco, like I said." He proffered a leather pouch.

Jeremy started to say he didn't use tobacco, but then he saw that he would hurt Charlie's feelings if he didn't allow him to give something in return for the coffee. "Thanks. I'm sorry about what happened to youse at Resaca."

"Sorry?" Charlie laughed. "Heck, we slowed y'all down pretty good, didn't we? Time y'all get to Atlanta, there ain't going to be no Yanks left. Er, present company excepted."

"But the way your men turned and ran . . ."

"Nobody turned and ran. I heard about your Indiana regiment that just lay down and wouldn't go forward, though. Not too good for Hooker's Ironsides."

"You call us Hooker's Ironsides?" said Jeremy.

"We do now. Y'all are pretty tough."

Jeremy couldn't wait to tell his messmates that the Rebs called them Hooker's Ironsides. "I heard Grant won a big victory at Spotsylvania, too," he told Charlie.

"Oh, you did, eh? I heard Lee is half a mile from Washington, and the White House has evacuated."

"I don't believe you!"

"It was in the newspaper," said Charlie.

"Some Reb newspaper?"

"Well, yeah. They're sort of always sayin' that Lee is half a mile from Washington." Charlie seemed to find this amusing. "I'll meet you next when you cross the Etowah. I reckon y'all are headed for Kingston. If y'all should camp near the Etowah, I got something I want to show you."

"What?" said Jeremy.

"Not going to tell you. But I guarantee you ain't never seen it before."

Jeremy did not like the sound of this. He reminded himself that Charlie was an enemy. For all he knew this something Charlie wanted to show him was the business end of an Enfield rifle. "Why can't you just tell me?"

"'Cause I wanna make you wonder about it, Yank," said Charlie. "Gotta run. Take care, buddy. Keep your head down and don't let nothing hit it."

"You too," said Jeremy, as Charlie splashed away across the creek. Somehow he had meant to be kind and sympathetic to Charlie about the Rebs' humiliating defeat, and Charlie had failed to be humiliated at all.

☆ ★ ★ FIFTEEN ★ ★ ☆

THEY WERE MARCHING ON CASSVILLE, GEORGIA, AND Jeremy was not afraid. He beat the drum and the men sang "John Brown's Body" as they marched along. It was a hot day—too hot, really.

"Double time!" came the order, and Jeremy beat his drum double-time and the men marched faster and stopped singing. Grasshoppers hopped up from the side of the road, and insects buzzed.

The night before there had been cannons firing— Union cannons, anyway. Jeremy and his messmates couldn't tell if the Secesh were firing back. Had the Rebs been driven back, or were they dug in at Cassville waiting to ambush the Twentieth Corps? Back in Syracuse, when Jeremy used to eagerly read newspaper articles about battles, he hadn't realized that soldiers in a battle don't know what battle they're in. After it happened it could be named the Battle of Some Place and you could read that the 107th marched down Such and Such Road and took Some Big

· 153 ·

Hill, but when it was happening the soldiers only knew that they were moving forward and hoping not to get shot.

They came to a log cabin beside the road. A little white girl about five years old stood on the porch. She was wearing an upside-down flour sack with holes cut in it for her head and arms. Jeremy smiled and nodded at her. She shrieked and ran into the cabin.

At the next cabin they came to there was a woman in the yard, hard and angular with a glare that could shrivel spinach. She had a baby on her hip.

"Yankee thieves!" she called. She came out into the road and shook her fist at them. "Thunderin' Yankee thieves! You-uns have took my cow, my pig, my chickens, my potatoes and carrots, and there ain't no milk for the baby!"

Jeremy looked away from her, and noticed the other soldiers were doing the same. It was called foraging, not thieving, and all soldiers did it, Yankee and Secesh both. It wasn't Jeremy's fault. But she kept following them, screaming.

"We-uns worked all spring to put in a crop and there ain't nothing left of it that you-uns haven't stole!"

Jeremy beat the drum louder to drown out her voice. Fortunately, she couldn't keep up because of the heavy baby in her arms, and they soon left her behind, though for a long time Jeremy could hear her in his head.

Before they got to Cassville, Jeremy smelled the smoke.

Then they looked down into the town. A riot seemed to be going on. One or two buildings were on fire. Men were running out of houses carrying frying pans, fruit, ladies' dresses—anything they could get their hands on.

The 107th halted.

"Right," said the lieutenant. "We're going to go down there and put a stop to that by whatever means necessary."

"They're our own men, sir," said a soldier.

"Yes, they are. And they're looting the Secesh. Looting isn't foraging. First of all, I need a squad to round up stragglers and send them on to their companies."

They went down into the town. It had been a nice old town, Jeremy saw. Now it was being destroyed by Federal soldiers, even though the Rebel army had abandoned it. Quickly the men of the Red Star Division stepped in, pointing guns at the looters and rounding them up into little huddles. Some of the Red Star men had been fire-fighters in New York City, and they moved in to put out the buildings that were on fire. Jeremy followed them. They didn't waste time looking around for fire engines but found some buckets and started pouring them onto the flames.

"You there," one of them said to Jeremy. "Go find us some sheets and blankets. Bring 'em back here and soak 'em in buckets of water."

Jeremy ran to do as he was told. Where was he supposed to get these things from? The houses, he supposed.

But wasn't that looting? No, it was foraging, because the things were needed to put out the fires. He ran into a house that had had its door smashed open.

A lady rushed forward with a broomstick and swung it at Jeremy. He darted past her. She wasn't in the mood for conversation, and it would be easier just to take the sheets than to ask for them. He ran upstairs and found a bedroom with a big four-poster bed in it. He pulled the sheets off the bed.

The lady followed him upstairs and came at him, wielding the broom. He ducked under it and ran back down the stairs, tripping over the dragging sheets and almost plummeting down the stairs, but he grabbed the banister and managed to save himself. He ran back to the fire. He shoved the sheets into a bucket of water. Then he ran to get more, hoping to find an unoccupied house this time. What were ladies doing staying in their houses when there was a war coming through?

In the fourth house, which fortunately was empty, he was pulling the sheets off a bed when he noticed that the closet door was open. A row of girls' dresses hung on hooks inside.

He looked at the dresses and he thought of Dulcie in her stained flour sacks. But if he took one of the dresses for Dulcie, was that looting or foraging? Foraging was taking what you needed. Looting was taking what you didn't need. It was generally understood that foraging usually meant only food.

He moved closer to the dresses and picked up a blue one. He took it off the hook and held it up to himself. It would fit him if he was a girl, and he was a little bigger than Dulcie, so it ought to fit her, more or less. There was a darn here and there. It wasn't like it was a *new* dress. But then, there was no such thing as a new dress in the Confederacy. Not since the blockade began in 1861. If he took this dress it would be missed.

There were seven dresses in the closet. For how many girls? Well, the girls, wherever they were, probably had dresses on now. Dulcie only had flour sacks.

Jeremy made up his mind—it was foraging. Dulcie needed this. But he didn't want to have to explain it to the soldiers down below, whose voices he could hear as they ran around arresting looters. He rolled the dress up as small as he could, stuck it under his shirt, and tucked it into his belt to keep it in place.

When he got downstairs he saw that the fires were out.

Nobody ever told you anything, at least not officially, but over time you figured it out. Originally General Sherman had hoped to march straight from Chattanooga to Atlanta with very little resistance. The Confederate Army had had different ideas, though, and there were thousands of Secesh between Sherman's army and Atlanta. Dulcie picked this up from the things she heard, from the men talking—it had become part of the general knowledge of the campaign, in all the hundreds of Union camps, among all the soldiers and all the people who followed them. There had been the battle at Resaca a week ago, and then a sort of business—not quite a battle—at Cassville, and now there was a time of rest, at the Etowah River, as the Union Armies of the Cumberland, the Tennessee, and the Ohio prepared to cross and make the final push to Atlanta against who-knew-how-many Rebel soldiers in their way. Everyone knew this, although no one had been told it.

They were very close to Dulcie's old home. And with the Union Army spread out over such a wide area, preparing to cut a wide swath, the war was undoubtedly going to go through there. Dulcie wondered what had become of Aunt Betsy and Uncle John. They'd said they would wait for the Union Army to come—was the Union Army there yet? Had they run away and joined them, or were they still waiting? Would the war hurt them when it went through? She had been treated well enough by the Union soldiers, but she knew that not everyone had been. She had heard a story about an escaped slave who had been made to dance on a red-hot piece of tin by Union soldiers. Dulcie hadn't met anyone who she thought would do something like that—well, maybe Lars and Jack—but she didn't doubt that there were such people among the tens of thousands of soldiers moving toward Atlanta. So she worried. But there was work to do.

Dulcie was making tourniquets. There was time now for this sort of task, while the army rested and waited.

A field surgeon's kit came with four tourniquets, and that wasn't nearly enough. Dulcie had used more than that herself at Resaca. But making them was easy enough—you had to find good, straight sticks and good, strong cloth, that was all. Dulcie was out searching for sticks beside the Etowah when she ran into Jeremy with a bundle in his arms.

"Dulcie! Er. I brought you this."

Dulcie took what he handed to her, suspicious because she had never known white people to give you anything without expecting a sight more in return. "What is it?"

"It's, you know. A dress."

Dulcie unfolded it and held it up. It was indeed a dress—what must surely be the world's most *sensible* dress. It was a severe dark blue, and there wasn't a bit of trim or lace or ribbon anywhere on it, nor so much as an extra tuck or a ruffle.

"Don't you like it?" Jeremy sounded hurt.

"It's beautiful!" said Dulcie.

Jeremy looked relieved. *Maybe he really doesn't expect anything in return,* Dulcie thought.

She stroked the cloth—this dress would be soft and smooth against her skin, not scratchy like every other dress she'd ever had. And all the darns and mends had been carefully done with thread exactly the same color, so that they hardly showed at all.

"Thank you," she said. "It's real nice. I never had anything made of cloth this good."

"Try it on and see if it fits," Jeremy said.

Dulcie looked around. They were in the woods near the river. There were no soldiers near, nobody but Jeremy, and a few birds chirping overhead. She went behind a clump of holly bushes. "Don't look."

"I ain't lookin'."

"Ain't looking at what?" another voice said. A rough sort of half-boy, half-man voice.

Dulcie, just out of her Union blouse, pulled the new dress over her head in a hurry.

"I've been looking for you everywhere, little buddy."

Dulcie peered through the holly leaves. She recognized Charlie, the boy who'd pulled her out of the river. How had he come and found Jeremy again?

She couldn't get the last button on the dress fastened in back, so she pulled the Union blouse on over it. The flour-sack petticoat would do to make tourniquets out of. She watched Jeremy and Charlie.

"There's Yanks invadin' across the Etowah at every bridge and ford, and some of y'all are just swimming it," said Charlie. "I been looking all among them and I didn't see you anywhere."

"We're resting here," said Jeremy. "Before the final push, where we drive youse back to Atlanta."

"I know," said Charlie.

There was a little pause then, as if Jeremy was waiting for Charlie to claim that nobody was going to be driven back to Atlanta. Charlie didn't.

"You ready to go see something you never seen be-fore?" said Charlie instead.

"Right now?"

"Yeah. I got a skiff and everything, c'mon."

"I got a friend with me," said Jeremy, gesturing toward the holly bushes where Dulcie was hiding.

Oh, thanks, Jeremy, Dulcie thought. They were between her and the camp anyway, but she could've slipped away after they'd gotten in the boat.

"How d'you do, Jeremy's friend," Charlie called cheer-fully to the holly bush.

"It's all right, Dulcie," Jeremy called.

That was the way he saw it, apparently! Him being friends with the enemy. Lips pressed tightly together in annoyance, Dulcie came out from her hiding place.

"That's the slave we pulled out of the river!" said Charlie.

"No, it ain't," Dulcie informed him coldly.

"Yes, it is, I recognize you. Never seen sharp little eyes like yours on nobody else."

"You didn't pull no slave out of the river, is what she means," said Jeremy. "You pulled out a freedman. Freedgirl."

Charlie and Dulcie gave each other a long, appraising look. Dulcie knew this type of boy. He smiled at you, sure, he was amused at everything, in his supercilious way, but you weren't more to him than his pet dog, which also amused him and would grieve him a sight more if it died.

And which he wouldn't dream of seeing whipped with a cowhide. He'd been brought up to think black people were animals, Dulcie thought. She didn't have to know him to know that.

"Well, bring her along too," said Charlie.

Oh, sure, to be handed over to the Secesh! "Where you going?" said Dulcie.

"Downriver."

"To what?" Dulcie said suspiciously.

"Somethin' I want to show the Yank."

Dulcie didn't like that at all. Why was Jeremy going off somewhere with the enemy? And Charlie wouldn't even say what he was going to show Jeremy! The thing about Jeremy was . . . he was nice. He was kind; he'd brought her a dress and he really didn't seem to expect anything in return. But he didn't seem to have a whole lot of common sense sometimes. He seemed to think the war was just a game.

"You going to show him the m—"

"Shh!" Charlie gave Dulcie a winning smile. "We're going to surprise him."

I bet, thought Dulcie.

"You coming along, Dulcie?" said Jeremy.

Dulcie was torn. On the one hand, she didn't want to go anywhere with Charlie. On the other hand, she didn't want Jeremy going off alone, trusting Charlie, not knowing any better.

Besides, she knew that they were very close to her old

home, which was just downriver, and if she didn't take the opportunity to find out if Aunt Betsy and Uncle John were all right, she would always wonder.

There was also the chance that Missus would be hurt by the soldiers. This didn't bother her at all, except that if Missus and Mas'r were hurt—all right, killed—then any chance of ever finding out what had become of Dulcie's mother would be gone.

"All right," she said.

"Capital! Come on then, Jeremy."

The skiff Jeremy had brought was a flat-bottomed boat, its many cracks and leaks stuffed tight with cotton. There was a can in the bottom for bailing, and as soon as they started moving they started bailing. Dulcie did it first, but Charlie said she was too slow and so Jeremy took over. The water was right up around their ankles. It felt pleasantly cool on her feet as they drifted between the hilly banks of the Etowah. She had to admit that she would have been having fun, if it wasn't for the fact that she didn't trust this enemy rowing the boat.

She trailed her hand in the water over the boat's side—the boat was sitting sort of low in the water. The boys talked as if she wasn't there.

"So where y'all figuring to cross the river?"

"Me and Dulcie ain't . . . Oh, the army, you mean. You said we was crossing everywheres."

"Y'all, though, from New York—where you crossing at?"

"The 107th, you mean? I dunno. No one's told us."

"Reckon y'all are headed for Dallas?"

"Dallas? I dunno."

"Don't nobody tell you nothin', Yank?"

"Nope."

Probably just as well they didn't, thought Dulcie, if he was going to turn around and tell it to the enemy.

They were pretty near the farm, Dulcie thought as she watched the trees and hills slip by. She couldn't have said how near, because she'd never traveled down the river like this—she'd only been out on it in a boat once or twice, and she didn't think she'd recognize the spot if she saw it. She was peering through the trees when she saw movement there, not rustly like an animal but smooth and deliberate like a human, and she wasn't sure what made her yell "Get down!"

She splashed down into the bilge at the bottom of the boat as she said it, and at the same instant the bullets began flying.

☆ ★ ★ SIXTEEN ★ ★ ☆

JEREMY AND CHARLIE DOVE INTO THE BOTTOM OF
the boat beside Dulcie. A bullet tore through the wooden
side of the skiff right beside Jeremy's face.

Charlie sloshed up out of the bilgewater and grabbed
the oars and started rowing as hard as he could.

"Are you crazy?" Dulcie yelled at him. She was ducking so low in the bilgewater that she swallowed a mouthful of it when she spoke, and choked on it.

"The skiff ain't no protection," Charlie said. "Gotta get
outta here."

At that Jeremy had to grab one of the oars from Charlie
and row—he wasn't going to stay down hiding if Charlie
wouldn't.

More shots. When you were the target you heard gunfire more with your stomach than with your ears. Another
bullet hit the side of the boat with a hard, splintery thud.
Then, finally, the shooting stopped. Jeremy supposed it had

only gone on for a minute or so, but it had seemed like years.

"They can't even tell who we are at this distance," said Charlie, out of breath. "Guess they don't wanna waste no more ammunition on them terms."

"Yours or ours, y'think?" said Jeremy.

"Reckon they're ours. Lookit us." Charlie tugged at the knee of his Union trousers. "We look like Union soldiers."

"Could've been ours. They wouldn't be able to see our uniforms good, and anyways, we're all red dust and mud," said Jeremy. "Besides, I *am* a Union soldier."

Dulcie got up off the bottom of the boat, dripping.

"It could've been anybody shooting," she said. "Yanks and Secesh! You think that's all that's running around in north Georgia these days? Could've been lots of folks. Could've been the slave patrollers, could've been the Home Guard, could've been the homegrown Yankees."

"The what?" said Jeremy.

"Don't you listen to her," said Charlie with his easy smile. "She's just talkin' through her hat."

"What're homegrown Yankees?" said Jeremy.

"Southerners who want the Union to win," said Dulcie. "There's scads of 'em in north Georgia."

"She's just makin' stuff up," said Charlie.

"Don't say 'she' like I ain't even here, Charlie," said Dulcie.

"Sorry." Charlie smiled big at her. "You're just makin' stuff up, Dulcie."

"I am not! I ran into homegrown Yanks when I was takin' my freedom." She turned to Jeremy. "They're all through Georgia, waiting to take up with the Union Army as soon as it comes along. Like us."

"Are they really Yankees, though?" said Jeremy, confused.

"No, they're Georgians who didn't want to quit the Union," said Dulcie. "They're for Georgia and the United States of America. Plenty of southerners didn't ever want to secede."

"Oh, that may be," said Charlie. "We didn't specially want to secede back home in North Carolina. But once it came about that there was going to be a fight, we stand with the South, of course. *All* of us."

They were talking to each other, Dulcie and Charlie, but they kept looking at Jeremy, as if the conversation was for his benefit. As if it was up to him to decide who was right.

"I thought North Carolina was the first state to secede," said Jeremy.

"*South* Carolina was," said Charlie, with an uncharacteristic flicker of irritation, as if he had had his home state mixed up with South Carolina a few more times than he could cheerfully tolerate. "Hey! Who's bailing?"

Nobody was, and the water was halfway up their calves. Dulcie grabbed the can, which was floating in the stern behind her, and started scooping as fast as she could. The water had reached the bullet holes and was gushing in. Jeremy snatched the can out of Dulcie's hands—he could bail faster than that, he thought. Dulcie went on bailing with her cupped hands.

"Stop those holes with something!" Charlie ordered.

Jeremy kept bailing—Dulcie started ripping strips off her old flour-sack petticoat and stuffing them into bullet holes.

The water was only a couple of inches beneath the tops of the gunwales. The boat was almost underwater.

"It's no good. We're going down. I'm going to try to make the shore," said Charlie.

Jeremy looked up and saw low hills covered with cotton.

"We're almost there anyway," said Dulcie.

"Almost there except you can't swim," said Charlie. "So I reckon we can try to get a little closer."

And then Jeremy felt the boat simply slip away from under him. The water settled in over the gunwales and the boat was lower, and lower, and no longer underneath them. He grabbed Dulcie's arm and started swimming toward shore. Charlie had ahold of her other arm. They fought through a thicket of river cane and scrambled up onto the clay bank.

They wrung river water out of their clothes as best they could, and then made their way through a small grove of persimmon and hickory trees.

"Those are some funny little hills," Jeremy commented

as they passed between two hillocks that looked like they hadn't been formed with the land but had popped out of the ground as an afterthought.

"Uh-huh. Here, this is what I brought you here to see," said Charlie, stopping.

"I seen cotton fields before."

"Keep lookin'," said Charlie, smiling. "Cause you ain't seen this before."

"Oh! It's like pyramids!" said Jeremy.

"They *are* pyramids," said Charlie.

"Only flat on top," said Jeremy.

"They're mounds," said Dulcie. "There used to be buildings on top. On the big mound there, there was a temple. And where we're standing now was a city."

Jeremy looked at the mounds. They were like the sudden hillocks they'd passed, only much bigger, towering high over their heads, and perfectly flat on top. Trees grew up the slopes of the mounds, but the tops had corn growing on them.

"Let's go up top," said Charlie.

The largest mound had a turf ramp built up the side of it. They walked up it. At the top, beside the cornfield, they turned and looked down. They could see the tops of the other pyramids below them, overgrown with trees but still discernibly pyramid-shaped. A long time ago a lot of people had worked hard here, maybe as hard as the soldiers digging into the night and throwing up great fortifications at Resaca. Jeremy imagined hundreds of people working, digging the heavy Georgia clay and building these mounds, month after month, maybe year after year.

"Who made this?" he asked.

"Indians," said Charlie.

"Why?"

"As a place for people to live in," said Charlie.

"As temples for the priests to live in," said Dulcie at almost the same time.

"They lived inside 'em? How do you get in?"

"I think they lived *on* 'em." Charlie frowned, narrowing his eyes as if looking at an old memory. "There was buildings up on top."

"There was a big war," said Dulcie. "A revolution. The people rose up and killed all the priests."

"The war was against invaders," said Charlie. "From outside. Spaniards."

"The *priests* were the invaders," said Dulcie. "They came up from somewhere—Mexico, I think—and there were Cherokees living here—"

"Creeks lived here," said Charlie, sounding amused.

"*Cherokees* lived here, and then these priests came in from some other tribe and made 'em build these here mounds. They enslaved 'em and made 'em build mounds."

Jeremy felt like his friends weren't really arguing about long-ago Indians but about the right-now South. He could feel the oldness of the place seeping into him now. He imagined he was really looking down at the ancient city, at a plaza and houses and ancient people moving among them, quarreling and making up and laughing at jokes he wouldn't have understood.

"Slaves built these mounds. Overseers whipped 'em." Dulcie frowned and looked down, and Jeremy suddenly felt like he could almost hear the crack of the whips as weary slaves dragged basket after basket of dirt up the ramp.

"They whipped 'em to make 'em build their temples," said Dulcie.

"Houses," said Charlie. "And then one day they looked out from here and they seen Spaniards coming, and they dug a big ditch. . . ."

"How'd they have time to dig a big ditch if they could already see the Spaniards?"

"All right, they had already dug the ditch before, and they stuck it around with spiked logs and fought off the Spaniards with flaming arrows and spears—for as long as they could."

"Then what happened?" said Jeremy, hoping he could get them to stop arguing about it.

"Then they had to give up," said Charlie. "Cause they couldn't fight forever."

"How do you know about it?" said Jeremy. He assumed Charlie's story was the correct one, because Charlie had been to school and Dulcie hadn't. But it was strange how he'd felt like he could hear the crack of the whips.

Charlie shrugged. "I don't know. It's an old story. I've always known it."

"Me too," said Dulcie. "I've always known the story too."

Only her story was different.

Jeremy looked at the woods below them. It was hard to imagine a war being fought in this quiet place by the river, blood being spilled over these square pyramids and the neat city squares they seemed to surround. But then, it was hard to imagine a city being here—priests, temples, and what must have been hundreds, maybe thousands, of people. What was once worth fighting a war over had become an old story, and nobody was sure of the details or even why they knew it.

A cloud passed over the sun, and Jeremy shivered. "Let's go," he said suddenly.

"There's something moving down there," said Charlie.

They all three hit the ground fast, and lay flat among the cornstalks.

"Maybe it's just slaves in the cotton field," said Dulcie.

"It wasn't in the cotton field," said Charlie. "It was over in the cane by the riverbank there."

Jeremy had thought he'd heard voices coming from the woods downriver from the cotton fields, but he didn't want to say so because he knew Charlie was a much more experienced soldier than he was.

"We're going to go down the mound among the trees over there," Charlie decided, pointing. "Then stay low under the cotton plants and head that way." He pointed.

"But I want to visit my old homeplace," said Dulcie.

"What?"

"My old homeplace. It's that way." She pointed the opposite direction from the way Charlie had pointed.

"Why do you want to do that?" said Jeremy.

"She misses her old mas'r and missus," Charlie supplied. "They're like family, to a slave."

"They are not!" Dulcie snapped. "I miss my real family. I want to find out what happened to my parents. And also to the other slaves."

"But they'll just grab you and put you back in slavery, won't they?" said Jeremy.

"How?"

Jeremy shrugged. He didn't know how slavery worked, but he imagined that there must be ways to force people into it or nobody would *be* in it. Anyway, lying on the ground here, with broken cornstalks digging into his belly, wondering where the enemy was, it seemed like a dumb thing to be arguing about, so he dropped it.

"How far is it to your homeplace?" said Charlie, sounding resigned.

"I don't know, half an hour or an hour. And it's on the way back anyway. Sort of."

They would have to walk back anyway, since their boat had sunk.

"Fine," said Charlie. "That way, then." He nodded toward the way Dulcie wanted to go. "And if you hear anything, freeze."

Moving silently down the side of the mound while remaining hidden was impossible. The sides were steep, never meant to be walked on, and the three of them slipped and slid, cracking twigs and rustling leaves as they went. Jeremy had always prided himself on his ability to move silently in the woods, but now with every step he seemed to make more noise than a regiment. There was no help for it, they were making a lot of noise and couldn't stop, and so Jeremy tried to move quickly. He grabbed a sapling that came out of the ground in his hand, and he tumbled the last ten feet or so, landing with a thud.

The others made their way down beside him, and, crouched over, they began walking through the cotton rows. Jeremy tried not to brush against the plants so that no movement would be visible in the fields from a distance.

". . . smart lot of homegrown Yanks around here last night . . . ," a voice said somewhere off to their right.

Jeremy froze, like Charlie had told him to, but Charlie gestured for them both to keep moving. After all, the voices weren't exactly coming from the direction they were going. Then a thought struck Jeremy and he froze again.

Charlie grabbed his sleeve to tug him onward. But Dulcie had stopped moving too.

"How do we know you ain't gonna hand us over to those Secesh?" she whispered.

"Tarnation, girl, don't you trust me?"

Dulcie answered this with a level gaze.

Charlie looked hurt, and Jeremy felt bad for him. Charlie wouldn't do that, would he? Would he?

"We trust you," he told Charlie.

Dulcie gave him a look that seemed to say that Jeremy could speak for himself, but not for her. Nonetheless, they moved on.

Then Charlie, leading the way, spread out his arms to stop them. The rows of cotton ended abruptly.

"There's the moat to cross," he whispered.

"Moat?"

"That the Indians dug around this place to protect it. It's full of water. We'll have to swim. Look, I'll take hold of the girl. . . ."

"I have a name," Dulcie said.

Charlie gave her a fed-up look. "Dulcie," he whispered, "and Jeremy, you just get down on your hands and knees and slide in there right smart and swim across with no noise."

"I can swim Dulcie across," said Jeremy, just because he wanted to point out that he could.

"I know you can. Now go."

Jeremy cast a doubtful look at Dulcie. He felt strongly that she was his responsibility, and he didn't like leaving her with a Reb, even for a minute. But he had to admit that Charlie was stronger than him and more likely to get her across the ditch silently.

He got down on his hands and knees and stuck his

head out quick to look all around. There was no one in sight. He slipped out of his shoes, crawled to the edge of the moat, and threw his shoes across. They landed with a thump on the other side, and Jeremy could imagine Charlie wincing at the unnecessary noise. He shouldn't have done it—his shoes were already pretty badly damaged by their dip in the Etowah. Too late now. He slipped into the water without a splash and dog-paddled cautiously, not letting his hands or feet above the surface. Pulling himself out the other side was harder, and he did make some noise with a wave of water sliding off him and splashing into the moat. He rolled over and found his shoes.

Charlie was swimming across with Dulcie clinging to his shoulders. They too managed to make almost no noise until they got to the edge. Then they both splashed climbing out—the dress he'd given Dulcie, Jeremy realized, was a real hindrance when it was wet, heavy and confining to her legs. Well, dresses weren't made for swimming in. Or doing much of anything in, he thought.

". . . heard something over here," said a voice in the woods. "Halt! Who goes there?"

All three of them stood stock-still and stared at each other.

Footsteps crunched through the woods. "Speak or I fire! Who goes there?"

"A friend without a countersign," Charlie called back. He pronounced *friend* "frayund" and *sign* "sahn," Jeremy noticed. He sounded more Southern than he usually sounded when he was talking to Jeremy.

"Come forward with your hands on your head."

Charlie put his hands on his head, and Jeremy did too. He saw Dulcie do the same. What was going to happen to them now? Was Charlie going to betray them after all? Was that why he'd brought them down here? Jeremy felt like a fool for trusting him. Why had Charlie said "a friend" just now, instead of "friends"?

They didn't have to move forward, though, because at that instant two Rebs came out of the forest. They were the raggediest-looking Rebs Jeremy had ever seen. It was impossible to tell whether their uniforms were Reb or Union, because all the clothes they had on were so completely covered in red clay dust that Jeremy doubted it could ever be washed out. And you wouldn't want to try to wash it out, because the clothes—what was left of them—would probably fall apart. Patches had been sewn on top of patches until the patches were not so much holding the clothes together as holding each other—the men were dressed in patches. They wore slouch hats and, instead of shoes, rawhide sandals that were crawling with flies.

Jeremy didn't notice this right away, though, because he was too busy staring down the barrels of the rifles that were pointing at the three of them. He clasped his fingers together extra-tight so that the Rebs would understand that he sure enough had his hands on top of his head and intended to keep them there. He felt much more frightened than he had felt at Resaca. These guns were pointed at *him,* not at the Union forces in general. Him and Dulcie and Charlie, of course.

And now everything depended on what Charlie chose to say about Jeremy and Dulcie.

"What outfit you with, 'friend'?" Both Rebs were as skinny as scarecrows, but if one of them was just a little less skinny than the other, it was that one who spoke.

"Fifty-eighth North Carolina," said Charlie, his southern accent even stronger.

"What about the—"

"She's my servant," said Charlie.

Jeremy wasn't sure if that was a good sign. Did it mean Charlie meant to stand by him and Dulcie, or was he making Dulcie a slave? He chanced a sidelong glance at Dulcie to see how she was taking this, and got a surprise. Instead of the defiance he expected to see in her bayonet-sharp eyes, he saw a completely changed Dulcie. She stood stooped over, her hands clasped on top of her head and her eyes downcast. Her face was expressionless, as if it was all one to her whether she was captured, let go, or shot. Dulcie was pretending to be a slave.

And he, by his silence, was pretending to be a Reb. At least until Charlie gave him away. Pretending, and hoping like anything that the men with the rifles didn't see through his pretense. He felt he ought to say something—

something defiant, like "The Union forever!" The Drummer Boy of Shiloh would have. But Jeremy looked at those rifle muzzles and stayed silent. His stomach hurt.

"Fifty-eighth North Carolina, are you?" said the skinnier Reb. "What about him?" He jerked his rifle barrel at Jeremy for emphasis.

Jeremy looked down at the ground and waited for Charlie to speak.

"Him too," said Charlie.

Jeremy let out a silent sigh of relief and hated himself for it.

"Can't he talk?"

"Nope," said Jeremy. "Struck dumb by a lightning bolt as an infant."

The Rebs looked as skeptical as this explanation deserved. But Jeremy had to give Charlie credit for trying—and he felt guilty for having doubted his friend.

"And how come he's got a U.S. belt buckle?" said the less-skinny Reb.

"Took it off a stiff 'un at Resaca," said Charlie.

"And you're 58th North Carolina, are you?"

"Yup."

"Think we should shoot 'em here or capture 'em?"

"Capture 'em. They're just kids."

"But there's three of 'em if you count the colored one."

"Who counts the colored ones?"

"They could turn on us, is what I'm saying."

Either they flat-out didn't believe Charlie—which was

pretty likely—or they weren't really Rebs but something else, homegrown Yanks or one of those other groups, Jeremy thought. Or they just didn't like people from North Carolina.

"Washington," said Charlie. "And I dreamed the boys was all coming home."

Jeremy looked at him to see if he had lost his mind. Charlie's lips were pressed tightly together, and he was staring right at the Rebs, and he looked perfectly sane.

The two Rebs exchanged a glance.

"And the Constitution," Charlie added.

"Do you know another name?" said the less-skinny Reb.

"Yes, I do," said Charlie.

"Tell me it, then."

"It ain't to be spoken," said Charlie.

"Can you spell it?"

"E," said Charlie.

"A," said the less-skinny Reb.

"C."

"E."

"P."

The guns were lowered. Charlie took his hands off his head. Cautiously, Jeremy and Dulcie did the same. Jeremy's hands were all pins and needles, and he was busy trying to figure out how you'd pronounce a name spelled E-A-C-E-P.

"Name's Bill," said the less-skinny Reb, sticking out a hand.

"Pleased to make your acquaintance, Bill." Charlie shook his hand. "I'm Charlie, and this here's my pardner Jeremy."

"Robby," said the skinnier Reb, and they shook hands all around—except Dulcie. Bill and Robby didn't ask her name, and Charlie didn't offer it. And Jeremy thought he was best off saying nothing at all while he tried to figure out what in tarnation was going on.

"What're you doing with a Yankee pardner?" asked Bill.

"Showing him around. I wanted him to see the mounds." Charlie nodded at the moat and the cotton field beyond.

"We was sent down here to wash out a nest of home-grown Yanks," said Bill. "Seen any around?"

"Nope."

"Well, if y'all see 'em tell 'em we're looking for 'em and they best dust off sharpish," said Bill.

"We'll do that," said Charlie.

"Hate to have 'em get hurt," Bill explained. He nodded. "Carry on, then."

"Any trouble up ahead?" said Charlie, pointing into the woods.

"Some more lookin' for the homegrowns. But just talk to them like you talked to us. They're fine."

Charlie nodded. "Much obliged, then."

"Hope to make your better acquaintance," said Bill.

"Likewise," said Robby, and Charlie said, "It was a pleasure makin' yours," and then the two Rebs turned and stalked off into the woods.

"What was that all about?" Jeremy whispered when he was sure they were out of earshot.

Charlie shook his head, not answering. "Let's go find this old homeplace of Dulcie's."

THE FARM LOOKED SMALLER THAN DULCIE REMEM-
bered. That wasn't surprising, she supposed—once, it had
been the whole world. Was that really only three weeks
ago? Now the world had grown infinitely more vast, full of
towns and railroads, mountains and rivers, and thousands
upon thousands of people. And now, with Mr. Lincoln's
soldiers invading, Dulcie could return without risk of
being recaptured. Maybe. She hoped.

The corn was coming along nicely, Dulcie saw, except
that the fields were overgrown with weeds. So was the garden. The barnyard was unkempt, the dooryard unswept—
so Aunt Betsy and Uncle John must have gone. They would
never let the yard look like that. There was no sign of the
chickens, the pigs, or the cow. They had either been impressed along with Begonia the horse or eaten by Yankees,
Dulcie supposed.

Missus sat alone on a rocking chair on the porch.
Dulcie didn't know what she felt as she walked across the

farmyard with the boys beside her—she had expected to feel anger, hate, maybe pride at Missus seeing she was free and out of reach forever. Fear she didn't feel. Fear was gone.

Missus looked up and saw Dulcie. Their eyes met. Dulcie stiffened. Behind her she felt Jeremy move closer to her, and though she should have been reassured she was annoyed instead. She had to stand up to Missus by herself. She was free and unafraid. She took a step forward.

"Come back, have you?" said Missus.

"I want to know where my parents are," said Dulcie.

"I knew you wouldn't be able to live on your own," said Missus, not listening. "Blacks say they want freedom. But what do they mean by it? Freedom from work, that's what. And you can't live if you don't work."

Dulcie noticed now that Missus's dress was dirty. There was a new rent down one side that had been inexpertly stitched up with the wrong color thread. Dulcie looked around the farmyard. Although the animals were gone the last evidences of them were still lying unremoved, mucking up the place. Usually the farmyard and the dooryard were swept into neat arc-shaped patterns at least once a week. Now they were just red dust.

"Where are Aunt Betsy and Uncle . . ."

"They run off. They run about a week after you did."

"So there's no one to take care of the place," said Dulcie. And, she realized, Missus didn't have a clue how to take care of it herself.

"I don't know how you blacks think you'll live on your

own. You're all like big children, really. You need looking after."

Against her will, Dulcie felt a wave of pity. "Look, Missus, you've got to take care of yourself." The words tasted funny in her mouth, and Dulcie realized she'd never called Missus "you" before. It wasn't how a slave talked. A slave would say, "Missus has to take care of herself."

Missus stared at Dulcie as if she'd never seen her before.

"You've got to," Dulcie repeated. "You've got to—well, to pull up those weeds in the vegetable garden, for one thing. Want me to show you which are the weeds?"

Missus's eyes narrowed. "You coming back to your rightful place, then?"

"No!" said Dulcie. "I mean, I'm in my rightful place now. I'm with the Union Army."

"She needs help," said Jeremy, softly, behind her. "Maybe you should stay and help her a little bit."

Dulcie wheeled on him, furious. His face showed pity for Missus. Dulcie might feel pity, but Jeremy—Jeremy had no idea! He just had no idea. "Come here," she told him. "I want to show you something."

She turned and marched toward the barn. She could hear footsteps crunching the dust behind her, and she didn't look to see who was following her. Behind the barn was a little house, made of logs, about the size of Dr. Flood's hospital tent. The door hung half-open and Dulcie, unable to suppress a shudder, marched inside.

Their breath told her the boys were both in there with

· 185 ·

her. She stood in silence, waiting for her eyes to become accustomed to the gloom. The place smelled of fear, sweat, and old blood.

She could tell Jeremy's eyes adjusted to the dark faster than hers, because she heard him gasp.

An iron bar ran across one wall, near the roof. Another ran along the floor. Three sets of iron shackles were fixed firmly to each bar. A long-handled whip still leaned against the wall and, next to it, a board with holes drilled through it.

"The board," Dulcie said, "they dip in boiling water, then beat you with it to raise blisters. Then they cut the blisters with a whip. Then they rub salt in."

"They don't do that all the time!" said Charlie.

"That Missus lady did this?" said Jeremy.

"Sometimes. Other times she'd hire a man in to do it. Once she hired a man to whip a slave—to whip Anne, I mean. He whipped Anne two hundred times. I watched."

"No man would do that!" said Jeremy.

"This one did."

"What did they whip her for?" said Charlie, challenging-like.

"For running away."

"She shouldn't have run away, then." But Charlie's voice didn't sound as sure as his words.

"And because Missus always hated her," Dulcie added. "Anne was very light-skinned, you see."

She hadn't understood this fully at the time, when she

was only five years old, but later she had understood. She'd put the rest of the story together from mutterings and whisperings around the fire in Aunt Betsy's cabin when they thought she was asleep, from remarks and glances and things only half-said. The adults would have said she was too young to understand, but she understood, all right.

"Mas'r has a very pointy nose," Dulcie said. "And there's sort of a little cleft at the end of it. And Anne had the same little cleft at the end of her nose."

Both the boys were perfectly silent at this. Jeremy was looking at her, but Charlie wouldn't.

"And then Anne had a little boy with curly blond hair and blue eyes. And after that Missus hated her even more than before and would whip her for anything at all. So Mas'r decided to sell her, but he wanted to keep the little boy. And that's when she ran away. With the little boy."

Charlie was now staring fixedly out the door of the shed with his face looking like he was somewhere far away. Dulcie wondered if he would run away from the sound of her voice and from her story.

"Mas'r had gone away. He said he had business to attend to in Milledgeville, but I think he just didn't want to be there when the slave factor came to buy Anne. Only just before that, Anne ran away, and they tracked her down with dogs and caught her."

Dulcie closed her eyes for a moment as the memory overwhelmed her—the cries, the baying of the dogs, the smell of fear and blood.

"They whipped her two hundred times and made all of us watch. Then Missus sold the baby away."

"Sold the baby? But you said he was white!"

"He wasn't white," said Charlie, turning from the door. His customary grin was gone and the expression in his eyes was unfathomable. "He was black."

"But she said he had blond—"

"It don't matter what he had," said Charlie. "One drop of black blood makes a person black."

"A child is a slave if its mother is a slave," said Dulcie. "It doesn't matter what the father was."

"But . . . but . . ." Jeremy looked completely baffled, and Dulcie had the curious sensation that she and Charlie were standing together, enemies, on the opposite side of a great chasm of understanding from Jeremy.

"What happened to the mother?" said Jeremy.

"To Anne? She died."

"But that's murder!" said Jeremy.

Dulcie just looked at him. She couldn't bring herself to say "No, it's not," and if Charlie said it, she thought, she would hit him. Charlie didn't say it.

"And you care what happens to that Missus woman now?" said Jeremy, angry. "We ought to bring her in here and chain her up!"

"No," said Dulcie.

"She deserves it! How can you not think she deserves it?" Jeremy was furious now.

"Nobody should have it done to them," Dulcie

explained. Suddenly she felt very tired. "Go ask Missus what happened to my parents," she said to Jeremy. "She's not gonna tell me."

"There'll be an account book," said Charlie suddenly. "Let's get the account book."

Dulcie looked at him, surprised. "How do you know?"

He shrugged. "Farmers keep account books. They write down . . . things they sell—I mean, livestock and like that—" He wouldn't meet Dulcie's eye.

Jeremy went up onto the porch, with Charlie beside him and Dulcie just behind. That Missus lady of Dulcie's was still sitting there, rocking.

"We want to know where Dulcie's mother is," said Jeremy.

"My husband takes care of all that. I wouldn't know a thing about it," said Missus. Her expression was vacant but her blue eyes were calculating. Jeremy imagined those eyes watching Anne be whipped two hundred times.

"Let us see the account book, then," said Charlie.

Jeremy was surprised. He'd learned in Tennessee that southern men took great pride in being polite to women. Charlie wasn't being polite, and for once he wasn't smiling. Maybe Dulcie's story about Anne had upset him more than he'd let on.

"And who are you, if I may ask?" said Missus. She looked at both of them. Dulcie wasn't in her line of view.

"One Hundred and Seventh New York Volunteer Infantry," said Jeremy. He didn't feel like he needed to give her his name. Not after what he'd just heard about Anne.

"And you?" said Missus, looking at Charlie.

"I don't know who I am," said Charlie.

Looking at Charlie's grim expression, Jeremy thought, *If he wasn't my friend I'd be scared of him.* Missus must've found Charlie scary too, because she got to her feet and went into the house. A minute later she emerged with a leather-bound ledger.

Jeremy sat down on the steps with the ledger on his lap and read through it, with Dulcie on one side of him and Charlie on the other. He was a little surprised that Dulcie couldn't read, but he guessed she had just never been taught how.

The ledger started in 1850. There were pages and pages about selling corn and cotton and watermelons. A steer named Harvey had been sold. A horse and a cow had been bought. There was nothing about hiring any slaves out. There was something about selling a woman and a boy, and then the woman was crossed out. Anne, Jeremy thought. Then more produce and livestock. He turned the page.

"I think that's it," said Charlie, leaning over and pointing. "October third, 1858."

Jeremy read aloud, "Sold to Jos. Butler of Milledgeville for $850, my negro wench Aed. about 30 years."

"But my mother was hired out, not sold!" Dulcie turned angrily to Missus. "You never said she was sold!"

Missus shrugged, not looking at any of them. "I don't know. My husband takes care of all that sort of thing. It's not my affair."

"Where is your husband?" said Jeremy. He hadn't even thought of the husband, who might show up suddenly with a gun and start shooting.

"In the barn," said Missus at the same time that Dulcie said, "He was drafted and sent to Atlanta."

Jeremy pointed at the ledger page. "Is this Dulcie's mother? Sold October third, 1858?"

Missus rocked. "I don't know. I don't remember when it happened."

"Eighteen fifty-eight," said Dulcie. "This is 1864. I was five, and now I'm eleven."

Jeremy looked at the following pages. "There's nothing else about any slaves in 1858."

Charlie took the book from Jeremy and flipped through it. "No, I reckon that's Dulcie's mother." He ripped the page out of the ledger and handed it to Dulcie.

Missus looked up at the sound of tearing paper. "You don't be coming in here tearing things up!" She got to her feet and looked at the barn. "James! James!"

Jeremy jumped up. Maybe the husband was in Atlanta, and maybe he was in the barn. He and Charlie and Dulcie dusted on out of there, Dulcie with the ledger page about her mother clutched in her hand.

When they got to the road they parted ways. Charlie headed back to the Reb camp, and Dulcie led the way back to the Union camp. Jeremy looked over his shoulder. There was no sound of pursuit, and he guessed that Missus had been lying and her husband was in Atlanta like Dulcie said.

But what if he had come out with a gun and told Charlie and Jeremy to leave and Dulcie to *stay*? Jeremy wondered what he would have done in that case. He hoped he would have done the right thing.

The meeting with the two Rebs in the forest had taught Jeremy that the right thing was hard to do when fear told you to do the wrong thing.

☆ ★ ★ EIGHTEEN ★ ★ ☆

THE 25TH OF MAY WAS A PERFECT, SUNSHINY DAY, NOT too hot. The Twentieth Corps were out of the mountains now, and the marching was easy along a dusty red Georgia wagon road. The 107th marched four abreast, and Jeremy beat time with his drum. There was no enemy in sight, and it seemed likely there would be no more opposition from the Rebels until they reached the fortifications of Atlanta.

"Can't wait to see them fortifications," said Nicholas. "We been hearing so much about 'em. What do you think they'll look like?"

"Like those red log-and-clay things we been seein', only mountain-tall," Dave guessed. "They've sent all the slaves to work on them; the things must be huge."

It was afternoon, and they'd marched all morning, stopped to eat, and marched on—they'd made several miles, and Jeremy began to wonder how much further it was till Atlanta and when they'd get there.

"I wonder if we'll take Atlanta just like that," he said. "We been driving the Rebs back right along the way. I think we'll drive 'em right out of Atlanta, too."

"Could be," said Nicholas.

"They can't stand up to the 107th!" said Dave.

"Nothing can!" said Jeremy.

"Nothing in a Reb uniform, anyways," said Lars.

"They don't wear Reb uniforms," said Nicholas. "They wear ours."

"It looks like it's going to storm, later on," said No-Joke.

"What are you talking about? There's not a cloud in the sky!"

"I don't know. It just feels like it. Like there's going to be a storm later."

"You and your megrims, No-Joke. Cheer up," said Nicholas. "Tell us what you're going to do when this cruel war is over."

"What are *you* going to do?" said No-Joke.

"Oh, I don't know. I thought about giving up the schoolteacher game and going to college."

"I'm going to move to the city," said Dave.

"What city?"

"I don't know. Maybe *New York,*" said Dave bravely. "I want to do something different. I don't want to go back to the farm." He cast a sidelong glance at Nicholas. "I bet there's colleges in New York." Then he added quickly, "What about you, Lars?"

Lars reddened. "What about you, LDB? What are you going to do?"

"I don't know." Jeremy hadn't thought about this. His plan had been to die nobly in battle. He didn't have a backup. He still doubted he was going to need one. "Might not *be* an after the war."

"You got the megrims worse than No-Joke," said Nicholas, waving a hand dismissively at him. "You didn't tell us what you're going to do, Lars."

Lars's face was brick red. He looked off to the horizon, toward the young green stalks of a distant cornfield, as if he found them fascinating. The tramp, tramp, tramp of the long marching column went on.

"Lars has a sweetheart," said Dave. "And he wants to marry her."

A whoop went up from the men around Lars, who turned so red that Jeremy thought he might have an apoplexy.

"Who told you that!"

Dave danced out of the way of Lars's fist and then fell back into step beside him. "Easy to guess. Nobody writes letters every single night." He chuckled, enjoying egging Lars. "For three solid hours. And haunts the chaplain all the time, asking him when the next mail is coming in."

The men laughed. Lars's face stayed red, but to Jeremy's surprise he didn't seem all that angry. Jeremy tried to imagine a woman who would want to marry Lars. A vision of an enormous woman, six feet tall with muscles like a cart horse and hair like polished brass, sprang into his head.

"I never noticed that he was writing for that long!"

"It's only lately," said Dave.

"She must have written him a nice letter, huh?"

"We're all coming to your shivaree, Lars!"

Jeremy grinned at the thought. If he could go to Lars's shivaree he could pay him back for a lot. Maybe that's what shivarees were all about. A lot of couples in the Northwoods got married secretly to avoid it—the young men outside the bridal couple's house all night long, beating kettles and drums and anything else that would make a loud noise, whooping and hollering and singing rude songs. It would be fun to do that to Lars.

"How about you, No-Joke?" asked Nicholas, taking pity on Lars at last. "You going to get married?"

"I told you. I'm going to start a school for freedmen."

"Oh! Why do that? Someone will teach those freedmen."

"Right. It doesn't have to be you. Let their old masters teach them. They owe 'em an education, at least."

"That would be a terrible idea!" said No-Joke. "How can slave owners teach slaves to be free?"

"Maybe they don't need to learn to be free."

"They need to be able to read and write," said No-Joke. "And cipher. And for some of them, more. Music. Theology. Law. Medicine!"

"I met a colored doctor when we was in Washington,"

said Dave. "A surgeon for one of the colored regiments. He was a real doctor, had went to college for it and everything."

"There will be more of them!" said No-Joke excitedly. "Thousands of colored doctors!"

"What do we need thousands of colored doctors for?" said Lars, who looked both relieved and disappointed that the subject had moved off of his sweetheart.

"Colored doctors, colored lawyers, colored teachers!" No-Joke's eyes shone. "And congressmen, and senators . . ."

"Whoa! Colored congressmen?"

"A whole great colored nation! Can't you see it?" No-Joke turned to them excitedly. "Can't you see it all around us?"

Jeremy wondered, not for the first time, if No-Joke might be a little touched in the head.

Lars grinned, and Dave and Nicholas were smiling, and Jeremy could tell that things were about to go badly for No-Joke. He was relieved not to be Lars's target for the moment.

"A colored nation, huh? Why not a colored president while you're at it? No-Joke, you must be . . ."

"Halt!" The order came down the line. Why were they stopping? They'd already taken their nooning.

"About-face, march! Double time!"

Jeremy drummed out the commands. With the swift ease of endless practice the men of the 107th New York turned around and marched back the way they had come.

"Why do you reckon we're going back?"

"That other road back there, maybe we took the wrong way."

"The whole division?"

"Why not?"

"So what's the hurry, then? Why double time?"

The long columns of men ahead double-timed down the road, and the 107th New York followed, in ranks of four.

"I don't like this," said Nicholas suddenly. "Every time we've had to reverse and march back double-time, it's been bad luck for the 107th."

"Did we do that at Antietam?"

"We did that at Gettysburg, I'm pretty sure."

It wasn't like Nicholas to be a pessimist, and now he was getting everyone else down. "I bet we just took the wrong road," said Jeremy. "And if the Rebs need to be taught another lesson before Atlanta, the 107th New York can do it!"

Jeremy remembered how they'd sent the Rebs running at Resaca. The 107th New York was invincible.

But No-Joke muttered, "I don't like this either."

The day felt hotter now that they were marching so fast. No-Joke had said it was going to storm, but Jeremy couldn't see so much as a cloud anywhere. He almost wished it *would* rain, to cool things off. At least he wished he still had his canteen.

They had marched back a mile or so when the column

turned off the road and began marching across a field. They crossed a small creek and then climbed a steep hill— still in step! Jeremy was proud to be a member of the 107th. They stayed in formation even as they reached the edge of a small ravine, and broke step only as long as it took to scramble down into it and up the other side. Climbing up, Jeremy grabbed something prickly, but he was a soldier, and tough. He ignored the sharp little thorns in his hands, because he had to keep drumming.

At the top of the hill, in the woods, they saw Union soldiers partly dug in behind hastily erected barricades of fallen logs. The artillery had unhitched the horses and were wrestling the cannons into position.

Meanwhile, the 107th was being ordered into line of battle, at the crest of the wooded hillside, part of a long blue line made up of the three brigades of the First Division, distinguished by the red, white, or blue stars on their hats. *Hooker's Ironsides,* Jeremy reminded himself. *And it's the Secesh who call us that!* Jeremy took his place in the line, his drumsticks clutched tightly in his hands. He no longer noticed the prickles in his hands. As far as he could see in either direction, Union soldiers were lined up, facing the woods. In the woods he could see nothing but trees.

"There's nobody there," he said under his breath.

"Oh, I reckon there's somebody there," said Lars. "But we'll soon have them wishing they weren't."

Behind them the cannons fired, making Jeremy jump. The shells screamed overhead and exploded red and orange in the forest beyond. Again the cannons fired. But they were all Union cannons. There was no answer from the forest.

Again Jeremy wondered if there was really anybody there.

"Attention!" Captain John F. Knox stood before them, his sword gleaming in his hand.

"This afternoon Generals Hooker and Geary with Geary's division encountered the enemy unexpectedly on Pumpkin Vine Creek, and they have driven them to ground here in this woods. It now remains for us to kill or capture the remainder of their force."

"They took a wrong turn," muttered No-Joke, next to Jeremy.

"What do you mean?" said Jeremy. "Who did?"

"Those generals. Geary and Hooker. We were on the road to Dallas. This road"—he nodded to a road that Jeremy could just make out going through the woods to their right—"is a different road."

"They took a wrong turn and stirred up a pile of rattle-snakes!" said Dave indignantly.

Nicholas shrugged. "What's the difference? We have to fight 'em somewhere."

Now came the part of warfare that Jeremy was becoming most familiar with. They waited. They stood in line, the men with their rifles on their shoulders, Jeremy with the drum strap digging into the back of his neck. The artillery went on shelling the woods ahead of them. The sound shook the earth under Jeremy's feet, and he began to get a headache and wished once more that his canteen hadn't been blown up.

The sun sank lower in the sky. It shouldn't be this dark yet, though, Jeremy thought—and then he looked up and saw dark clouds gathering in a yellow sky. It looked like No-Joke was right. There was going to be a storm.

At last the skirmishers were ordered forward, men who moved out in front of the attack. They had a dangerous job. The rest of the soldiers, shoulder to shoulder, would follow after. Their job was nearly as dangerous, because moving forward in formation, they were very easy to shoot. Except Jeremy still doubted there were any Rebels in the woods. It must be hours now since the skirmish at Pumpkin Vine Creek. He bet the Rebels had all run away. Absquatulated. He savored the word in his head.

"Attention! Forward, double-quick!"

The bugles blew the command; the drummers drummed it. Jeremy beat his drum and marched forward with the company, all in line, all together, the men with their rifles on their shoulders, Jeremy with his drum before him.

"Center on the colors! Close in on the right!"

They were not formed in ranks, one behind the other, as they had been at Resaca. After the skirmishers, the soldiers were ranked in long, long lines of men stretching as far as Jeremy could see to his left and right. The 107th was toward the right end of the line, near the road, but not close enough to the end that Jeremy could actually see it. The officers wanted the men close together. It seemed to Jeremy that if the Rebs fired a shot they couldn't fail to hit somebody. But they had yet to fire a shot—if they were even really there.

Ahead of them the skirmishers were firing; the rifle shots echoed among the trees. The smell of powder from the cannon smoke and the rifles filled Jeremy's nostrils— the smell of war. He moved forward eagerly. He could see the Union skirmishers. "Double-quick!"

But the line of men began to slow—barely perceptibly, and still perfectly in step. The Union skirmishers ahead were slowing down. The rattle of gunfire ahead grew louder—was it just Union skirmishers firing? Jeremy saw one of them suddenly lifted off his feet, his body arching as he flew backward and landed limp on the ground.

So the Rebs were there after all, and the 107th was closing in on them. They'd soon have those Rebs on the run.

Ahead, the Union skirmishers had stopped moving forward. Why were they stopping? Then they waved madly, gesturing to the men behind them to stop. Jeremy hesitated. Should they stop? But there had been no command to stop, and the men of the 107th and all the rest of the men in the long, long line pressed on. So Jeremy pressed on too, of course. Anything else would have been unthinkable. He kept beating his drum.

And yet he wondered why the skirmishers had wanted them to stop. If there were Secesh up ahead, well, that was what the First Division was here for, wasn't it? To send them packing. Why should they stop?

And then he saw.

In a moment they had caught up with their own skirmishers. Ahead Jeremy could see the red clay mass of fortifications. Fortifications everywhere, bristling with Confederate cannons, far closer than seemed possible. There was no way to retreat. . . . They could not outrun the guns. Their only hope was forward—to overtake those huge fortifications.

The Union soldiers brought down their rifles from their shoulders and fired. There had been no order to fire. There didn't need to be. They grabbed cartridges out of their pockets, bit them open, loaded, and fired again. Grab, bite, load, fire. And then the return fire came. Bullets whizzed all around like angry metal bees. Jeremy heard a cry beside him and the thud of a body falling to the ground. Jeremy had nothing to fire, and he slid backward, letting the men get ahead of him.

A storm of shells, minié balls, grapeshot, and canister burst from the Rebel fortifications. In an instant a fourth of the men in front of Jeremy were lying on the ground—some still moving, some not. Jeremy blinked and coughed, his lungs full of gun smoke. He tried to beat his drum, but found he no longer had his drumsticks. He looked down for them and then dropped to his knees. He felt unable to get up again.

He hadn't been hit. He hadn't been injured. It was just

that when his brain tried to tell his legs to stand up, his legs wouldn't obey. He hated himself! He was a coward, not a Drummer Boy of Shiloh! Every second there seemed to be more men lying on the ground before him, and the sound of bodies hitting the ground and the moans of the wounded weren't quite drowned out by the explosions all around. The men in the line kept closing up ranks, covering the gaps left by each fresh barrage from the Rebel fortification.

"On, men! The 107th! York State and the Union!" Captain Knox still had his sword in his hand, and Jeremy looked up from his knees in time to see the brilliant white flash of an exploding shell in the space where the captain was standing. Jeremy felt himself thrown into the air and then hit the ground again, hard. He opened his eyes and decided he wasn't dead, although he suddenly couldn't hear anything. His drum was gone. He got to his hands and knees and looked around. He was staring at a bare foot, lying on the ground. It didn't seem to be attached to anybody. Just beyond it was a bright blue flower, growing up near the toes. Captain Knox was no longer there.

"Out of cartridges!" someone yelled, and Jeremy realized his hearing had returned. "Get me more cartridges!"

That was one of a drummer boy's duties. But where could he get them from? Jeremy looked at the bodies lying around him. He crawled up to one, found the metal ammunition box on its belt, felt in the pockets for more cartridges. He found them, stumbled toward the man who had yelled, and dumped the cartridges into his hands. Then he went back to find more.

As he scrambled about, his courage returned. Not suddenly, the way it had left him, but quietly and matter-of-factly. There was a job to be done, and he was doing it. All around him men were dead and dying, and the threshold between life and death did not seem very great or very frightening, and so he turned his attention to finding dead men who still had cartridges and getting those cartridges to the men who were still standing.

The air was so full of exploded gunpowder that he could taste it in his mouth, and his eyes stung with it. He didn't have time to think of this. He needed to get cartridges to his men. He had no thought now that Charlie might be on the other side, that the bullets he was finding might hit Charlie. The other side was the enemy, pure and simple.

Quickly he lost any feeling of distaste for what he was doing, and he stopped looking at the powder-blackened faces of the dead. When the men whose pockets he was rifling stirred, he ignored that, too. His job was to get ammunition to those still on their feet. The sky grew darker overhead, and he heard thunder under the cannon fire. Again a shell exploded near him. The one that hit him, he thought, he would probably never know about. He hoped not anyway. He knew now that there would be no gathered circle of kneeling comrades, pressing a Bible into his hands. That was a song, and made up, and a lie. He would just keep going until the moment of nothingness came, as it had come for so many of the men lying around him.

There was no line of soldiers anymore. The survivors hid behind trees or clung to the ground, like Jeremy. Two things could happen now, Jeremy realized. Either more Union soldiers could arrive to relieve the First Division, or the Rebs could come swarming over those fortifications and finish off the surviving Union soldiers.

And then the gathering storm overhead burst. Hot flickers of lightning rippled over the battlefield, and thunder crashed. The trees bent over, their branches thrashing in sudden wild gusts of wind, the leaves turning over white against the steel-dark sky. Then rain poured down in torrents. The firing stuttered to a stop, and the Rebs behind the barricade cheered.

Jeremy crawled back the way they had marched—it wasn't even dark yet; had it been only an hour before? He couldn't see anything through the pouring rain anyway. He just kept crawling in the mud that soaked through the knees of his breeches. His clothes were wet and slowed his dragging pace. Finally he stood up. His legs were shaking. He heard marching and orders being given—had he crawled into Rebel territory? No, those were northern accents he heard. The Union Army had arrived to relieve them at last.

Jeremy stumbled on. Maybe the First Division was being ordered to fall back now that their relief had arrived. He had heard no command, and was not sure there was anyone left to give one. There were no bugles and no drums—Jeremy had lost his. For all he knew he could be deserting.

Through a bright triple flash of lightning he saw other soldiers in blue moving in, marching in formation, not a step wrong, just as the First Division had marched a short time before. Jeremy found it hard to even care. He felt numb.

☆ ★ ★ N I N E T E E N ★ ★ ☆

THEY HADN'T BEEN EXPECTING A BATTLE. DULCIE HAD been dozing on top of a stack of canvas in the medical wagon as it clopped along. She still hadn't completely recovered from the sleepless nights at Resaca. The shots ahead woke her up, but she went right back to sleep again, though she felt the wagon turning around and heading back the other way. The cannon fire that had frightened her back on the farm long ago was too common a noise to worry her anymore.

When the wagon jolted to a stop Dulcie stirred and opened her eyes. It was late afternoon, she could tell by the sun. Now she heard guns firing up ahead. Someone was in battle, or skirmishing, or something. A fly landed on her mouth, its tiny feet crawling over her lips. Revolted, Dulcie swatted it away and then lay rubbing her lip furiously. There was no more disgusting sensation in the world than having a fly land on your mouth.

"Get out of there! We need to set up!" Dulcie recognized

Bill's hectoring voice. He was a soldier who'd never fully recovered from a bout of camp fever, and so had been put on medical detail.

"Look at her, asleep in the afternoon!" Bill stuck his head into the wagon and his voice echoed louder. "Blacks are lazy."

Dulcie sat up, crawled out over the crates and rolls of canvas, and jumped down onto the ground. She turned to face him. She was really angry. "You shut up!"

"Ooh," said Bill, putting his hands to his face and pretending to be scared. A couple of men laughed.

"You don't know all black people. You know *me*! *I'm* lazy!" Dulcie pointed at her chest. "Me, Dulcie, *I'm* lazy! Don't say black people are lazy! Say I'm lazy!"

"We don't have time for this," said Seth. "Dulcie's not lazy, Bill, you saw her at Resaca. Let's get this set up." He turned to Dulcie and explained briefly, "The fun's started and we're in it."

Dulcie gulped. The sound of guns wasn't just some anonymous soldiers skirmishing—the 107th was in battle. *Her* regiment. At Resaca they had known days ahead of time. At Cassville they'd known a day or two in advance, and then the battle hadn't happened. Now there was a battle going on with no time to set up a field hospital, no time to set yellow flags to guide the wounded soldiers in. She helped drag the canvas and the crates out of the wagon. They assembled stretchers. The day darkened overhead. There was a roll of thunder. Dulcie took the buckets and went to look for water. They would need lots of it soon—to clean wounds, to wipe down instruments, to drink. The sound of guns ahead of them, she now knew, was the sound of work being made for the medical corps.

After she had filled all the buckets Dulcie dug out the pile of yellow flags. She needed to find where the soldiers would be coming from. She started walking toward the battlefield. Somewhere behind her she could hear the drums and the march of approaching troops—reinforcements. The sky had grown dark, and the trees whipped around wildly in a sudden wind. A bullet whined over Dulcie's head. She was going in the right direction, anyway. Toward the bullets. Then it began to rain.

The shooting stopped, but the groans and cries of the wounded echoed from the broken forest. Dulcie moved forward cautiously, her bare feet slipping in the wet Georgia clay. She felt a wave of dread. The agonized moans from the woods reminded her of Anne being whipped. Two hundred lashes. Dulcie cringed, and each new groan felt like a lash against her own flesh.

It was raining harder, and she could see people all around her, people moving and talking in the twilight, but she couldn't tell who they were.

"Where are the stretcher bearers?"

"Are the Rebs letting us collect our wounded?"

"Who cares what the Rebs are allowing? Let's get 'em."

"Where's the dressing station?"

"Where are the surgeons?"

"John! John! John, you old cauliflower, where are you?" The panicked voice broke off at the end in a sob.

"It's darker than a stack of black cats out there."

"I don't care, I'm going in."

There was confusion, chaos, men stumbling everywhere, calling out for each other in voices that were fear-filled or mournful but not loud. The moans of the wounded came from somewhere up ahead—somewhere to the east. The rain pounded down. A long, pained howl rose above all the rest, for a while, and then it stopped and did not start again.

Dulcie saw that the men around her were moving toward the woods, and with a gulp she went too. She had to. She was the surgeon's servant. No, she *chose* to. She was a free woman.

She tripped over something soft, and fell. A body. She crept close to it. She touched it gingerly. The body's owner shrugged her hand off and snored. He was wrapped in a rubber blanket and asleep. In the rain, amid the groans and calls, asleep! How could anyone sleep in this?

As Dulcie's eyes adjusted to the darkness she saw that many men were asleep, just like this one. Some were wrapped in rubber blankets, others in rain-soaked woolen blankets, others in nothing but their sodden clothes.

"Dulcie, is that you?"

Dulcie recognized Jeremy's voice and turned. She

could make out a boy-sized figure through the driving rain. "Yes, it's me."

"Where are the others? Where's Nicholas and Dave and them?"

"I just got here. Come on. I'm going in."

To her surprise she felt Jeremy's hand grip hers. They moved forward together.

"There's a creek here," said Jeremy.

Dulcie hitched her skirt up with one hand, and together they stepped into it. The cold water rushed around her ankles and reminded her of the night she ran away.

They came to a ravine. They let go of each other's hands as they climbed down into it. Dulcie's bare foot groped for the bottom and met unresisting flesh. Hastily she stepped off of the body and onto the floor of the ravine.

"Do youse have rattlesnakes in Georgia?" asked Jeremy.

"Yes," said Dulcie. "There's a body here."

"I know." She heard Jeremy kneel beside it. "Can't tell who it is. Can't see anything."

They climbed up out of the ravine again. The woods beyond were full of men's voices calling over the groans.

"Algie!"

"Hiram! Hi, where you at, you old fool?"

"Possum! Anybody seen Possum?"

In the darkness a cluster of tiny lights seemed to float along toward them. Dulcie blinked. The lights stopped before them and spoke.

"Do you need a lantern?"

"Thank you," said Dulcie, accepting the tin lantern. Candlelight shone through the nail holes poked in the side.

The tower of lanterns moved away.

"We can't see as good now we have the lantern," said Jeremy.

It was true. The light drew their eyes and made the darkness around them darker. Dulcie slid the door over the light holes, and they were in darkness again.

"The lantern will come in handy when we find someone," she said.

"We're looking for Dave and Nicholas," said Jeremy. "And No-Joke."

Dulcie mentally counted the members of Jeremy's mess. "Lars and Jack are all right, then?"

"Oh, and Lars and Jack," Jeremy admitted.

The next man they found was lying facedown on the ground. Dulcie knelt beside him and opened the lantern door. Yellow dots of light flickered on a face with a gingery mustache. The man had a tintype photograph of a little girl clutched in his hand.

"He's dead," said Jeremy.

They moved on. Other lanterns were flickering among the trees. Voices called out, and men groaned in pain. A man stumbled past carrying another man over his shoulder. Where were the stretcher crews? Dulcie wondered.

They came to another body and shone a light on it.

"This one's still breathing," said Dulcie.

"Who is he?"

"It doesn't matter who he is, Jeremy! Look, his leg's shot up." Dulcie hadn't brought a tourniquet. "Jeremy, take his belt off."

With an impatient huff, Jeremy knelt and undid the belt buckle. He wanted to be looking for his messmates, not helping men he didn't know, Dulcie thought. But she was in the medical corps, and any wounded soldier was her problem. Even a Secesh would have been her problem. She took the belt from him and cinched it around the man's leg. "Help me pull it tight, Jeremy. No, tighter."

"His leg will come off!"

"It has to be really, really tight." Dulcie didn't tell him that the man's leg would have to come off anyway. The man appeared to be unconscious, but he might still be able to hear, Dulcie knew.

"Good," she told Jeremy, putting the lantern close to the tourniquet. He had made it so tight that it bit deep into the flesh. The bleeding from the wound had stopped. "Now we have to find a way to get him out of here."

"We have to go look for Dave and Nicholas and them!" said Jeremy.

Dulcie hesitated. They couldn't carry this soldier between them. He was a big man.

"He's not bleeding anymore!" Jeremy said. "Dave and them could be dying and no one's helped them!"

Dulcie looked around her. There were hundreds of lanterns, hundreds of voices calling, but the calls of the injured seemed to outnumber them. The rain had slowed.

"All right," she said. "But remember where he is."

As soon as they moved on she knew that that was impossible. The moon came out briefly through an opening in the clouds. They could see a little bit. What Dulcie saw was a horror of broken trees, shell craters, and slumped bodies everywhere.

"We're not even in the worst of it, I don't think," Jeremy said. "There was a place, like a line, didn't nobody get past it. Only it wasn't a real line, only it turned into a line of bodies."

"Jeremy?"

A lantern shone in their faces suddenly, and Dulcie blinked her eyes shut against the sudden light.

"Is that you, Jeremy?"

"Dave?"

"I can't find Nicholas!"

Dulcie's eyes adjusted to the light. Dave's face was pale and frantic in the yellow light from his lantern.

"I can't find him!" Dave repeated.

"If you can't find him maybe he ain't here." Jeremy was trying to comfort Dave, but Dave looked even more panicked.

Dulcie reached out and put a hand on Dave's trembling arm. "Come with us," she said. "We'll look for him together."

Shots stuttered in the woods up ahead. They looked up and saw the answering fire—orange blazes cutting through the darkness.

"Is the battle starting again?" said Dulcie.

"Skirmish, probably," said Jeremy.

A bullet smacked into a tree above Dulcie's head.

"Nicholas is still out there!" Dave cried.

Dulcie's knees felt weak. She hadn't come under fire before except for that business in the rowboat. But there was a job to do. She gripped the lantern. Ducking low as the bullets flew overhead, they moved toward another body.

Dulcie opened the lantern.

"Dead," said Jeremy. "Wait, I know him! His name is John Decker—he's in our regiment."

There was nothing to be done for John Decker, and they moved on.

A shape lurched toward them.

"Nicholas!" Dave cried gladly.

Dulcie wondered how he could tell the moving dark shadow was Nicholas. But a moment later the man stepped into the lamplight and she saw it was—Nicholas, his face black with powder, his wet hair plastered down on his head. He staggered under the weight of a body on his shoulder.

"'S No-Joke," he said. "I think he's still alive. Where's the dressing station?"

"I don't know," Dulcie admitted. Someone must have set one up by now, surely?

"Need to get him out of here."

A bullet burrowed into the ground beside Nicholas, emphasizing his point.

Together they moved back toward the creek, Dulcie and Dave lighting the way with their lanterns. There were still wounded men calling out around them. Dulcie knew she should be back helping Dr. Flood, if she could find him.

When they got to the ravine, Dave and Jeremy slid down first to take No-Joke from Nicholas. Dulcie followed with the light. Then they clambered up the other side and Nicholas handed No-Joke up to them. No-Joke let out a groan as he was lifted. Dulcie couldn't tell if he was conscious. The specks of light shone on a black line of blood trickling down from the corner of his mouth.

A silver-white mist hung over the creek, glowing weirdly in the moonlight. They splashed across the creek, struggling to keep No-Joke out of the water, and made their way in the dark toward the light of campfires that the soldiers had managed to start despite the wet ground and soggy firewood. Dulcie saw the house shape of a wall tent, glowing with candlelight from inside.

"There. That'll be the dressing station," she said.

They stumbled up to it. It wasn't the 107th's tent, and it wasn't Dr. Flood inside. Instead they saw a doctor Dulcie didn't know, a bearded young man with his sleeves rolled up and his arms spattered with blood.

The man didn't turn around. "Set him down there."

"But he's our pardner!" said Dave.

"Everybody's somebody's pardner." The doctor was surrounded by candles. He knelt on the ground. A soldier who looked about sixteen lay on a sheet, staring up at the doctor in terror. The soldier's leg had a tight tourniquet around it, done with a belt just like the one Dulcie and Jeremy had used.

The doctor frowned at Dulcie. "Didn't I see you around the field hospital in Resaca?"

"Yes, sir," said Dulcie. Nicholas had laid No-Joke down inside the tent. Dulcie helped the men try to arrange him comfortably.

"I need you to anesthetize this patient," said the doctor.

Dulcie stared at him. "Me? I don't know how, sir!"

"I'll show you how." The doctor held up a tin canister. "It's not difficult. I had a drummer boy doing it for me at Resaca."

Dulcie was horrified. She knew that people could die under anesthetic. She didn't say this, though, because she could see that the soldier whose leg was about to be amputated was frightened enough. But she didn't want any part of anesthetizing him. And she needed to go find Dr. Flood—he would need her help. Except that she had no idea where he was, in the dark chaos outside the tent.

"What's your name, girl?" said the doctor. His face was gray with weariness already.

"Dulcie, sir."

"Well, Dulcie, if I can do these amputations tonight, most of my patients will live. If I have to wait till tomorrow, most of them will die. It's up to you."

When it was put like that Dulcie saw there was only

one choice to be made. She left No-Joke and reached for the tin canister. "Show me what to do."

"That's the spirit." The doctor looked at Jeremy. "You, drummer boy. Bring me some water, please." He nodded at a pair of buckets beside the tent opening.

Nicholas and Dave went back to search for Lars and Jack. Dulcie wished she didn't have to be the one giving the anesthetic. It was a frightening responsibility. But she did her best not to show her fear to the patient, because she knew he needed her calm.

"It's all right, soldier," she said. She knelt by his head and took the canister as the doctor showed her. She lowered it gently over the soldier's face. She trickled chloroform into it as she had seen Seth do at Resaca, and gradually the soldier's stiff body relaxed. He was asleep.

Through the hours that followed Dulcie just concentrated on the tin canister and the brown bottles of chloroform. When one was empty she laid it aside and grabbed another. Soldiers were brought in and out. Legs and arms piled up near the tent door, and after a while Jeremy was given the unenviable task of taking them out and burying them. Birds sang, and the new day dawned. Firing began again in the distance, and that was the first time Dulcie noticed that it had ever stopped. Once, Jeremy put a dipper to her mouth, as if she had been a patient, and she drank the cool water gratefully. Her legs under her were asleep from kneeling so long. The supply of patients never seemed to let up. Dulcie never looked at the surgery, but the sound of the knives and saws and the smell of blood filled her head.

Long after daylight she felt someone taking the chloroform canister from her hands. It was the doctor. She still didn't know his name.

"We've done all we can, Dulcie. The rest is up to God," said the doctor.

Dulcie tried to get to her feet but couldn't. Her legs were too stiff. She stretched them out in front of her and endured the painful tickle of pins and needles as they slowly woke up.

She turned to the tent door. No-Joke was still there.

She looked accusingly at the doctor. The doctor looked sad.

Dulcie got up on her hands and knees and crawled over to No-Joke. "He's still alive!" she said.

"Yes, but . . . ," said the doctor wearily.

No-Joke's eyelids fluttered but didn't open. "Dulcie?"

"You're all right, No-Joke." She wished she knew his real name. She knew it helped patients to hear their names spoken.

"No, I'm not." The ghost of a smile flickered across No-Joke's face. "Take—"

Dulcie could see he was struggling to move his arm. She reached out and took his hand. It was cold. "Take what, No-Joke?"

"Picture . . . pocket . . ."

With her free hand Dulcie unbuttoned the pocket of

No-Joke's Union blouse. The metal-backed photograph he had shown her was in there. Dulcie drew it out and held it up for No-Joke to see. His eyes were still closed.

"Here's the picture, No-Joke."

Dulcie watched him. His hollow cheeks were pale; even his lips were almost white.

She looked at the family in the picture, their black eyes like No-Joke's, the mother and the older sister with their hollowed-out cheeks like No-Joke's.

Then No-Joke's eyes flew open, and he looked at the picture of his family for a moment. And suddenly, looking at the picture, Dulcie knew No-Joke's real name. But she didn't say it. . . . It seemed too impossibly strange to disturb him with in his very last moment of life.

"Hattie won't know . . ."

The little sister in the picture. "I'll make sure she finds out," said Dulcie.

"But you don't know . . ." He trailed off again.

"I do. And I will," said Dulcie. "Don't worry. I will."

No-Joke closed his eyes, and Dulcie squeezed his hand. But his hand was limp in hers, and Dulcie knew that he was gone.

When the burial detail came for No-Joke, Dulcie had already cleaned out his pockets. She would make sure that everything in them got to Hattie, the little sister in the tintype photograph that she took from his pocket. She had no idea how she'd accomplish this. Perhaps she could get his last name from the company roster—if he'd enlisted under his real last name. It was hard to see how she could keep this promise without telling No-Joke's secret to at least one person. Maybe Jeremy. She also took a handkerchief, a little book that she assumed was a Bible, a pocketknife, a bone-handled toothbrush, and a folding spoon. Somehow she would have to give these things to No-Joke's family. She'd promised.

Suddenly there was a tin bowl of soup being held in front of her face, and Dulcie looked up and saw the doctor.

"Eat this, Dulcie."

Dulcie took the bowl and spoon from him.

"I'm sorry about your friend," said the doctor. "There was nothing I could have done. He was—"

"Bleeding internally," said Dulcie. She had interrupted him. That was practically sassing and would have gotten her the cowhide before she was free. Too tired to apologize, she spooned up the soup that he had given her instead.

"Are you working for someone?" said the doctor.

"Dr. Flood."

"You're a good little medic. You have the knack. If you ever get tired of working for him, come work for me."

Dulcie was too tired to answer. She ate her soup. It was warm and comforting, with lumps of potato and shreds of salt beef in it. She mulled over the thought that she could leave Dr. Flood if she got tired of working for him, and that nobody would send dogs to hunt her down—nobody would even think it was particularly strange. She was at home with this thought now. Freedom was easy to get used to.

After she ate she went to find the burial detail. On the way she picked up a stave from an empty barrel that had been broken open.

They hadn't filled in the long trench yet. Dulcie found No-Joke in the middle of the long row of white-faced soldiers, each laid down carefully, feet together, hands crossed.

She knelt beside the trench and picked up a sharp rock. Pressing as hard as she could, she scratched a cross into the gray barrel stave. Then she stood and drove it into the ground, working it through the red clay until it stood up on its own.

It wouldn't stand long, she knew. Dulcie still had her promise to keep, even if she didn't know *how* she was going to find No-Joke's family. But No-Joke would probably stay in this mass grave forever, unmarked and unidentified.

And only Dulcie knew that his name was probably Eliza.

IT HAD BEEN THREE DAYS SINCE THAT HOUR ABOVE Pumpkin Vine Creek, and the First Division had not moved. The battle was still going on, and it didn't have a name yet, but the men were calling what had happened on May 25 the Hell-Hole. The two armies were entrenched in the woods, and the firing went on all day long. The weather had been unrelievedly hot since the storm the night of the Hell-Hole, and the stench of the still-unrecovered dead hung heavy over the lines. Everyone was jittery. People didn't laugh all the time anymore, and when they did laugh there was a ragged, desperate edge to it. Jeremy expected the firing to break out into another slaughter at any moment. Whatever he was doing, whatever he was thinking about, he always had one ear on the gunfire, ready to notice any change in intensity.

His stomach hurt.

The frayed edges of the 107th had gradually joined together again. Half the men were gone, although not all of these were dead. There were a lot of injured who had been sent back in ambulances to Cartersville, Georgia, where hospitals had been set up in some houses.

The battlefield had spread, Jeremy heard. The rest of Sherman's army was engaged—such an innocent-sounding word that was, *engaged*—just to the north, and the cannon fire pounding in the distance told Jeremy that the fighting up there was much hotter. The area around and behind the battlefield was such a maze of trenches and pathways that it was easy to get lost in it, and there were rumors already of men wandering into the wrong camp and being captured.

"There are no more to bury right now," said Dulcie.

"That's good," said Jeremy wearily. One of his many duties since he lost his drum had been burying arms and legs.

"Come and eat something."

He followed her to the fire. A cauldron hung over it on a tripod—the medical corps had been allowed to bring heavy equipment like this. She scooped up a tin bowl of soup for him and one for herself. They sat down on the ground.

"Did they find Lars yet?" he asked, more out of a feeling of obligation than any real worry. It was honestly hard to like Lars any better now that he was among the missing. (Jack had turned up a few hours after the battle, and Jeremy wasn't altogether sure he'd been in it.)

"No."

Jeremy took his spoon out of his pocket and ate the soup. "This ain't as bad as what we usually get," he said.

"Thank you."

"Oh, you made it?"

She nodded.

"Oh, well, it's good, then. Where did you get potatoes from?"

"They sent them from Nashville for the hospitals. To prevent scurvy."

Jeremy savored the potatoes. He held a chunk of one between his teeth and bit it slowly, enjoying the mealiness of it. Potatoes were something the soldiers were supposed to get in their rations, but never did.

"At least you've seen the elephant now."

Jeremy managed to smile. He could tell she was trying to cheer him up, but he really didn't care about the elephant anymore.

"I want you to help me find No-Joke's people," she said. "I promised to let them know he was dead."

"I'm sure the colonel or somebody has them in the muster book. He's probably written them already."

"I don't think No-Joke enlisted under his real name. In fact, I'm sure he didn't."

She sounded very serious. Jeremy looked at her.

"No-Joke was a woman," said Dulcie.

"You've no right to say that about him!" Jeremy set his empty bowl down with an angry clatter. He thought of No-Joke, the only one of them who had joined up to free

· 226 ·

the slaves and for no other reason. "He was a good soldier!"

"Who ever said he wasn't? Here."

Jeremy took the tintype Dulcie handed him. He looked at the hollow-cheeked, unsmiling young woman with No-Joke's serious eyes. "That's his sister Eliza."

"Then how come you knew right away what I meant?"

Jeremy looked at the picture again. The dark-clad family of four stared somberly back at him, posed and frozen, their heads held stiff for the photographer. When No-Joke showed him the picture, Jeremy had assumed that his family had just sent it to him in the mail. But come to think of it, No-Joke never got any mail. At least Jeremy had never seen him get any. He was like Jeremy in that.

"He wasn't one of the old 107th," he said aloud. "He was one of the 145th, from New York City. They were broken up and put into different regiments."

"So nobody knew him," said Dulcie.

"Someone had to know him," said Jeremy. "There are lots of men from the 145th in the 107th."

"New York City has 800,000 people," said Dulcie, who had learned this from Miss Lottie's attempts to memorize geography lessons. "I bet no one knew him. And he made sure his pardners were men who weren't from the city."

Jeremy hardly listened to her. He was staring at Eliza, who stared back at him with No-Joke's burning black eyes.

Take away the long hair—Jeremy blinked. Now he was having trouble seeing the woman *not* as No-Joke.

"Besides, look at his pocketknife."

Jeremy took the open knife she handed him but didn't look at it. He was in shock. He didn't have anything against females. It wasn't that. It was just that they were supposed to do female things, darning and tatting and . . . and whatever it was they did. They weren't supposed to be marching through Georgia with General Sherman. Well, there was Dulcie, of course, but she was contraband. That was different.

And if No-Joke was a woman, he realized with growing horror, then *anybody* could be a woman. Well, not Lars, maybe—he had that big golden beard. *Had* had.

"There's no razor edge on that knife," Dulcie explained.

Jeremy looked down at the knife blade in his hand. It was true, but . . . "Hah! I've seen him shave."

"You've seen him put soap lather on his face, maybe. And then scrape it off with the back edge of a knife."

Jeremy remembered his messmates had once laughed at No-Joke shaving, saying he looked the same before and after and that he had as much reason to shave as Jeremy did.

"All right," he said finally. "Say he's a woman. Why'd he, she, why'd she do it?"

"Because he was an abolitionist," said Dulcie. "She, I mean. She wanted to fight for freedom."

"But why couldn't she do something else? Like be a nurse or, or a cook or something?"

"Because that wasn't what she wanted to do," Dulcie explained patiently. "What does it say on the back of the photograph?"

Jeremy flipped it over. "It's just the name of a photographer's shop. In Brooklyn, New York."

"Well, I guess that's where we start looking, then."

"How? Brooklyn's probably huge. And we're not in it."

"Well, we know his sister's name. Hattie. And his name might have been Eliza. Hers, I mean."

"And the photographer's name." Jeremy thought. He could see that this was going to be an enormous task, but he was already beginning to like the sound of it. He'd never been to Brooklyn. He wasn't too thrilled about bringing bad news to the dark-clad family in the tintype, but they might have been wondering what had become of him—her—for years. At least they would know. And Jeremy would have a purpose in life besides dying gloriously. The thought of the search interested him as nothing else had since that hour in the Hell-Hole.

"All right, let's do it," he said. "After the war."

"When the war's over I want to go and find my ma and pa."

"We'll find your ma and pa, and then we'll go to New York."

"If they want to."

"Are you just handing the job over to me? You said you promised!"

"But it's easier for you."

"But you're the one who promised!"

"Jeremy, they're my ma and pa! Wouldn't you want to find your ma and pa?"

Jeremy thought of his pa, in Auburn Prison, and his ma, who he didn't know anything about. He should know something about his ma, he thought angrily. His pa should have told him. He would ask him. He would write to him and ask him.

"If I write to my pa, Old Silas will find out."

"Who?"

Jeremy hadn't realized he'd spoken aloud. "Old Silas. He's my—well, I guess you could call him my master."

"White people have masters?"

"Well, I do. Did. I was a bound-boy. I was bound to Old Silas until I'm twenty-one, but he didn't treat me right and I ran away."

"Can he come after you with dogs?"

"Dogs? I don't think so, no."

"Then don't worry about it," said Dulcie. "You're a Union soldier. He can't take you from the Union Army. If you know where your pa is you should write to him. I would if he was my pa. If I could write."

"Oh, I know where he is," said Jeremy. "I know exactly where he is."

Jeremy was lost.

He had been to the front to deliver a message and was coming back to the rear, or thought he was, but he'd gotten turned around in the woods somehow. He didn't know where he was or where he should be going. The staccato of gunfire was all around, and he couldn't tell his direction from it.

He heard a branch snap behind him. He spun around, fists raised.

"Where did you spring from, Yank?"

Jeremy looked at Charlie's smiling face and saw the flashes of fire in the Hell-Hole and heard the bodies hitting the ground around him. Charlie's smile was a lie. Charlie was a killer.

"You've seen the elephant," said Charlie, not smiling.

"I've seen *you*. I've seen you Secesh, what you do."

"Hey, I thought we were friends."

"I didn't know then what you could do," said Jeremy. He thought of No-Joke and he wanted to punch Charlie.

"What I could do? Pardner, I ain't never shot a man, and that's the truth."

"Sure you haven't."

"Fixed fact. Can't do it." Charlie sounded proud of it. "I reckon there's lots of men who can't. Probably even on your side," he added generously.

Jeremy remembered realizing, when he first met Charlie, that there was no way he could stick his knife into him. Yes, but shooting someone would be easier, surely. The Drummer Boy of Chickamauga had done it. You didn't have to touch the person. You only had to look at them.

Not even that, he realized. Crouched behind a log bunker, all you really had to do was shoot. Fire your gun, or better yet your cannon, in the general direction of the enemy and don't think about the results. He wondered if Charlie had done that. He suspected he had.

"All you have to do is squeeze a trigger," said Jeremy.

"It's a little more complicated than that."

"And it hits a person. You don't have to see that part of it."

"Well, sure you do, buddy. Especially after. And then, you know, in the night. You have to listen."

Jeremy remembered the night after the Hell-Hole, and the screams and groans in the woods as he and Dulcie had searched for his messmates. Had that been as hard for the Rebs to listen to as it had been for him? Then why had they fired into the First Division so relentlessly? Why had they cheered?

Because we would have killed them otherwise. There are two sides to every story. What was it Nicholas had said? A hundred sides.

"One of my messmates died," he said.

"Yes," said Charlie. Jeremy looked at him, wondering what kind of answer that was—Yes?—and saw a very old look on Charlie's face that didn't belong there, and he didn't like it. Charlie must have had a lot of pardners die since Shiloh.

"I'm sorry," said Charlie. "About your pardner, I mean."

Jeremy realized that he couldn't start hating Charlie now for being a Confederate soldier. He'd been that when they met.

"I lost my drum," he said.

"Ain't seen it." Charlie put his usual breezy, self-assured face back on, and it was a relief to both of them. "Is that what you're doing over here? Looking for your drum?"

"What do you mean, 'over here'?"

"You're inside our lines, pardner."

"Oh."

"Lucky you're in uniform or they might shoot you for a spy."

"Of course I'm in uniform!" said Jeremy indignantly. His thoughts were catching up with him. They'd have to capture him first, of course. But a Reb soldier was standing right there in front of him. But it was Charlie. And anyway, Charlie didn't have a gun. But he was bigger than Jeremy. And he probably had a knife. Should Jeremy run? But he didn't even know which way to run. The multitude of pathways and trenches that had snaked their way through the forest in the last few days was too confusing.

"Oh, I ain't gonna capture you," said Charlie, smiling. "I got enough troubles of my own."

"What are you doing over here, then?"

"I'm in my territory, pard. Just looking around. There's a wounded Federal over there." He nodded to his left.

"What? One of ours? Where?"

"I was just going to get help to carry him in."

"You were going to capture him?"

"Better than leaving him here to die."

"You can't capture him! I'll . . ."

"How 'bout you help me carry him? If we can shift him. He's a mighty big fellow."

It was Lars.

He had been shot in the leg and must have crawled here to take refuge behind a fallen tree. He'd made a tourniquet of his belt on his leg. He was conscious when they got to him, and looked at them blearily. An over-powering smell of rot came from his wounded leg.

"He needs to be operated on right away!" said Jeremy.

"I know. Come on, pardner, help us out here. Can you stand up?" said Charlie.

"He can't. We need to go for help," said Jeremy.

"If we go for help they'll capture you," Charlie pointed out.

Or maybe kill me, Jeremy thought, but he didn't say it aloud, even though he wondered if Charlie was thinking it too.

Charlie crouched down and put one of Lars's arms around his shoulders. "Here, do like I'm doing."

They got him upright. Lars let out a moan. His eyes glinted through narrow slits of puffed eyelid but didn't seem to focus on anything. Together they stumbled forward. Most of Lars's weight was going on Charlie's shoulders, because Charlie was taller, but even so Jeremy found each step a tremendous effort, his whole body braced to keep the huge man upright. Lars swayed and lurched like a drunken man, and his bad leg dragged on the ground. With every step they took Lars let out a moan of pain that hurt Jeremy's bones.

"Let's tie his leg up," said Jeremy.

So they stopped and used Lars's shirt to make a sling to keep the leg off the ground. Jeremy turned his head away in nausea. Lars's leg had become a horrible thing, something Jeremy couldn't even have imagined before he saw it. Maggots were involved.

With the leg tied up they got on more easily, and sometimes Lars even helped them, giving a little hop. But Jeremy's back ached and he was dizzy from the smell of infection by the time they reached the hospital tent.

"Whush! This is *our* camp!" Jeremy said.

The tent ahead of them, with its yellow hospital flag, had Union soldiers all around it. Charlie seemed unconcerned. "Had to be yours. Our surgeons are out of chloroform. Out of everything, really."

The soldiers were coming forward now, taking Lars from their arms, carrying him into the tent. Jeremy fell to his knees, exhausted.

"You want a drink of water, is what you want," said Charlie, going to the bucket beside the tent.

Jeremy took the dipper that Charlie brought him and drank. Why was Charlie still here? If he'd been Charlie he'd have dusted off to the woods as soon as the soldiers came to take Lars. A soldier in an enemy camp risked capture. But then Jeremy looked at Charlie. Charlie didn't look like an enemy, did he? He was wearing Union trousers and Union shoes and had now acquired a Union blouse.

"Are you deserting?" Jeremy blurted.

Charlie shushed him and then smiled. "Not so loud, pardner. No, of course I ain't. I'd be much obliged if you don't draw attention to me."

Charlie pronounced *I'd* "ah-eed" like a northerner instead of "odd" like a southerner. Maybe he was speaking with a northern accent all of a sudden so nobody would notice him. But nobody was paying any attention to them anyway, of course. They were just boys.

"I need to go tell my messmates that we found Lars," said Jeremy.

"I'll tag along."

TWENTY-ONE

DULCIE WAS GLAD THAT NOBODY HAD DECIDED burying amputated limbs was a suitable job for her. She felt sorry for whoever had to bury Lars's leg. She hoped it wouldn't be Jeremy.

When Lars came out of the chloroform-induced sleep, Dulcie was there with a dose of morphine. She'd learned to give this to her patients quickly, and also to smear topical opium on the wound before they awoke. That reduced the pain. Nothing reduced the shock of finding themselves with one less limb (or sometimes two or three less). And they often claimed to still feel pain in the missing limb, and no amount of morphine could make it go away, and there was no way to put opium on a leg that wasn't there—although if she hadn't been warned repeatedly not to waste the stuff, she might have tried.

Lars was unusually calm. He clenched his teeth, opened his eyes, and looked down at his body. Then he tried to move his right leg and winced.

"How long was I out there?"

"Four days," said Dulcie.

"Four days? And no one came looking for me?"

"They did," said Dulcie. "But they couldn't find you."

"I need to write a letter."

Dulcie went and found him a pencil and a piece of paper, but she wasn't too surprised that when he tried to take hold of the pencil his fingers wouldn't close around it.

"Write it for me," he said.

"I can't," said Dulcie. It was a problem she'd run into several times while tending wounded soldiers. "But if you tell me the letter I can remember it."

He looked at her like she was crazy.

"Just tell me," she said. "You can tell me the address, too. I'll remember it all, and someone else will write it down for you."

Jeremy found his messmates playing cards by a fire that had died down to embers. A pot perched in glowing coals had a little coffee simmering in it, but there was nothing else to cook. The rations had been slow in coming in since they'd moved away from the railroad line. General Sherman meant for them to live off the land, but it was hard to feed a whole army off of the land, especially when the land objected. Nicholas had managed to get a chicken yesterday, but the lady whose house he foraged it from fired off a shotgun and nearly took his head off—Nicholas had showed them all the nick in his kepi.

"Pull up a piece of ground," said Nicholas. "Who's your friend?"

"His name's Charlie," said Jeremy. "We found Lars!"

The men sat upright and laid their cards facedown. "Alive or dead?"

"Alive! Well, for now, I mean. His leg is a mess. They're taking it off now, I think."

"Poor old cuss," said Dave.

"I should probably get over there and help," said Seth.

"I think Dulcie's doing it," said Jeremy. This earned him a sour look from Seth, and Jeremy realized Seth might be jealous of Dulcie. "It was Charlie here who found him, really."

"Nice work, Charlie," said Nicholas. His usual casual friendliness seemed somehow pinned on, as if he didn't really mean it.

Jeremy realized he should say something now, mention that, incidentally, Charlie was the enemy. But what would happen then? Would they take Charlie prisoner? Would Charlie end up getting shot because he was mostly in a Union uniform and therefore, according to the law, a spy?

"What regiment you with, Charlie?" said Nicholas.

Jeremy looked at Charlie uncomfortably. But Charlie just smiled and said, "Not any of the ones you know, I reckon."

"Ah," said Dave.

"Hmph," said Seth.

"Jeremy," said Jack, "that there's an enemy. You might not understand this, but in a war you got your own side, and then you got the enemy."

Jeremy felt his face burning. He couldn't look at his messmates, and he couldn't look at Charlie. It wasn't Jeremy's fault Charlie had insisted on coming to meet his messmates.

"Stow it, Jack," said Nicholas. "Charlie's been savin' Lars."

"Probably shot him too," said Jack under his breath, not loud enough for Nicholas to hear.

"Jeremy, why'ncha help Charlie to some coffee," said Nicholas. "'Tain't fresh, but there's a little in the pot there." He nodded at the fire.

"I'd be much obliged," said Charlie. Jeremy found a dipper beside the fire. He pulled his cuff down over his hand as a pot holder and took the pot off the embers. A sour smell of burnt coffee came up to his nose when he poured, but then coffee always smelled pretty bad, as far as he was concerned. He handed the dipper to Charlie. They sat down on the ground.

"What did Lars say? Was he conscious?"

"Not hardly," said Charlie. "He didn't rightly say anything." Jeremy noticed that his pronunciation was not just northern but York State. In fact, he sounded like he came from the Northwoods. He sounded like Jeremy. "I found him over our way, but it seemed like he'd have a better chance if your surgeons worked at him."

Nicholas nodded, accepting this.

"Not that our surgeons are *bad,* only they're out of everything."

"I heard them Reb surgeons like to experiment on Yankee prisoners," said Jack.

Charlie shrugged. "'Tain't true."

"Maybe not, but you'd send him to one of your prisons like Andersonville and he'd die anyway," said Seth.

"I heard your prison up to Elmira is pretty bad," said Charlie with a smile.

"You want to go and see?" said Jack.

"Jack, Jack, the man's a guest," said Nicholas.

Charlie sipped his coffee and looked like he was struggling not to make a face. "Ah. That's the real Simon Pure, that is."

"I heard youse make coffee out of sweet potatoes," said Dave.

"Sweet potatoes, chicory, roasted rye—'bout anything, really."

"How's that taste?"

"Brown," said Charlie. "You cook anything long enough it'll be brown, and you can make a drink that's brown. Course, so's mud."

Charlie still sounded like a born Yorker. It was giving Jeremy a headache listening to him.

"How many soldiers youse got over there?" Seth nodded toward the woods.

"Fair number." Charlie took another sip of the coffee.

Seth laid his cards down again. "I'm folding. I can see Jack's got two kings there."

The other men laid their cards down as well. Jack looked furious.

"Those two kings are from another deck," said Seth. "Ink's lighter on the back." He turned to Charlie. "So how much longer are youse going to fight for?"

"I don't know," said Charlie, to Jeremy's surprise. "I don't have slaves myself, and I'm tired of fightin' for other men's. Most the men just want to get home to their wives and sweethearts, and they don't care if school keeps or not."

"Whush," said Jeremy. "If everyone feels that way why are we still fighting?"

He remembered when he'd first met Charlie, Charlie had told him the Rebs were going to chase the Yankees right back out of Georgia. Lately Charlie hadn't seemed so sure of that.

"Don't know if everyone feels that way," said Charlie. "Just a lot of folks. And we don't know what happens if we surrender, either. Are we enemy soldiers or traitors?"

"Don't see how you can all be traitors," said Dave. "Wouldn't be enough rope."

"And there wouldn't be no folks left in the South," said Nicholas.

"There'd still be the blacks," said Seth. "We could give the land to them to farm."

"See, that's what folks are worried about," Charlie explained. "Are you going to respect our property or not?"

"Not if your property is people," said Nicholas.

The other men nodded slowly. Jeremy thought of No-Joke, and just for an instant it seemed like No-Joke was sitting among his messmates, pleased with their response.

"I don't see why we should respect their property, anyway!" said Seth. "They're a lot of thunderin' traitors!"

"Well, yeah, that's the thing, isn't it," said Charlie.

"You admit it!"

"I admit that's how you folks see it. That's why we wonder what'll happen to us."

"Should've wondered that before you started this dog-and-pony show," said Seth.

"A smart lot of rich men started it," said Charlie, looking at his hands. "Told us we had to stand by the South. Then they went home to their families, to watch their slaves makin' money for 'em."

He said it like he was thinking out loud, and for the first time since they'd met Jeremy had the impression that Charlie was saying exactly what he thought and nothing else.

"That's pretty thin, bein' in a war that you don't even know why you're in it," said Jack.

"Seems to me if I was from the South," said Dave, "that would mean something to me, standing with the South. That'd be reason enough."

"Seems to *me*," said Nicholas, "that we've wondered our own selves why we're in this blamed war."

Jeremy remembered that conversation. He remembered No-Joke being the only one who was sure that the war was to end slavery. He wondered if his messmates felt differently about that now.

"I'ma go check on Lars now." Seth reached for his crutches. Charlie sprang up and handed them to him, and then held them steady as Seth used them to pull himself upright.

"You manage right well on those crutches," said Charlie. "But wouldn't a wooden leg be easier?"

"A wooden leg! A wooden leg! I thunderin' well never thought of that! A wooden leg!" Seth thumped off, and Charlie looked after him, nonplussed.

"He ain't ready for one yet," Nicholas explained. "The stump ain't all healed yet. I'ma make him one when he is ready."

"Nicholas carves wood really well," said Dave.

Jeremy hadn't known why Seth didn't have a wooden leg. "Doesn't the government give them out?"

"Nah, they say if they did that, they'd be in the wooden leg business and never do nothin' else," said Dave.

"Oh." Charlie looked around him. "Well, it's been a pleasure making y'all—youse's acquaintance, but I had better be going back before they shoot me for desertion."

"Better see your friend out of the camp," said Nicholas.

"Case he should run into anybody less hospitable than our-selves."

Jeremy remembered the man at Resaca who had casually spoken of using up twenty-three Reb prisoners. He didn't want Charlie to run into anybody like that. And then he remembered that No-Joke had thought that that man was right. He wondered what No-Joke would have thought of Jeremy being friends with Charlie.

"Reckon this is where it turns into our territory," said Charlie, when they reached a patch of woods that looked exactly like the woods they'd been walking through. "'Less the line has shifted while we been visiting."

Jeremy stopped. "Well, I'll see you . . ."

". . . when you see me," said Charlie, raising a hand in farewell. Then he walked away.

He didn't say anything about the next river or about Jeremy bringing him some coffee beans or anything. Jeremy felt rather hurt by this.

When Jeremy returned to the campfire, his messmates' eyes were all on him. He had the feeling they were not pleased.

"We were just discussin'," said Nicholas, "whether you knew your friend there was a spy."

"A spy?" Jeremy was astonished that they could think this. "Charlie ain't no spy!"

"Oh, really? He's an enemy soldier, he came into camp wearing our uniform. . . ."

"Even a U.S. belt buckle!"

"He's got a C.S. belt buckle!" said Jeremy. But he had only noticed that when he'd first met Charlie. He wasn't very good at noticing small details usually. Seth and Dave were both good at it. They had that kind of eyes.

"Said U.S. to my eyes," said Dave. "And he speaks with a York State accent, except now and then when he forgets to."

"How long have you known him?" said Nicholas.

"Just—since before Resaca."

"Resaca. Uh-huh. And what-all have you told him?"

"I don't know! Nothing important! He never asked me anything important! He's been—friendly—" It didn't sound very convincing, now that he thought about it. Why wouldn't a spy be friendly? But Charlie wasn't a spy! "He saved Dulcie from the river when I found her."

"Dulcie's probably worth at least six hunnerd dollars to him."

"Well, I see I shouldn't have brought him to meet youse! But he was only over here because he helped me bring Lars! I could never of done it by myself."

"Why didn't you come and get us, then?"

"Because—because he was right there. It was him that found him. Besides, it was in enemy territory."

"What were you doing in enemy territory?"

"I was lost!"

Nicholas stood up and took hold of Jeremy's arm. For the first time, he looked very schoolmasterish, and Jeremy would have liked to step back if he could have, because this was the way schoolmasters looked when they were about to reach for a hickory stick. "Listen up good, Jeremy. This is a war, not an excursion trip. Your friend Charlie is just as loyal to his side as you are to yours, and if he finds out anything from you he will use it against us."

"Didn't you hear what he was saying?" Jeremy cried. "He just told us he doesn't care if the South wins or loses!"

"He told us what he thought we'd want to hear. What I want to know is, what did you tell him? Anything about the route we were taking? How many of us there are? What supplies we have? Weapons?"

Jeremy looked at the ground. In the course of their conversations all those things had probably come up. It seemed like he remembered Charlie asking him things like where the army was headed next, where they were going to cross the mountains or the rivers—but Jeremy had thought it had been so that they could meet up again. Had he told Charlie anything important? And he *had* had his doubts about Charlie; again and again he'd had them.

"Just think about it," said Nicholas.

He let go of Jeremy's arm, and Jeremy rubbed it. He didn't look at the other men. He turned around and walked away. He didn't *want* to think about it.

☆ ★ ★ T W E N T Y - T W O ★ ★ ☆

"PLEASE TELL CHALKIE TO BE A GOOD GIRL SO THAT
her daddy will get all better," said Dulcie.

Jeremy dipped his pen in an inkwell and wrote this on
a piece of Union stationery. "Got it."

"Tell Davis I am so proud he made head of the class
and spelled down the whole school even though I knew he
could do it."

Jeremy wrote this, too. He wondered how old Davis
was. Jeremy himself had once spelled down the whole
school, and he had only been seven when he did it. It
seemed like a childish thing to be proud of now, and he
wouldn't have actually *told* anyone about it, but he was
proud of it nonetheless.

"I don't like what he said to Chalkie," Jeremy said.
"What if he doesn't get better? What was wrong with him,
anyway?"

"This one? Shot in the hand."

"Will he get better?"

· 248 ·

"I don't know, probably. It depends on whether gangrene sets in."

"Well, what if he doesn't? And then Chalkie thinks it's because she hasn't been good enough?"

"I don't know." Dulcie shrugged. "They all say that."

It was true, they did, or at least all the ones with children. Jeremy had been writing letters for days. It amazed him how Dulcie could remember everything the soldiers wanted written, and even the addresses. The Christian Commission was helping them out with the postage. They were supplying paper, too, although sometimes they ran out and Jeremy had to go around asking for more from the soldiers. He had not yet approached his own pardners. He hadn't been back to his mess since that day he'd taken Charlie there. He didn't want to face his messmates again, and he wasn't entirely sure why. All right, maybe he did know why, but he didn't want to think about it. The fact was, it was awful being told you were wrong, especially in front of other people, and he wasn't sure if he was angrier because he'd been wrong to make friends with Charlie or because he'd been *told* he was wrong.

"With affectionate regards, I remain, your father, Hiram," said Dulcie.

Jeremy wrote it down and signed "Hiram" with a flourish, even though it wasn't his name. Writing with a flourish had been the next most important part of his formal education after spelling and memorizing. A really good writer could make a capital letter take up the width of a page, once all the swirls and scrolls were worked into it.

He blew on the ink to dry it and reached for an envelope.

"What's it say?" said Dulcie.

Jeremy looked down at the envelope. There was a picture stamped on it in red and blue ink of a ragged colored man with an enormous grin.

"It's got the address on it you told me to write," he said guardedly.

"No, underneath the picture on the envelope."

Charlie looked at the envelope. "It says, 'The Latest Contraband of War,'" he admitted reluctantly. "And then it says—that's supposed to be the man talking—'Dis chile ain't nebber gwine back to Massa, dat's what's de matter!'"

"Ah," said Dulcie.

"It's supposed to be funny," Jeremy said. "See, because—"

"I understand it," said Dulcie.

"We're short of paper anyway," said Jeremy.

"Yes, I know. All right. 'Dearest Maddie, I take pen in hand to acquaint you with the events of May 25th, 1864, at New Hope Church near Dallas, Georgia.'"

Jeremy took another piece of paper and wrote.

He wasn't entirely sure what his job was, now that he no longer had a drum. It was possible he no longer had a job. The 107th had been relieved the night before—Jeremy could imagine his messmates making jokes about how very, very relieved they had been—from the position they'd helped hold at New Hope Church ever since the Hell-Hole. They'd marched in the sweltering heat to Picket's Mill, which seemed to Jeremy to be another part of the same long battle, six miles away. They were behind the front lines here. The war pounded on ahead of them, and Jeremy stayed around the field hospital and made himself as useful as he could. As far as he knew no one was looking for him. Anyway, it wasn't like he had deserted. He just couldn't face his pardners after the way Nicholas had scolded him in front of all of them.

Besides, he saw Seth once or twice in the distance, and so he assumed Seth had seen him too and had told his messmates where he was. If they'd wondered.

It was raining. A few days ago, when the rain began, they had all welcomed it. It had been a break from the unrelenting heat. But it hadn't stopped. It had rained and rained and rained. There were no tents, of course, except for the hospitals. The trenches were knee-deep in water and slimy red mud. Everyone's boots and shoes were full of water, and their clothes had been soaked for so long that it almost seemed like they were made that way, spun wet, woven wet, cut wet, and sewn together wet. Jeremy had stopped writing letters because the paper was all soggy and the ink bled in brown blobs across the page. Instead he was tending the sick, of whom there seemed to be more every day, and the wounded, who poured in steadily from the front lines.

Funny that they had once supposed that they would march straight to Atlanta without opposition. Now it seemed as though the whole Confederate Army was between them and Atlanta, even though he knew this wasn't true. A large part of both armies was up in Virginia, and news of one terrible battle after another trickled through the newspapers and the grapevine telegraph. Much of it turned out, with the next round of news, to have been wrong. Victories were reported in battles that had never even happened.

Sometimes rumors came through that the war was over—sometimes General Lee was about to surrender the Confederate forces, and other times General Grant was about to surrender the Union—and Jeremy was always disappointed when it turned out not to be true. Right now he felt, traitorously, that he would gladly trade the Union for a pair of dry socks.

A letter had come from Lars.

"It's addressed to Nicholas," said Jeremy

"Well, take it to him, then," said Dulcie.

They were inside the medical tent, and the never-ending rain rattled down on the canvas over their heads.

"Seth can take it. He goes back and forth a lot."

"Nicholas will want to read the letter *now*," said Dulcie. "Besides, Seth does too much. In fact, I can't believe you'd let Seth take it!"

He still looked reluctant, and Dulcie almost offered to carry it to the front line herself. But she didn't, because she knew Jeremy was afraid and she thought it was time he got over it. Not afraid of the front line, of course. He'd seen the elephant and battle was just a job to him now. But Dulcie could tell he was afraid of his former messmates. She didn't know what that was about, but she reckoned he'd better make it up with them, whatever it was. Because what if one of them got killed in battle and he never had made it up? Dulcie had seen enough now to know that this was pretty likely. And how would Jeremy feel then?

"Better take it right smart," Dulcie suggested. "They probably want to know how he's doing."

She had helped to bundle Lars into the ambulance over a week ago. It was the last she saw of her patients, their departure laid out flat in the painfully jolting, mule-drawn wagons. After that she had no way of knowing what became of them. She knew that Lars had had a very fine infection when he left, which was considered promising. But sometimes infections made things worse instead of better. Nobody knew why.

Once, a couple of days after the Hell-Hole, she had seen a man with a wound that didn't produce any pus at all. The flesh stayed the same color as healthy flesh, and the slash in the man's arm had healed without the help of any infection at all. This, Dr. Flood had told her, was called "healing by first intention." Nobody knew what caused it.

"But couldn't we find out?" Dulcie had asked. Dr. Flood had smiled and called her a good medic.

He'd been annoyed with her, though, a week or two ago. That night of the Hell-Hole—or the next morning, rather.

"Where were you?" he'd demanded. "I was operating all night."

"So was I," said Dulcie. "Sir. I couldn't find you, and another doctor asked me to help."

And the bloodstains on her apron and the exhaustion on her face backed her up, she knew that. But it occurred to her for the first time that, while she could leave Dr. Flood if she got tired of him, she would also have to leave him if *he* got tired of *her*. So she added, "I'm sorry."

And then, to remind him that there was more than one side to every story, she'd added, "The other surgeon offered me a job, but I told him I was already working for you."

And Dr. Flood had nodded and said, "I see," and no more had been mentioned about it.

Seth helped Dr. Flood a lot too. But Dulcie was worried about Seth. He ought to have been in one of the invalid regiments, or been mustered out. The stump of his leg had never finished healing, and now he seemed feverish and exhausted, although he kept working all the same. He just took more and more morphine to keep him going.

Nicholas was out on the skirmish line. Jeremy was relieved at that. It meant he could just leave the letter with someone else.

"Can I leave it with you, sir?" he asked Sergeant Kinney, the man who had told him this.

"You can take it right out to him," said Sergeant Kinney, squinting at Jeremy through the pouring rain. "There's an agreement not to fire."

"Er, an agreement with who? Sir?"

"With the enemy. They want to get home to their families same as we do." He nodded across an open field. "You'll find 'em overt'other side of them trees."

Jeremy squelched off across the field. It seemed like an odd way to conduct a war. But then, why not? He and Charlie had met several times without fighting each other, and as far as he was concerned it was nothing to be ashamed of. It was maybe even a good thing. So if the rest of the 107th, and the rest of Sherman's army, learned to do the same—well, then maybe everyone would get home safe.

He smiled to himself at the thought that he had once wanted to die in battle. There were plenty of more useful things a person could do—he knew that now.

He found Nicholas sitting on a log under a loblolly pine, playing cards with a soldier Jeremy did not know. They both had rifles propped up beside them, with bayonets fixed. Raindrops splashed on the guns and the cards and the cardplayers.

"Er," said Jeremy.

Somewhere in the distance there was the sound of a gunshot.

Nicholas looked up. "Are we starting up again?"

"Ah reckon not," said the other soldier. "Ah told you we'd warn you if we got orders to shoot, and we ain't had none."

Jeremy stared at Nicholas, who had the grace to look embarrassed.

"You're playing cards with the enemy!"

Nicholas gave Jeremy his easy smile. "Oh, it's all right. We ain't playin' for money."

The enemy grinned. "Couldn't get no one to play for *my* money. It ain't fit to start a fire with." He reached into his pocket and pulled out a purse made of blue cloth, with the words *Confederate States of America* embroidered on it in red. He took out a crisp, blue-printed bill and handed it to Jeremy. "There's a little souvenir for you, kid."

"But it's two dollars!" said Jeremy. He tried to give it back. You couldn't take money from the enemy. It would be like taking a bribe.

"Naw, it ain't. Don't believe everything you read, kid. Who steals my purse steals trash." He seemed to consider the whole thing a pleasant joke. "Well, the contents, any-way. I'm right proud of the purse."

Jeremy figured the Reb had made the purse himself. The Reb was wearing Union blue breeches and a Union blouse that had been dyed some sort of color that you couldn't really put a name to. The Confederates called it "butternut." Anyway, it was not blue.

"Give it to your grandkids," said the Reb. "Tell 'em it's a souvenir of when you fought in the Second War of Independence."

Jeremy tried again to give the bill back, but the Reb wouldn't take it. Jeremy didn't want to hurt the man's feel-ings, so he said, "Thank you, sir," and pocketed it.

He looked accusingly at Nicholas again. Jeremy wasn't embarrassed at all anymore. He didn't feel he'd been child-ish to trust Charlie, because here was Nicholas the school-master, playing cards with the enemy.

"Everyone's doing it now," said Nicholas easily.

"Here's a letter from Lars," said Jeremy.

"Give it here!" Nicholas set his cards facedown and ripped the envelope open. He scanned the contents quickly. "He's in Tennessee," he reported. "The sweetheart is on her way down by rail—Oh! I guess that makes it official, eh? That louse, he's gonna get married on the sly and cheat us out of our shivaree. Still in the hospital. Doesn't know how long."

"Is he going to be all right?" said Jeremy.

"Who knows?" Nicholas shook his head. "He's all

right now, but anything can happen—he's got a healthy infection. Could get better, could get worse."

"I sure do hope he pulls through," said the man who for all any of them knew had shot Lars himself. "Shame he didn't marry the girl he was sparking before he left."

"Didn't have her then," said Nicholas. "We think it came about through letters."

"Ah." The Reb touched his shirt pocket. "We have letters like that on our side too."

"*Why* is everyone doing it now?" said Jeremy.

"What, writing love letters?" said Nicholas. "I'm not. Can't speak for the others."

"No, I mean *this*. What *you* told *me* not to do," said Jeremy meaningly.

"Oh, this. Well, along the skirmish lines, we agreed that we won't shoot if they don't."

"So we pass the time," said the Reb. He had an easy smile, like Charlie's. Like Nicholas's, for that matter.

Jeremy took his leave of them, deep in thought. He'd been scolded for passing time with Charlie, and now everyone was passing time with Rebs. Hmph. And they'd called Charlie a spy. They'd been angry at Jeremy just because they could be, because he was young and they wanted to remind him that he was just a drummer boy and not a full-in soldier.

Jeremy wondered if this sort of visiting across the lines happened in every war. He'd never read about it in the newspapers or the dime novels, but he suspected it might.

After all, who had more in common with soldiers in the field than the soldiers on the other side of the line?

He tried to remember the things Charlie had talked about when he'd sat and sipped coffee with Jeremy's messmates. The memory was a little rusty, because Jeremy had been trying not to think about it, but everything he could remember Charlie saying had seemed more like giving information *to* the Union. Nicholas could say Charlie had just been saying what he thought they wanted to hear, but the fact was, Charlie had told them that the Rebs were tired of the war, that they were out of supplies, that they were curious about what kind of terms they would get if they surrendered.

If Charlie was a spy, then which side was he a spy for?

☆ ★ ★ TWENTY-THREE ★ ★ ☆

DULCIE WENT INTO THE TENT TO GET SOME FRESH bandages.

Seth was sitting beside the medicine chest. He froze when she came in. Just for a second. Then he began counting bottles and writing things down on a list. He was taking inventory. He could do that, because he could write. Dulcie couldn't, but she did remember exactly how many bottles there were of each medicine.

And one thing she knew was that there were often fewer bottles of morphine after Seth had been in the tent than there had been before.

She didn't worry about this very much. She knew Seth had to take morphine for the pain in his leg. She wondered if he was taking more than he ought to. She knew that if she gave a patient too much chloroform, it could kill him. But was there such a thing as too much morphine? That she didn't know.

She did know that they didn't want to run out of morphine. But she also knew that Seth didn't entirely like her. He'd been kind to her when she was a runaway slave, but now that she was a person with a job he didn't seem to like her so much. So she didn't say anything about the morphine.

"Jeremy! Git in here out of the rain!"

Dave was sitting in a shelter woven of loblolly pine branches, the kind of lean-to that Jeremy had sometimes made in the Northwoods when he was far from the farm and it came on to rain or snow unexpectedly.

Jeremy scrunched in beside Dave. He looked at his messmate sideways, not sure what to say. He hadn't spoken to Dave in a week either. They sat in silence for a moment and watched the rain pound down. Now and then a raindrop made its way through the woven pine branches and hit Jeremy in the face.

"Been keepin' yourself busy?" said Dave.

"I've been writing letters for injured soldiers. Oh—we just got a letter from Lars," said Jeremy. "I took it to Nicholas."

Dave sat up straighter, interested. "He still alive, that ol' cuss? I knew he was too mean to die!"

"He's getting married to his sweetheart."

"Hah! I knew it!" Dave punched the air, and Jeremy

ducked out of his way and got his head stuck out in the rain for a second. "He figures on cheatin' us out of our shivaree, too. Reckon we oughta beat the Johnnies right now so we can go back and surprise him."

"I got a Confederate two-dollar bill," said Jeremy. He took it out of his pocket and handed it to Dave, who examined it with interest.

"The soldier who gave it to me said it wasn't worth nothin'," he added.

Dave gave him a sharp look. "You still consortin' with the enemy?"

"Nicholas is!" said Jeremy, indignant. "He's over there"—he pointed out into the rain—"playin' cards with a Secesh! He went and slangwhanged me for the same thing, and now he's doin' it! He's an old hypocrite!"

It wasn't till he got to the end of this speech that Jeremy remembered Dave was Nicholas's best pardner. Jeremy had probably brought his horse to the wrong market, saying all that, but it made him mad.

"Nicholas is A-1," said Dave, not looking particularly mad. "But you gotta understand—he reckons there shouldn't be no kids in this war." He looked at Jeremy sideways, like he was worried Jeremy might take offense. "He don't want no kids at all here, not even drummer boys, not even no contraband like Dulcie. Says war's men's business."

"Oh," said Jeremy.

"There been kids killed in this war, you know," said Dave. "Makes Nicholas mad."

"The Drummer Boy of Shiloh," said Jeremy.

Dave frowned. "Wasn't never no Drummer Boy of Shiloh."

"Yes, there was! There's a song about him."

"I know. Kinda song that would make people wanna join up, right? Some fool's always writin' songs like that. But it didn't happen."

"How would you know? You weren't at Shiloh." Jeremy knew this sounded rude, but it annoyed him that Dave sounded so sure.

"No, but I read all about Shiloh. Read everything I could about the war. I wanted to get in it so bad. I kind of wanted to—" Dave stopped, and laughed.

"Die for your country?" With weeping comrades kneeling all around.

"Yeah! So I joined up with the 107th at Elmira, and they sent us to D.C. and a month later we was at Antietam." He shook his head. "Antietam was worse than Shiloh. Don't let nobody tell you different."

Jeremy didn't say anything—he could see from Dave's face that Dave was back at Antietam and Jeremy's voice wouldn't reach him there.

"Only thing Antietam was like was hog-killin' time back at the farm," said Dave. "And after I seen that, I didn't want to die for my country no more. I just wanted to—"

He stopped talking, looked at Jeremy, and seemed suddenly back in the present and like he was thinking whatever he'd been going to say wasn't such a good idea.

"You wanted to desert?" said Jeremy, carefully.

"What? No! I would never desert. I just wanted to be dead." Dave stared out at the rain. "If people could do things like that to each other, I didn't want to be a person no more. Only Nicholas, see, he came and talked me out of that."

"You saw the elephant," said Jeremy.

"Yeah. Reckon you seen him too now."

"Yeah." Somehow it didn't seem that important anymore.

"Oh, about that song. We was in Tennessee last winter, and I talked to some of the western soldiers that was at Shiloh. Asked 'em about it. There just wasn't no stories about no drummer boy dyin' there. It didn't happen."

"Oh." Jeremy held the Drummer Boy of Shiloh in his head for a minute, and then let him go. It wasn't as hard as you'd think. He'd seen battle, and he knew it wasn't anything like that song.

The thing was, he'd joined up over a lie, and now he wasn't so sure how he felt about that.

"You wish you wasn't in it now?" he asked Dave.

Dave thought about this for so long that Jeremy reckoned he wasn't going to answer.

"I wish it was over," Dave said at last. "And some days I don't care who wins, just so's it'd be over. But you know, I hated the farm. The men always called me"—he stopped, took a deep breath—"things, and threw me in the creek and like that. Now I know I ain't so different from anybody else, Nicholas told me that, and I ain't never going back home."

"Oh," said Jeremy. He remembered he had thought that Dave was the kind of person who got treated like that, but he sort of hated hearing about it and hoped Dave wouldn't tell him any more.

"Most days, I want us to win," said Dave. "Cause, you know, if we lost, then what would happen to the slaves, and the contraband? Dulcie and them other kids and stuff?"

With a twinge of shame Jeremy realized that his Drummer Boy of Shiloh dream had been a dream about himself. He had wanted to be important, to have the war be somehow about him. That wasn't a cause at all. It wasn't ending slavery and it wasn't preserving the Union. It was just selfishness.

"How about you, Jeremy? Sorry you joined up?"

"No!" said Jeremy. "Sure is different from how I thought, though."

Dave smiled, understanding. "Ain't no Drummer Boys of Shiloh nowhere. Ain't no dyin' surrounded by weepin' comrades, ain't no glory and no bein' a hero. Just a lot of rain and mud and trying to stay alive."

"It's no good dying gloriously when there's work to be done," said Jeremy.

"You got that right," said Dave. "There oughta be a song about *that*."

They looked out at a puddle that was forming in front of their lean-to.

"Now I come to think of it, there *was* a kid that died at Shiloh," said Dave.

"Really?" Jeremy wasn't sure, now that he'd gotten over the Drummer Boy of Shiloh, that he wanted him back.

"On the other side. Boy twelve or thirteen years old. Read about it in a Reb newspaper right after Antietam."

"How did you get a Reb paper?"

"From a Reb, of course. Same place you got your shinplaster." He nodded at Jeremy's two-dollar bill, which still lay in his lap. "The newspaper was printed on old wallpaper."

"Wait, you mean you were talking to the enemy as long ago as that?"

"Sure. We always been talking to the enemy."

"Hah," said Jeremy.

"It was a sad story. See, the Johnnies, when they made their army, they brought a lot of boys in from military schools to be drill sergeants. Then they sent 'em all back to school, but this one kid, Charlie Jackson, he wouldn't go. And he was killed at Shiloh."

Jeremy stared at him. "What did you say his name was?"

"Charlie Jackson."

"And he was killed at Shiloh? You're sure?"

"It was in their newspaper."

Jeremy's mind was racing. All right, maybe Charlie

Jackson wasn't that rare a name. But how many military-school boys named Charlie Jackson could there have been fighting at Shiloh? But Jeremy's Charlie had *not* been killed at Shiloh—he was most demonstrably alive. Or had been the last time Jeremy had seen him.

"Here comes that fellow Ambrose Bierce," said Dave. "He 'bout scares me mortally to death."

Jeremy looked up through the rain at the lieutenant approaching them. He saw what Dave meant. The man looked like something in a ghost story. He held himself stiff and white and distant, as if he was a corpse in the business of appearing nightly and demanding revenge on his murderers. You could almost believe the rain was passing right through him. And he had odd, piercing blue eyes that didn't seem to look at you so much as at something he was imagining. He was, however, pretty much alive, and very wet. Jeremy and Dave saluted, but didn't bother to stand up because that would have meant leaving their lean-to.

Lieutenant Bierce returned their salute. He peered down at them through the rain. "Hundred and Seventh New York, eh? Your regiment has just caught a spy."

Jeremy felt as if he'd been hit by a minié ball. "What kind of spy?"

"Quite a young one," said Lieutenant Bierce. "But not too young to shoot." The lieutenant smiled a thin, not-very-nice smile. "Why are you worried about a spy?"

"He's not, he's just feelin' ill, sir," Dave said. Jeremy didn't hear the lieutenant's reply, because he was sloshing as fast as he could toward the 107th's camp. And a moment later he heard Dave splashing along behind him.

It was Charlie. Of course it was Charlie. And if he had been the 107th's prisoner to start with, he had drawn a much wider audience now. When Jeremy and Dave arrived Charlie was trying hard to smile his usual seeing-the-joke smile, but in spite of himself he was looking a little nervous in the midst of a crowd that included Jeremy's messmates, some other men from the 107th New York, and many other men Jeremy didn't recognize.

Jeremy pushed and threaded his way through the crowd until he was part of the ring that was right around Charlie. The rest of his messmates were in the ring. Even Nicholas, who must have come in off the skirmish—to bring in his prisoner? Jeremy wondered.

Charlie's hands were tied behind his back with a belt. The end of the belt was in Jack's hand, and Jack was smiling.

Jeremy hated Jack.

Jeremy looked at Charlie and Charlie didn't look back.

"I told y'all," Charlie said. "I was coming over here to surrender. Look, I'll take the oath of allegiance. I said I would."

"Sure you will. You'll wear a Union uniform too, won't

you? Wearing one already," said Jack. He gave the belt in his hands a yank, and Charlie winced.

"That's enough of that, Jack," said Nicholas.

"He's a spy! Shoot him already!" someone called from behind Jeremy.

"Remember the Hell-Hole!"

"But what was he doing?" Jeremy demanded.

Across from him, Nicholas looked at Jeremy. He pursed his lips and shook his head, once. Jeremy understood. Don't say anything, that was what he understood. Charlie was going to be shot, and Nicholas was not going to tell anybody that Jeremy knew Charlie. None of Jeremy's messmates were going to tell, except possibly Jack. Charlie himself wasn't going to tell. He'd pretended not to see Jeremy. Jack actually hadn't seen Jeremy yet.

Jeremy shut his mouth as tightly as Nicholas across from him was demonstrating.

But Jeremy had spoken, and so Jack looked at him now. He gave Jeremy the kind of smile that he reserved for times of special cruelty. "I think he was sneaking into the camp to visit somebody, Jeremy. Durned if I know who."

"If we're going to shoot him let's do it already," said Dave loudly. Nicholas glared at him and Dave looked at the ground, ashamed. He'd said it to save Jeremy from Jack, Jeremy realized. And earned Nicholas's displeasure, which for Dave had to be about the worst thing in the world.

"Maybe we should ask him who he was coming to visit," said Jack, still smiling.

"I wasn't coming to visit anybody. I was coming to surrender. I do surrender," said Charlie. "Do you kill men who are surrendering?"

"Why not? The Rebs do," said a voice somewhere behind Jeremy.

"We kill *spies,*" said someone else.

"Enough already! Somebody shoot him!"

There were cries of agreement.

Jeremy gulped. Nearly everyone around him was armed. In a minute or so somebody was going to shoot Charlie. Maybe sooner. Maybe several people. The crowd was pressed tight all around, and it was likely Charlie wouldn't be the only person killed once the firing started.

Jeremy took a deep breath.

"He was coming to see me," he said.

Dave gasped. Nicholas winced. Charlie looked at Jeremy, and then away, quickly.

Well, he'd done it. And now he was probably going to die. But he couldn't let his friend be shot right here in front of him no matter what side he was on. Not without saying anything. That wasn't being a hero—the Drummer Boy of Shiloh wouldn't have understood it. If he had ever existed. But there it was.

"He was coming to visit me because he's my friend," said Jeremy. "Not because he's a spy. He isn't. He's been my friend since before Resaca. Since we came into Georgia."

Dave put his hand to his head in despair.

Nicholas said, "Shut up, Jeremy."

"Anyway, everybody else does it," said Jeremy. He looked at Nicholas as he said it. Nicholas shook his head and scowled. Not because he didn't want Jeremy to give him away. Because he didn't want Jeremy to give *himself* away. But it was too late to stop now.

"His name's Charlie," said Jeremy. "Or at least I think it is. Charlie Jackson." He looked at Charlie. "Why do you call yourself Charlie Jackson?"

He bit his tongue as soon as he said it. He hadn't meant to admit in front of this hostile crowd that Charlie was lying about his name. Probably. Maybe.

Charlie smiled at him. "What are you going on about, young fella? I don't know you from Adam."

"Yes, you do," said Jeremy.

Jack was grinning as if he'd never expected to see such a good show.

"Your name's Charlie Jackson and you were at a military school and they brought military-school boys in to be drill sergeants to train rebel troops and then you wouldn't go back to school and then you . . ." Jeremy trailed off. According to Dave's story, Charlie Jackson had died at Shiloh.

"And then I what?" said Charlie.

"I don't know," said Jeremy. The Charlie standing in front of him was clearly not dead. Yet.

An odd thing had happened to the shape of the crowd. Jeremy had somehow ended up in the middle of it, next to Charlie and Jack, and angry men surrounded all three of them now. Angry men and one girl. Dulcie had worked her way to the center ring of the crowd.

"That Reb hasn't been to any military school," said Dulcie.

"How do you know?" said Charlie, still sounding amused. Jeremy wondered if Charlie was as terrified underneath as Jeremy was.

"Because military schools are for the better sort," said Dulcie. "All schools are for the better sort. And you're not the better sort."

"The better sort!" someone in the crowd laughed. "As if any Reb could be the better sort."

"I've studied white folks since I was this high," said Dulcie, holding her hand about waist level. "Didn't have any choice. And I know what you are."

Jeremy turned to look at Charlie, who had turned brick red. Why should he care about not being the better sort? Especially at a moment like this? Jeremy wasn't the better sort, and he'd never cared about it.

"Sounds like the little colored girl knows you too, Reb," said Jack maliciously. "You comin' to visit her?"

Nicholas reached over and grabbed Dulcie by the back of her dress. "You get out of here now. Nobody asked your opinion." Then he grabbed Jeremy by the collar. "You too." He raised his voice. "This boy does nothing but lie! I'm tired of it!"

Jeremy turned angrily to retort, but Nicholas gave him a shove that sent him into the crowd, and people stepped aside to let him land sprawling in the mud. Before he could get up someone had grabbed him again, and he was hauled to his feet and rushed struggling and protesting through the crowd, away from Charlie and whatever was about to happen to him.

When they got clear of the crowd he saw that it was Dave, who was clutching Jeremy in one hand and Dulcie in the other and marching them both along so fast that their feet got tangled up and they would both have fallen if Dave hadn't been holding them up.

"I hate Nicholas!" said Jeremy.

"Don't be an idiot," said Dave. "He's savin' your life."

BLAM-BLAM. A shot, then another, so close after it they almost sounded like one.

Dave stopped in his tracks and stared back through the rain at the crowd.

Jeremy felt the shot echo through him. His legs trembled and he almost fell. The shot had not hit *him*. He almost wished it had.

He turned to run back through the rain. Dave and Dulcie each grabbed one of his arms, and he couldn't shake or punch or kick them off. They wouldn't let go no matter how Jeremy pulled and struggled. Through the rain he heard shouts and angry cries—he thought he heard Nicholas's voice among the fray.

"Charlie!" Jeremy cried.

☆ ★ ★ TWENTY-FOUR ★ ★ ☆

THE TENT SMELLED OF MILDEW. THE RAIN HADN'T stopped for days. They were running out of morphine. Dulcie told Jeremy that Seth was stealing it. Jeremy couldn't decide if he hated Nicholas or not. He knew that what Dave said was perfectly true and that Nicholas had only been trying to save him.

People were complicated. If there were a hundred sides to every story, there had to be a thousand sides to every person. And Jeremy needed to find a different side of Dulcie.

Only two shots had been fired from the crowd around Charlie, probably because of the rain. No one knew who had fired them. Two people had decided at once that it was time to shoot Charlie. It could have been much worse, in that tightly packed crowd. But it could have been better— Nicholas might say that not one bullet in a hundred hit a person, but both these bullets had. One had hit Jack, and both had hit Charlie.

One bullet passed through Jack's left hand to hit Charlie in the left arm. The other had hit Charlie in the left shoulder.

"Shot in the hand, that's nothing," Jeremy had said.

"One of the soldiers that was shot in the hand at the Hell-Hole died," said Dulcie.

Jeremy had only said it because Jack was making such a fuss, as if no one had ever been injured before, and just because his hand was infected now. It was *supposed* to be infected. Dulcie and Dr. Flood and Seth had all told him so.

Charlie's wounds, oddly, were not infected. Jeremy worried about this. They were much deeper than Jack's, especially the one in his shoulder, which still had the bullet in it, buried deep inside somewhere. Nobody had tried to take it out. Dulcie said this was because they were afraid the bullet might be too close to his heart.

"I figure they're just waitin' on me to die," said Charlie, with his customary sardonic smile.

Jeremy had just finished writing a letter for Jack, who was having trouble holding a pen even in his unshot hand, for some reason. Jack and Charlie were side by side in one of the tents that had been brought for the injured. Usually the wounded were moved to the rear, but Jack wasn't considered badly enough wounded and Charlie, of course, was a prisoner. He would have to be sent back under guard.

"Destination Elmira, I reckon," said Charlie. "Think the prison's as bad as they say?"

"Nah," said Jeremy, thinking it probably was.

"You do me a favor and send me some of that hard-tack, will you? I heard they don't feed the prisoners over-much up there."

"All right," said Jeremy. This was the first time he'd talked to Charlie since he'd been captured, and that was three days ago. Jeremy had been busy caring for other patients, with Seth and Dulcie. Two of the orderlies had deserted after the Hell-Hole, including one named Bill who Dulcie had apparently not liked much. There were a lot of people coming down with sickness from the constant rain.

"Send me a blanket, too. I hear us southern boys keep dyin' from the cold up there."

"What name should I send it to?" said Jeremy.

Charlie grinned. "Charlie Jackson'll do fine."

"What's your real name?"

"Charlie Jackson."

"Then who's the boy who died at Shiloh?"

"Can't two people be named Charlie Jackson?"

Jeremy didn't answer this. He had thought that Charlie was his friend and that he could trust him. Now he didn't know what to think.

"I'm supposed to change your bandages," he said instead.

Beside them Jack groaned in his sleep and muttered something Jeremy didn't catch.

"Where'd you get them bandages from?" said Charlie,

trying to see the rags Jeremy was holding without moving his head too much, because that would mean moving his shoulder, which Jeremy could tell hurt him a lot.

"Off a stiff 'un that died yesterday. Don't worry, Dulcie rinsed 'em out."

"No thanks. I'll scream bloody murder if you touch me."

"That's what you did yesterday, Seth said."

"Yup. It's what I'll do tomorrow, too. Ain't nobody changin' no bandages on me."

Jeremy looked at the gray mass of bandages reaching from Charlie's shoulder around his chest and down his left arm to the wrist. They were crusted brown with dried blood. Jeremy waved his hand at the flies that crept all over them, and the flies buzzed off and immediately landed again. "You can't expect to get better without no doctorin'," he said, a little too heartily because he knew people weren't expecting Charlie to get better at all.

"Had less doctorin' than Friend there," said Charlie, through clenched teeth. "And look at him." He meant Jack, who was still asleep but had gone a hot red color. Jeremy reached out and put his hand on Jack's forehead. It felt much too warm. Jack had a high fever. Jeremy wasn't sure if that was supposed to be part of healing, like the infection, or not.

He turned back to Charlie. "There's nothing wrong with two fellas being named Charlie Jackson," he said. "But you're tellin' me there was two military-school boys at Shiloh, both named Charlie Jackson. And that they was both brought out of school to act as drill sergeants and wouldn't go back." Jeremy pursed his lips and shook his head to let Charlie know he didn't believe a word of it.

There was silence between them for a moment, broken only by the rattle of rain on the tent and the rasp of Jack's breathing.

"Seemed like Charlie Jackson didn't need his name no more after Shiloh, so I took it," said Charlie.

"Why?"

"Don't recall now."

This was so plainly a lie that Jeremy would have liked to call Charlie a liar right to his face, but that was a fightin' word back in the Northwoods and Charlie was in no condition to fight. It wouldn't be fair. Jeremy noticed there were tears in the corners of Charlie's eyes. "I'll get you more morphine," he said.

"Ain't no more," said Charlie.

"Let me ask," said Jeremy.

The truth was, he couldn't stand being around Charlie's pain, and Jack's fever was scaring him. Dulcie was a sight better at this sort of thing than Jeremy was. Jeremy would never make a great medic. But a drummer boy without a drum had to do something.

He went and found Dulcie lining an ambulance wagon with pine boughs.

"There's no more morphine," said Dulcie. "Not till supplies come in. Maybe tomorrow."

"Are we sending the wounded to the rear yet?" said Jeremy.

"Soon as we can. Dr. Flood is writing up the passes now."

"They need passes? Even if they're wounded?"

"Course. Can't go to the rear without a pass. That's desertion."

"Are Jack and Charlie going to be sent to the rear?"

"Jack ain't badly wounded enough."

"Dulcie, have you seen him?"

"Saw him yesterday."

"I wish you'd go see him." Jeremy didn't like Jack much—all right, he didn't like him at all—but a pardner was a pardner and you saved his life as often as you could. Jeremy suspected getting Jack to a real hospital was becoming a matter of life and death.

"He had a good infection."

"I think it's turned into a bad infection. Dulcie, you got to get Dr. Flood to send him to the hospital."

"All right," said Dulcie. "I'll ask him for a pass for Jack."

"And for Charlie. Charlie's hurt bad."

"I know that. They're just giving him time." She didn't say "to die," which Jeremy appreciated.

"I think he can get better."

"Better for him if he don't," said Dulcie baldly.

Jeremy bit back an angry retort. This was the side of Dulcie he was fighting with now. The side that didn't like Charlie, not in the way that Jeremy didn't like Jack but in a deeper, colder way that was much older and much harder to argue with.

"He's my friend," said Jeremy. "Dulcie, please."

Dulcie shut her mouth tight, and said nothing, and walked away toward the tent Jeremy had just left. She was going to check on Jack. Jeremy didn't follow her. He didn't know how to get through to that cold, old part of her and make it see that Charlie was a person and his friend—whoever he was and whatever his real name was—and needed saving. He would have to do it himself.

He started toward the field hospital tent. Maybe he could get Dr. Flood to see it his way. He stopped. Dr. Flood would see it Dulcie's way. He was waiting for Charlie to die too. And if Charlie didn't die it was the Elmira prison camp for Charlie. What Charlie needed was to escape.

Jeremy turned around and walked back the other way. Charlie needed to escape, and Jeremy needed to help him. But how could he get Charlie back to the enemy lines when Charlie couldn't even turn his head without crying in pain? Much less walk. And then there would be the Reb hospitals, which Charlie hadn't wanted to take Lars to because they were out of drugs and out of everything. Charlie might say he didn't want doctoring, but Jeremy didn't think he should be without it.

He turned and started back to Dr. Flood's tent. Surely he could make the doctor understand.

No. Nobody was going to see it Jeremy's way. To the

other men in the regiment Jeremy was what Nicholas had called him—just a boy who made them tired.

The only person who could possibly help him was Dulcie, and Dulcie wasn't about to.

It was Jeremy's task to go and tell his messmates that Jack was much worse. As Dulcie said, they couldn't leave it to Seth, whose crutches slipped and slid in the mud from the constant rain. And when Jeremy found them sheltered under a lean-to, he realized just how few of his messmates were left. Lars was gone, minus a leg but perhaps plus a new wife by now. No-Joke had been left at the Hell-Hole, a few miles back, forever. There was Seth, of course, back at the hospital. And Jeremy and, at least for now, Jack.

That left Nicholas and Dave, trying to keep a fire going in the driving rain, trying to brew up a pot of coffee.

Jeremy watched them through the rain as he walked toward them. He thought how different his messmates were from what he had imagined back in the Northwoods. The flashy U.S. uniforms he had pictured had become mud-soaked rags. The valiant do-or-die charges had become agreements between the two sides not to fire, as long as they didn't have orders to. And his noble comrades, the very flower of American manhood, were these two muddy men who looked like they would far rather be in a dry tent than in a battle, no matter how noble or valiant a battle it might be. He had never imagined a war would have so much rain in it.

"Jeremy." Nicholas smiled a friendly greeting, and it looked sincere enough. "Good to see you, pardner."

Jeremy turned to Dave. "Jack's worse," he said. "I think it might be time to—"

"Say goodbye?" said Nicholas.

"Yeah," said Jeremy, still looking at Dave but not seeing how he could avoid answering a direct question from Nicholas.

The two men got to their feet wearily and trudged after Jeremy toward the growing forest of medical tents.

"Hey, Jeremy." Nicholas's hand landed on Jeremy's shoulder. "Hang on a minute."

Jeremy stopped and looked up at Nicholas. Dave went slogging on ahead of them.

"I hope you know I didn't mean none of that stuff I said the other day."

"Yeah, all right," said Jeremy.

"I was trying to keep you out of trouble. You know that, right?"

"Yeah. All right." Jeremy wasn't sure if he believed Nicholas, but he knew that he really didn't feel like talking about it. He just wanted Nicholas to shut up.

"You're a good soldier, pardner. You done good at the Hell-Hole, and you done good when you brought Lars back, and you're doing good right now."

Nicholas sounded like he meant it. Jeremy suddenly

wasn't all that angry with him anymore. Nicholas was all right. He almost wanted to thank Nicholas for trying to save him—all right, for saving him—from the angry crowd that had shot Charlie. Almost. But mostly he didn't want to talk about it.

"Yeah," he said. "Thanks."

There was one thing he had to know, though. "Was it you who captured Charlie?"

"Me? No. It was a coupla fellas from B Company."

"Oh. Good."

And they went to see Jack.

Jack did not regain consciousness. Nicholas said he would write the letter to tell Jack's family, which Jeremy was relieved at, because he would have hated to write it himself. Later there would be another letter, probably, written by an officer, but a letter from a pardner was important because it told so much more that was real. Not really real, of course—Jeremy doubted that Nicholas would write exactly what had happened that day or tell them that Jack had been shot by a Union soldier. There would probably be something about it having happened in the course of apprehending a spy, something like that. Nicholas would make it sound heroic.

Dulcie removed Jack's things from his pocket. Nicholas would send them on with the letter. A pocketknife, a folded letter with a lock of hair inside, a leather pouch half-full of ground coffee mixed with sugar, a St. George medal. Jeremy wondered if Jack's family knew where he was. Probably they did. Jack had gotten mail and written letters. It was only Jeremy and No-Joke who hadn't.

Jeremy had promised Dulcie that he would write to Pa, because she'd nagged him until he promised. He just hadn't done it yet. He didn't know what to say. He'd had lots of practice writing letters now, with all the ones that Dulcie had dictated to him, but those letters all seemed to be between family who knew each other a sight better than Jeremy and Pa did.

Jeremy was almost too busy to notice Jack's death. Seth had finally been ordered to the rear, and that meant much more work for Jeremy and for Dulcie. It had taken the combined efforts of Dr. Flood, Nicholas, and Dave to convince Seth that he had no choice but to obey General Sherman's orders. Finally Seth had been sent off, on foot and crutches, along the road among the many others like him whom Sherman wanted away from the battle line— men with one leg, or one arm, or one hand, who were felt to be hindering the army's progress by insisting on staying with their regiments.

"I know it ain't fair," said Dave. "You ain't hinderin' nothing. But orders are orders, pardner."

Jeremy thought of the rapidly disappearing new supply of morphine and thought that with Seth gone, at least they wouldn't run out of it as fast. But he was a good medic, Seth was.

"Just be sure and write me when you're ready for that wooden leg," said Nicholas. "I wouldn't want it whittled by some fool who doesn't know his business."

Jeremy had figured it out. There was only one way for Charlie to escape, and that was for him to be sent to a hospital in an ambulance, disguised as a Union soldier. The problem was, it needed Dulcie's help, and this she absolutely, completely, and firmly refused to give.

"You have Jack's pass, don't you?" Jeremy urged. "And Jack ain't gonna be using it. Why can't you just give it to Charlie and ship him out as Jack?"

"Because," said Dulcie. "That would be wrong."

"That ain't why," said Jeremy. "It's because you don't like Charlie."

"It would still be wrong." And this was the point from which he could not budge her. He thought about trying to wrest the pass from her by main force, but of course she would just go and tell Dr. Flood.

He decided to try again in front of Charlie, just in case Charlie could be of any help. There did seem to be some kind of understanding between Charlie and Dulcie that Jeremy couldn't entirely account for. Maybe it was because they were both southerners. But if it was an understanding it definitely wasn't a friendly one.

Dulcie had just given Charlie a dose of morphine and Charlie was a little fuzzy from it, but at least not in so much pain, and he managed his usual smile. "Dulcie doesn't want to help. Dulcie's just waitin' on me to die," he told Jeremy.

"You're not going to die," said Dulcie automatically. It was a thing she said to wounded soldiers.

"I don't figure on it," Charlie said. "Not for another eighty years at least."

"All you have to do is let him have Jack's pass," said Jeremy. Of course, the rest would be difficult too—Charlie was still flat on his back and couldn't raise his head more than an inch or two.

"And then I'll be out of your hair forever," said Charlie.

Dulcie narrowed her eyes at Charlie. "My mama had family in North Carolina. What part you from?"

"Eastern part," said Charlie guardedly.

"Down around near Wilmington?"

"No, not that far east."

"Fayetteville way?"

"Sort of near there. Not real near."

Jeremy was not sure what this was all about. They were both speaking in much thicker southern accents than either of them ever addressed to him, and he felt cut out of the conversation.

"Seem like you took it kind of funny when I told y'all about Anne."

"Sad story," said Charlie.

"Where's your mother at?"

"She died from fever."

"What about your pa?"

Charlie looked like he wanted to turn away, but he couldn't move his head. "I run off."

"Why'd you join the Secesh?"

"What else was there to do?"

"Why you call yourself Charlie Jackson? It ain't your name, is it?"

"Easiest way to change regiments."

"Wasn't no North Carolina regiments at Shiloh," said Dulcie. "I heard all about Shiloh."

"Changed a couple times before that."

Jeremy wondered why Charlie had changed regiments so many times—most people only changed if they were forced to. Your regiment was who you *were*. But Dulcie didn't seem to think it was strange.

"What does E-A-C-E-P spell?" she asked.

Charlie grinned. "Thought you didn't know your letters."

"I heard that, I remembered it."

"Spells 'peace.'"

"No it don't," said Jeremy automatically.

"It's the signs and countersigns for the Peace Society," said Charlie.

"You in the Peace Society?" Dulcie sounded dubious.

"Yup."

"What's the Peace Society?" Jeremy broke in.

"Sort of like the homegrown Yanks," said Dulcie.

"Not that much like," Charlie contradicted. "Just a secret society of Confederate soldiers that want the Union to win."

"Oh," said Jeremy. Up north there were people who wanted the South to win, and what they were called was Copperheads, at least by everybody but themselves. But there were no *Union soldiers* that wanted the South to win. Not that Jeremy had ever heard of. Certainly not enough to form a secret society.

"We want to rejoin the Union," said Charlie. He sounded tired, and Jeremy thought the morphine would put him to sleep soon.

"Why?"

"'Cause life was better in the Union. 'Cause we weren't fightin' and dyin' for no rich man's slaves while he stayed home and got richer growin' cotton he wasn't supposed to be growin'."

He looked at Dulcie and said, "'Sides, th'Union don't want no more slavery. I don't either."

Dulcie looked at Charlie for a moment in thought. Her look wasn't quite as cold as it had been, and Jeremy hoped maybe she was making up her mind to help Charlie. He wondered if Charlie would stay awake long enough for her to decide.

"All right," she said finally. "I'll do it. On one condition." She glared at Charlie.

Charlie looked at her through half-closed eyes. "What c'dition?" he murmured.

"You tell Jeremy who you are."

Charlie's eyes opened all the way, startled wide awake. It was clear to Jeremy that Dulcie was suddenly holding all the cards and that Charlie hadn't even realized she'd been dealt a hand.

"What's that mean, Charlie?" Jeremy asked.

"Tell him," said Dulcie. "Or I don't help."

Charlie gave Dulcie a thoroughly fed-up look and then looked at Jeremy with the expression of a man letting another man know that the two of them would just have to put up with this woman's whims.

"All right. She wants me to tell you I'm black," he said.

"You're what?"

"Black."

Jeremy laughed, not wanting Charlie to think he didn't get the joke, although he didn't. "No you're not."

Charlie looked back at Dulcie. "Well, I told him. All right?"

"That's *what* you are. I think we both got a right to know *who* you are."

"Does it really matter that much?"

Dulcie nodded.

"All right. My name was Bruno. But I like Charlie better. An' I aim to like Jack better still." The morphine was slurring his speech again.

Dulcie gave him a meaning look.

"What, everything? All right, my father owned a farm in North Carolina. A farm, and a house, and some slaves. And me. 'S near the sandhill country. Doesn't really matter where. And I ran away."

"I don't understand," said Jeremy.

Charlie smiled up at him. "No, you wouldn't. Can't wait to get up North. Won't nobody understand. Gonna love it, up North."

"What's your father's name?" said Dulcie.

"That doesn't matter," said Charlie. "He ain't no father to me anyway. Like I said, I ran away. And then I found the war, and then after Shiloh I decided to be Charlie."

Jeremy felt even more that he didn't understand. He was very confused. He was still looking at Charlie and trying to figure out what was black about him. Not even his hair was black. Jeremy's hair was black. But Charlie's would be a sort of sandy color, if it was clean. Jeremy hadn't seen clean hair since he'd left Shelbyville. If you cleaned Charlie up could you tell he was black? Jeremy didn't understand any of this.

Charlie lifted a finger from the blanket where his unbandaged arm lay. "One drop of blood," he murmured, still smiling, and fell asleep.

Jeremy looked at Dulcie. She looked vindicated, and Jeremy still didn't understand what Charlie had just told him and why it mattered so much to Dulcie. But he said, "So you'll help, then?"

Dulcie nodded, and Jeremy felt a rush of gratitude. "But I don't know how we're going to get him into an ambulance," he said, moving on quickly to the next stage of the problem before she could change her mind. "Because he can't hardly lift his head, let alone walk, and he's too heavy for the two of us to carry."

This had been troubling him ever since he'd thought of the plan. He had considered but discarded the idea of getting Nicholas and Dave to help—it almost amounted to treason, some ways of looking at it, and he couldn't ask that of his pardners even if they would have agreed to it.

"The stretcher bearers will move him to the ambulance," said Dulcie.

"But they'll know he's not Jack."

"Only if they know Jack."

"Well, they probably do, don't they? I mean, aren't they the 107th's own stretcher bearers?"

Dulcie frowned. "Might be. Things get a little mixed up sometimes, but they might be." She thought for a minute. "I know. Leave it to me."

"And they'll know Jack's dead."

"I said leave it to me."

And with that Jeremy had to be content, because she wouldn't say any more about it.

Dulcie could not have said exactly why it was so important to her that Jeremy know that Charlie was black. Maybe it was because of the way Jeremy had been to her— kind, and a good friend, but really, just a little bit proprietorial, as if he was somehow responsible for Dulcie, maybe because she was a girl but probably also because she was black. He hadn't acted that way to Charlie. And if he knew about Charlie would he understand a little better? Would he treat Dulcie like she had as much brains as he did? That was part of it.

The other part was, it made her angry that Charlie would lie. Would she have done the same thing if she could have gotten away with it? Well, that wasn't really the question. Would she have joined the Confederate Army and fought for slavery? *That* was the question.

Who did Charlie think he was, anyway?

Dulcie kept all this in her own head as she carefully bandaged Charlie's. He wasn't much help, hardly able to turn his head or to lift it a little bit when she told him to so that she could get the bandage underneath as she wound it around and around, from his chin to the top of his hair.

"At least leave me room to breathe." His voice came muffled through the bandages.

"I am."

"What about my eyes?"

"Very delicate. That shell exploded right in front of you. The least little bit of light before they're healed could blind you."

She saw him smile through the slit she'd left for his mouth. "What happens when they take the bandage off and see I'm not injured underneath?"

"I'm sure you'll think of a good explanation."

He smiled again. He was sure he would too, Dulcie thought.

The stretcher bearers and Jeremy arrived at the same time.

"Where's his pass?" one of the bearers asked Dulcie.

"In my pocket." Charlie's voice came through the bandages.

The other stretcher bearer dug the folded paper out of Charlie's pocket, read it, and frowned. "I thought this Jack fella died last week. It was in a newspaper from home."

Dulcie sighed. "They got it wrong again? Those newspaper lists are always wrong."

"That's the truth," said one of the stretcher bearers with feeling. "The paper back home said I died at Chancellorsville, and my mother nearly went into a decline before she found out I was alive."

"They printed that my cousin John was wounded in the thumb," said the other stretcher bearer. "Come to find out it was another John that was wounded in the thumb, and my cousin was wounded in the head. It having been shot off."

Dulcie nodded. She hadn't thought she'd have any trouble convincing the stretcher bearers that there'd been an error in the casualty reports. There were errors in them all the time.

"Hey, Ch—Jack. Write to us when you get there," Jeremy said, leaning down so Charlie could hear him through the bandages.

"I'll do that, little buddy. Thanks."

They lifted him onto the stretcher and carried him away, but not before Dulcie heard him add, "You too, Dulcie—thanks. For everything."

TWENTY-FIVE

THE REAR STRETCHED BACK FOR MILES, AND GENERAL
Sherman kept sending anyone he could back to it. Atlanta
lay ahead, and he wanted only fighting men at the front.
And the people whom the army couldn't do without,
which included medics like Dulcie. At the rear were the
contraband, thousands upon thousands of them. Every
mile that Sherman moved through Georgia it seemed another thousand slaves joined behind him. He didn't want
them to follow him, Dulcie knew. But that didn't matter.

It was among these thousands that she finally found
Uncle John, standing on top of a hill and holding a spyglass.

"Where's Aunt Betsy?" Dulcie asked him, when they
had exchanged greetings.

He waved at the mountain in the distance, where
Dulcie knew the Secesh lay in wait. Another battle was
brewing, over that mountain.

"In the Secesh camp," he said.

"You mean she didn't get away?" Dulcie found it hard to believe that Uncle John would have escaped without Aunt Betsy, and she wondered how it could have happened.

"Oh, she got away. And then she went back to do laundry for the Secesh generals." He smiled.

"But . . . why?"

In answer Uncle John handed Dulcie the spyglass. "Train that over there on that mountain, girl, and tell me if you can find Aunt Betsy doing laundry."

Dulcie took the heavy spyglass in both hands. It was hard to hold it steady at her eye, and when she finally did the distant mountain leapt up close, as if it had only been a few feet away—a green blur became individual trees. There was a buzzard sitting in one of them, waiting for the next battle. The tiniest move of the spyglass caused many trees to whiz dizzyingly past, and finally Uncle John had to take it from her hands, look through it, and then hold it steady for her.

"Now look," he said.

"I see a woman hanging up washing on a line. Is that Aunt Betsy?" She couldn't see her clearly enough to tell.

"Yup. Now tell me about the laundry."

"The laundry? It looks like, er, drawers."

"What color?"

"Gray, mostly." She saw this wasn't enough for him, so she added, feeling a little annoyed, "Two white pairs, a gray pair, a red pair, three more gray pairs. No, now she's moving the red pair to the end. After the three gray pairs. Now she's moving it back again! Why's she doing that?"

"No battle today," said Uncle John, putting down the spyglass. "I'ma go tell the captain that."

"How do you know?"

"Aunt Betsy does the laundry, that's how I know. She does it right behind the Secesh generals' tents, and she listens to what they say, and then she takes and hangs it on the line, and all I have to do is look for it."

"What—"

"We worked out a code, before she left. She moves the drawers to tell me what the Secesh are planning."

Dulcie marveled at this.

"Oh, we ain't the only ones doing it. If them Secesh generals knew all the news that was being carried across the lines by their drawers flappin' in the breeze, I reckon they'd rather keep wearing them drawers dirty till they fall apart."

"Nicholas!"

Nicholas looked up from the letter he was reading. "Evenin', Jeremy." He folded the letter and put it in his pocket.

"I didn't mean to interrupt your letter," said Jeremy. He sat down on a log beside the fire. He really wanted to ask Nicholas's advice about what was bothering him. Dave said you could trust Nicholas. But Nicholas had said some pretty harsh things to Jeremy, even if he had sort of mostly apologized. And could you trust Nicholas to stand by you when you were pretty much breaking the law?

"Oh, it's my third time reading it," said Nicholas. "It's from my sister."

"Oh." Jeremy realized he'd never thought about Nicholas having a sister or anything like that.

"I heard that Secesh friend of yours escaped," said Nicholas.

"Did he?" said Jeremy.

"Yup. No one knows how. There's no flies on you, Jeremy."

Jeremy wanted to say that Dulcie had helped, but then he also didn't think he should admit that either of them had had anything to do with Charlie escaping—even though he could see Nicholas already knew.

"You have to help out your pardners," said Nicholas. "No matter what side they're on."

"I think Charlie's on our side now," said Jeremy. "He told me he's black."

Nicholas looked surprised. "Didn't look black to me."

"Me either. But he said something about one drop of blood."

He told Nicholas what Charlie and Dulcie had said to each other, although he left out the part where Dulcie had agreed to help Charlie escape.

"I just didn't know he was black," said Jeremy. "I mean, I never thought of it."

"So?"

"So, I don't know. What did he want to fight on the Secesh side for?"

"Probably didn't know why he was doing it," said Nicholas. "I think a lot of people got into this war not knowing why."

That was for sure.

"Time he visited with us, it sounded like he was starting to make up his mind about things," said Nicholas.

"Yeah. Maybe."

"You going to tell me how you did it?" said Nicholas.

"Did what?" said Jeremy.

Nicholas laughed. "All right. Maybe you'll tell me after this cruel war is over, eh?"

"I have to write to my pa," said Jeremy. "He's in prison."

"That can happen to a man."

Jeremy had to trust Nicholas or he couldn't ask his advice. "I'm afraid to write to him because I ran away from my master."

"You have a master?"

"Back in York State I was bound over to a man named Old Silas. But he treated me bad, and so I ran away."

There, now his life was in Nicholas's hands, so he sure hoped Dave was right. But you had to trust your pardners.

"What's that got to do with writing to your pa?" said Nicholas.

"Well, if I write to him Old Silas might find out where I am and come and get me."

"Come and get a Union soldier? I'd like to see him try. Anyway, you say he treated you bad. Didn't it say in your indenture that he would treat you good?"

Jeremy knew what an indenture was—it was a legal paper. "He never signed no paper."

"He didn't? Are you sure?"

"Yeah."

"There was no paper at all?"

"I said there wasn't," said Jeremy.

"Then you aren't a bound-boy." Nicholas dismissed Old Silas from Jeremy's life with a wave of his hand.

Jeremy couldn't believe it could be that simple. "Are you sure?"

"I got a book to home called *Every Man His Own Lawyer*. It's all in there."

"Oh."

"So I reckon you can write to your pa."

Jeremy noticed that Nicholas didn't tell Jeremy he *had* to write to his pa. It was up to Jeremy.

There was going to be another battle. It was in the air. It might happen today, it might not happen for a week, but Dulcie and Jeremy both knew it was a mountain that lay ahead of them, another mountain to be fought over, another mountain to be climbed, before Atlanta. And then there would be Atlanta. And after that, who knew? How much longer could the war go on? All wars ended eventually. After them came a broken world that had to be fitted together again, as best it could be, and scattered, broken people to be fitted into it somehow. That would be a long work.

It might be a world with no room in it for people like Charlie, Jeremy thought, but Charlie would make room for himself. Charlie would land on his feet even if he was flat on his back. That was Charlie.

There was no room in the world for Dulcie, not yet, but room would have to be made.

"Dr. Flood's going back to Tennessee after the war to work in the contraband camps," said Dulcie. "There's a plan for turning them into freedmen's camps, to help the freedmen find jobs and places to live and each other—their families, I mean. He wants me to go with him. He said I could work as a medic."

"Are you going to?" Jeremy asked.

"I don't know," said Dulcie. "I have to find my mother and father first."

Pa, Jeremy thought, was another person that there wasn't much of a place for in this world. It was going to be hard for Pa coming out of prison, if he ever did. Jeremy had not written to him yet. He would do it today. After all, tomorrow there might be a battle, and then it might be too late.

Jeremy thought of his two remaining messmates, Nicholas and Dave. In a way that he sensed more than understood, the world didn't seem to have a place in it for them, either. But they, like Charlie and Dulcie, would make one. Assuming they all survived.

"You could come to New York with me," Jeremy said. "If you don't want to go to Tennessee. We could find No-Joke's family."

"I know." Dulcie smiled big at him, and the light of the setting sun glowed on her face and lit up her smile. "We can do whatever we have to, and whatever we want."

The 107th New York was recruited mainly from Steuben, Allegany, Chemung, and Schuyler counties. Except for Jeremy and his messmates, the soldiers mentioned in this book were real people. Captain Knox died at New Hope Church. Dr. Flood worked in freedmen's camps after the war, then became mayor of Elmira, New York. Lieutenant Tuttle kept a journal that was published in 2006.

The story about Charlie Jackson that Dave tells Jeremy in chapter twenty-three is true, but the Charlie in this book is fictional. Laws ensuring that slavery "followed the condition of the mother" kept people in slavery even when their owner was their father.

General Benjamin Butler first had the idea of claiming runaway slaves as "contraband of war." The Emancipation Proclamation made them legally free, but soldiers still called them contraband. Dulcie is fictional, but many freedchildren stayed with the army and were hired to work.

Thousands of underage boys served as soldiers on both sides in the Civil War. They only had to say that they were eighteen—and many weren't even asked. Hundreds of women claiming to be men also served, and at least one girl enlisted as a drummer boy. There was no minimum age for drummer boys until 1864.

Over 180,000 African Americans served in the Union Army. None appear in this book because none marched in the Atlanta campaign. General Sherman didn't allow them to.

The "bonnie blue flag" in the song in chapter seven was an early, unofficial flag of the Confederacy.

There were many pro-Union groups in the Confederacy, and at least two peace societies in the Confederate Army. There are numerous records of Confederate and Union soldiers meeting to trade, talk, and play cards. Sometimes they even invited each other to dinner.

☆★★ SELECTED SOURCES FOR ★★☆
THE STORM BEFORE ATLANTA

Billings, John D. *Hard Tack and Coffee.* 1887. Reprint, Konecky and Konecky.

Blight, David W. *A Slave No More.* New York: Harcourt, 2007.

Castel, Albert. *Decision in the West: The Atlanta Campaign of 1864.* Lawrence: University Press of Kansas, 1992.

Conklin, Henry. *Through "Poverty's Vale": A Hardscrabble Boyhood in Upstate New York 1832–1862.* Edited by Wendell Tripp. Syracuse, NY: Syracuse University Press, 1974.

Kennett, Lee. *Marching Through Georgia.* New York: HarperCollins, 1995.

Marten, James. *The Children's Civil War.* Chapel Hill: University of North Carolina Press, 1998.

Rutkow, Ira M. *Bleeding Blue and Gray: Civil War Surgery and the Evolution of American Medicine.* New York: Random House, 2005.

Scaife, William R. *The Campaign for Atlanta.* Atlanta: self-published, 1993.

Supplement to the Official Records of the Union and Confederate Armies. Pt. 2, vol. 46, pp. 93–138, "Record of Events for One Hundred Seventh New York Infantry, August 1862–May 1865." Wilmington, NC: Broadfoot, 1997.

Swanson, Mark. *Atlas of the Civil War Month by Month*. Athens: University of Georgia Press, 2004.

Taylor, Susie King. *A Black Woman's Civil War Memoirs*. 1902. Reprint, Princeton, NJ: Markus Weiner, 1999.

Tsui, Bonnie. *She Went to the Field: Women Soldiers of the Civil War*. Guilford, CT: TwoDot, 2006.

Tuttle, Russell M. *The Civil War Journal of Lt. Russell M. Tuttle, 107th New York Volunteer Infantry*. Edited by George H. Tappan. Jefferson, NC: McFarland, 2006.

Wickersham, John T. *Boy Soldier of the Confederacy: The Memoir of Johnnie Wickersham*. Edited by Kathleen Gorman. Carbondale: Southern Illinois University Press, 2006.

Wiley, Bell Irvin. *The Life of Billy Yank*. New York: Doubleday, 1971.

Wiley, Bell Irvin, and Hirst D. Milhollen. *They Who Fought Here*. New York: Macmillan, 1959.

Williams, David, et al. *Plain Folk in a Rich Man's War: Class and Dissent in Confederate Georgia*. Gainesville: University Press of Florida, 2002.

Wise, Arthur, and Francis A. Lord. *Bands and Drummer Boys of the Civil War*. New York: Thomas Yoseloff, 1966.

Wright, John D. *The Language of the Civil War*. Westport, CT: Oryx Press, 2001.

☆ ★ ★ ACKNOWLEDGMENTS ★ ★ ☆

I would like to thank Jenny Peer and Elisa Leone of the Savona Free Library; Ken Akins, manager of the Etowah Indian Mounds State Historic Site; Keith Beason, past president of the Friends of Resaca Battlefield, Inc.; Aaron, Jennifer, and Deborah Schwabach; Suzy Capozzi; and Joanna Stampfel-Volpe. Any errors that remain are my own.

★ YEARLING!

Looking for more great books to read?
Check these out!

- ❏ *All-of-a-Kind Family* by Sydney Taylor
- ❏ *Are You There God? It's Me, Margaret* by Judy Blume
- ❏ *Blubber* by Judy Blume
- ❏ *The City of Ember* by Jeanne DuPrau
- ❏ *Crash* by Jerry Spinelli
- ❏ *The Girl Who Threw Butterflies* by Mick Cochrane
- ❏ *The Gypsy Game* by Zilpha Keatley Snyder
- ❏ *Heart of a Shepherd* by Rosanne Parry
- ❏ *The King of Mulberry Street* by Donna Jo Napoli
- ❏ *The Mailbox* by Audrey Shafer

- ❏ *Me, Mop, and the Moondance Kid* by Walter Dean Myers
- ❏ *My One Hundred Adventures* by Polly Horvath
- ❏ *The Penderwicks* by Jeanne Birdsall
- ❏ *Skellig* by David Almond
- ❏ *Soft Rain* by Cornelia Cornelissen
- ❏ *Stealing Freedom* by Elisa Carbone
- ❏ *Toys Go Out* by Emily Jenkins
- ❏ *A Traitor Among the Boys* by Phyllis Reynolds Naylor
- ❏ *Two Hot Dogs with Everything* by Paul Haven
- ❏ *When My Name Was Keoko* by Linda Sue Park

Visit **www.randomhouse.com/kids** for additional reading suggestions in fantasy, adventure, mystery, and humor!